FIERCE MAGIC

Fierce Magic

A VICTORIAN FAERIE TALE

E.B. WHEELER

Rowan Ridge
Press

ISBN: 978-1-960033-13-0

First printing: August 2024

Published by Rowan Ridge Press, Utah

Cover design by Lauren Makena

Cover and interior design © Rowan Ridge Press

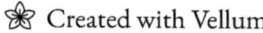 Created with Vellum

For everyone who shines a light into the darkness

Chapter One

Energy hummed through the glens and rills of the Scottish woods on the Winter Solstice, wilder than in the tamed landscapes of England. But weaker, too, thready and quick like the pulse of a man hovering near death. Skeletal oaks reached twisted limbs in the faint moonlight to snag Henry's coat, as if entreating him to linger. The odor of moss and decaying leaves filled his lungs, cloying, almost sickening. He would swear the trees whispered to him, just below his hearing. The trees didn't like the darkness—or at least whatever threat lurked in the night.

"I ain't convinced the Grigori even came this way." Jairus Hale's drawl broke the quiet.

"Indeed," Domin said softly. "I believe they have evaded us once again."

Henry tore his gaze from the trees. The Grigori. Of course. He and his friends had ventured to this isolated corner of Scotland tracking the occultists who sought to harness magic. The Leannan they had summoned a few months previously had exacted a toll of blood from London, and now the Grigori snuck about the countryside, plotting some new scheme.

But that wasn't the threat that spoke to Henry at the moment—the one that thrummed in his bones. A deeper wrongness murmured to him from the shadows. Something Fay. He feared he would never escape them. Their magic wove through him, binding him to their will and echoing with memories of homes destroyed and people tormented—Henry's magic used as a weapon by his Faerie masters. Now, he fought to take his magic back and make it his own. And tonight, it spoke to him.

"Wait," Henry said, half to himself and half to his friends.

He should be glad to give up the hunt. He longed to return to Edinburgh to meet Cassandra and prepare for their wedding. He and Cassandra had a few precious days over Christmas when they could be together. A few precious days to marry in secret in Scotland, safe from the English laws that required marriages to be publicly announced. He and Cassandra could dream those few days of a human life, joyful and free. Titania, the Faerie Lady of the Woods who held Henry by a silken thread of magic, would never forgive him for daring to fall in love, much less for marrying without her permission. She would destroy them both if she knew.

Yet Cassandra insisted they not live in fear. She trusted Henry and his magic. She would tell him to heed the warning he felt.

A flash of white bounded through the trees.

"There!" Henry dodged after the Fay creature, deeper into the tangle of trees. He hoped he would not fail Cassandra. Not leave her alone in Edinburgh, wondering what became of him.

Jairus and Domin followed, not bothering with stealth.

The white form drew ahead of them, and the night swallowed it.

They slowed and spread out, searching for its trail.

"Here!" Jairus held up a small miner's lamp, which cast a wan orange glow. "Something big moved this way. It broke the branches. I'd say it's the size of a horse."

Domin stood behind Jairus, frowning. "Scotland has many water horse Fay. None of them are friendly."

"Fitzhugh rides a kelpie," Henry said. "Could he be here?"

Domin was quiet for a moment. "I cannot tell if there is Unseelie magic present."

Henry winced inwardly and reproved himself. He had come to rely on Domin knowing...everything, it seemed. But their world was shifting. Domin still had centuries of knowledge at his disposal, but since Spring-heeled Jack had stabbed him, leaving a shard of an enchanted dagger lodged just over his heart, his magical senses were dulled and fading quickly.

Jairus knelt to study the ground. "Might be a headless horseman. I chased one through Texas once."

"Do ghosts break branches?" Henry scoffed.

Jairus stood and brushed his hand off on his trousers. "These days, I'm not sure. All the time, I'm seeing things that walk between the living worlds and the dead." He said it lightly, but concern flashed in his eyes, and he clenched his fist with the demon mark that drew the dead to him.

They pushed their way through to a clearing in the trees.

"Where now?" Henry asked.

"Something approaches." Domin pivoted to face the darkness.

Henry and Jairus turned, too. After a moment, Henry heard it: the fast approach of hoofbeats. The shriveled leaves clinging to the winter trees shivered. A breeze picked up, rattling the dry husks like chattering teeth.

Jairus pulled out his shotgun—the one loaded with iron shot. Henry gripped the rowan wood stake he'd taken to carrying and willed the cold in the air to concentrate until the stout weapon grew a tip of ice.

A huge white stag burst through the brush in front of them. Its leg oozed blood where Rushford, the leader of the Grigori, had shot it the previous year. Henry lowered his icy weapon. What was the stag doing so far from the old woods of Drixton? Mary's changeling sister had warned them that the Fay were hunting it—that it was a messenger from the mysterious Fisher King.

The stag's steps faltered, its injured leg trembling with fatigue. It fixed its dark eyes on Henry and lowered its great horned head. Henry returned the bow and stepped forward.

A strange cry rang through the trees, sending prickles down Henry's spine. A reddish glow like the embers of a dying fire flooded the clearing. The stench of decay and a shiver of something Unseelie washed over Henry. It reminded him of the Otherworld. It reminded him of...

"Jane Tudor," he said under his breath.

He didn't know why the Fay wanted the Fisher King's stag, but he knew they shouldn't have it. And especially not Jane, who had also tried to control the Wild Hunt. He rushed to intercept her.

Domin grabbed his arm, jolting him to a halt. Domin's magic might be fading, but he still had the supernatural strength of the Fay.

"It could be a trap," Domin hissed in his ear.

Henry winced. He was being reckless again.

Jairus shuttered his lantern and hoisted his shotgun. He positioned himself to the side of the clearing, readying an ambush. The red light gave his scarred face an eerie cast. He beckoned the others closer.

Henry crept forward, carefully this time. The dim light illuminated the silhouette of an otherworldly black stag trotting toward them along a deer trail. The red radiated from fissures in the stag's form like embers in a fire-blackened log. Jane Tudor rode the beast, trapped astride as she would always be in the mortal realm.

Jairus's shotgun blasted away the quiet.

The stag shrieked and reared. Jane maintained her seat on the creature, and she locked eyes with Henry. She howled in rage, and lightning raked the black sky, momentarily blinding Henry. He blinked away the streaks of color and scrambled aside as the black stag's hoofbeats approached.

Jane's blonde hair twisted in the wind like angry serpents, and her stag stomped its hooves. Thunder boomed, and the ancient trees trembled.

The white stag limped for the other side of the clearing. Another blast of lightning exploded in front of it, igniting a dead tree.

The white stag shied away, then turned back to face Jane's stag, ears back and antlers lowered.

Thick smoke filled the clearing, and the trees quavered as if shrinking from the flames. Henry quelched the fire with a motion.

Jairus emptied the other barrel of his gun, hitting Jane's stag solidly in the chest. Dark red light poured over the clearing, and the stag bellowed its pain and fury.

Henry called the frigid winter air and whipped a whirlwind

of ice into Jane's face. She raised her arm to shield herself. Henry charged her stag with his ice dirk. Domin leapt for Jane. The stag twisted, dodging Henry and flinging Domin aside. It kicked Domin with a solid crack that sent him reeling to the ground.

Henry's hair rose on end, and a metallic taste filled his mouth. A crackling sound vibrated over Jairus's gun.

"Lightning!" Henry shouted.

Jairus dropped his gun and scrambled back from it.

Henry tried to seize control of the lightning, but it was wild with Jane's unbalanced energy. The electricity slashed through the clearing and exploded on the ground. Some of the energy raced through Henry, a burst of natural and faerie energy. He screamed. Jairus and Domin cried out as well. A thousand scalpel cuts sliced Henry's legs, and then he collapsed. His head throbbed and his teeth buzzed. Jairus also lay on the ground. Domin was nowhere in sight. Henry groaned. What of the white stag?

The Fisher King's stag had fallen to its front knees as though prostrating itself before Jane. Henry tried to rise, tried to grasp some of the energy flittering about the clearing, but he could do nothing more than breathe.

The ground stirred. Jane's final blow against them, maybe a fissure in the earth to swallow them all.

But Jane's stag backed away from the disturbance rippling in the center of the clearing. Jane fixed her eyes on the white stag and urged her mount forward.

The writhing forest floor burst open, and roots encircled Jane's stag like cords. This was some woodland magic that Henry did not know.

Jane and her mount roared as one. The stag tried to rear

free, and Jane grabbed her dagger to attack the roots vining around her legs and worming their way up her body.

Jane snarled at Henry. "What strange trick have you mastered? I will make it mine."

Henry wanted to laugh at her false assumption, but all he could manage was sitting up.

Jane cut away several of the roots holding her, and she laughed in triumph. "You are not so powerful."

Jairus raised his pistol and fired. The silver bullet hit Jane in the ribs. She shrieked and dropped her dagger, clawing at the injury. It wouldn't kill her or stop her magic, but the pain was real.

"I will pour your blood on my lady's altar," Jane yelled at Henry. "You and everyone you love."

Henry went still. Cassandra. Jane could never know how much Cassandra meant to him, or she would be the first the Unseelie Court destroyed.

"You talk too much." Jairus raised his pistol again.

A blast of icy air tore through the clearing—again not Henry's doing—and brought a churning mass of clouds with it.

Henry summoned the winter wind, whisking the clouds away, but when they thinned, blackness had swallowed the clearing again, and there was no sign of Jane or her stag. Henry blinked hard, trying to adjust to the darkness.

Jairus retrieved his lamp and opened the shutter, returning a faint wash of light to the clearing. He swore. "She's gone."

The white stag remained in the clearing, and a young man knelt before it—or rather, a Fay, given the man's green-tinted skin. The one behind the forest magic, no doubt. The Fay whispered something to the white stag and gently stroked its face.

Henry noticed Domin walking unsteadily toward them. "You're injured."

"Several broken ribs. They will heal."

Domin should have been able to heal himself, but not any longer.

"I'll bind them," Henry said.

Domin shrugged, as if broken ribs were of little importance.

Henry turned to the young Fay man. "I think we owe you our lives."

The Fay broke from his study of the stag to look at Henry. Long, dark tendrils of hair hung around his face, and upon closer examination, his clothes appeared to be made of scraps of whatever he had found in the woods: moss, strips of bark, patches of leaves. His face was smooth and unlined, but his eyes were old and sad.

"Ghillie Dubh," Domin said, nodding to the Fay.

The Ghillie Dubh stood and inclined his head. "Domin." His voice was raspy, as though he were not used to speaking. "It has been many years."

Domin nodded.

"I do not know if I saved your life," the Ghillie Dubh said to Henry. "I only know I should have been able to stop that Unseelie rider long before I did. But my strength is waning. The magic here is not what it once was, and so I begin to fade."

Henry shivered, careful not to glance at Domin. He did not want to think of his friend fading. Instead, Henry studied the Ghillie Dubh. This was another solitary Fay—old and powerful enough to live apart from the Faerie courts and retain his magic, though he did not seem particularly strong standing there, his shoulders drooping and his eyes weary.

The white stag struggled to its feet, limping into the deep nighttime shadows of the trees. Henry watched it go, struck by a sudden sense of loss. He was certain it had been calling to him for help against Jane, but he wished he could know more of the creature and the King it served—one with a deep connection to the land and its magic.

"Did you come here tonight seeking the stag?" the Ghillie Dubh asked, seeing Henry's interest.

Domin shook his head. "We were tracking a different prey before we were distracted by Jane's hunt. Humans. Adult males. We think they came to these ancient woods for dark purposes, but we do not know what or why."

The Ghillie Dubh wrinkled his forehead. "Perhaps I saw those whom you seek yesterday. I watched them. They had strange instruments made of glass and metal, and they studied the oldest of my oaks. But they departed. They seemed disappointed. I do not know what they hoped to find, but I believe they left without it."

Henry groaned. They had been so close to the Grigori. "Then we have let two enemies slip away from us this night."

"You have many adversaries," the Ghillie Dubh said quietly.

"It keeps things interesting," Jairus quipped.

The Ghillie Dubh gestured to several deer trails cutting through the clearing. "But you can only walk one path. Eventually, you must choose the way you will follow."

Henry considered that. Jane had escaped, but the white stag evaded her. For the moment. The Fay built their schemes slowly and on a larger scale. The Grigori were likely to strike again soon. It was like choosing between the crushing power of a landslide or the piercing jab of a dagger.

"We regroup." Jairus gathered his weapons. "Back to Edinburgh."

Henry nodded. Given the chance, Jane would harm the people Henry cared about—not just on the solstice, but every night. Jane, and Titania, and the Grigori, too. Many adversaries, as the Ghillie Dubh said. But if Henry could return to Edinburgh in time, he could marry Cassandra and make certain he was always there to protect her. Henry might not be able to walk more than one path, but that didn't mean he had to walk the one that the Fay or the human world laid out for him.

Chapter Two

Cassandra had never thought much about visiting Scotland. She had never imagined eloping there. But Edinburgh was fast approaching.

Mary dozed fitfully beside Cassandra, the Faerie changeling no doubt oppressed by the constant presence of the iron wheels and rails of the train.

Cassandra didn't let the train's rocking lull her to sleep. The protections on Amy's London home kept dark creatures at bay, but outside of it, the demon mark burned into her hand drew wicked things to her dreams. The previous night, she'd had visions of a rotting tree spreading huge branches that oozed blood across all of England, until its shadow swallowed each of her sisters and friends. She shivered and pushed the image aside.

Amy sat across from Cassandra and Mary in their private first-class train carriage. Her perfect elfin features looked pinched and wan in the fading light, and her fingers twisted a handkerchief until Cassandra was certain the threads would snap.

"At least it's Edinburgh and not Gretna Green," Amy said, her voice as tight as her smile. "And it's a legal marriage, even if it's an irregular one. Henry has resided here for over a month now, after all, and you're traveling with chaperones. Witnesses. It's not the most respectable way to start a life, but once you're settled into married life, no one will ask..." She gave the handkerchief another vicious twist. "The important thing...the most important thing..."

Cassandra smiled and leaned forward to rest a hand over Amy's. The elf's fingers were cold. "The most important thing is that Henry and I will be married and none of our enemies will know."

The words felt so unreal. Cassandra expected to wake up and find herself back in Amy's London home.

Amy let out a slow breath, loosening her grip on the battered handkerchief. "Yes. You're right. My mother would... would kill you if she knew, and then torture Henry for daring to marry against her will. This is the safest way, though it cannot be what you prefer."

"It's not," Cassandra admitted. She touched the little iron rose pin her sister Georgina had painted for her—the one she had once used to stab the Dark Lady. "I wish my family could be here. I wish they could know. But for them to be safe—for Henry to be safe—we can't have banns read and newspaper announcements and everything that would come with a regular marriage. The Fay would find out."

They would punish Henry or threaten Cassandra to manipulate him. Cassandra never wanted to be the cause of Henry's suffering. Yet Cassandra did not think it right to hold their happiness hostage to a change—a freedom—that might never come.

As much as she hated eloping to Scotland, the alternatives were worse.

Cassandra forced a smile. "A Christmas Eve wedding seems auspicious, at least."

Amy buried her face in her handkerchief, her blonde curls falling forward. "I'm helping you elope. I am a terrible chaperone!"

Cassandra laughed. "Not at all! You're here with me, aren't you? Not letting me do this alone."

And Amy had taken the role of mother—or at least older sister—and had a frank discussion with Cassandra about the intimacies of married life. It had left Mary wide-eyed and Cassandra feeling flustered, yet also intrigued.

In fact, this was probably the best chaperoning Amy had done while Cassandra stayed with her. This was merely an elopement leading to a respectable marriage. It wasn't walking into the lands of the dead or facing the Wild Hunt or fighting a mad changeling in the streets of London. No, taken all together, this was one of the more *normal* adventures that Cassandra had enjoyed since leaving home. Her sisters would be scandalized to know she had eloped, but it would be something they could understand—if Cassandra was ever able to tell them. The rest of it... It didn't matter. They could never know about her dealings with the Fay or they would be in even more danger.

The train slowed, approaching Waverly Station. Cassandra gawked out the window. After London's relative flatness, the gas lamps illuminating Edinburgh's steep hills looked like fallen stars trying to climb back to heaven. The constellation of lights glowed against the deep winter darkness falling over the city, though it was still only evening.

Mary stirred and rubbed her eyes, and Amy folded her much-abused handkerchief and tucked it into her reticule. Cassandra wanted to shout with relief at the thought of finally being free from the train, and the iron didn't hurt her as it did her friends. She could only be grateful that they were willing to accompany her, not leave her to travel alone on this outrageous outing.

Flutters multiplied in her stomach. She was getting married. To Henry—her dear Henry. She scanned the train platform, hoping to see him waiting for her, but strange, indifferent faces met her gaze. Her throat tightened. She hadn't heard from him for a week or more, but certainly, he would be there.

She stood and straightened the bustle of her dress—the new one Amy had insisted on buying. Not a wedding gown, exactly, but at least a fine new dress in a very flattering shade of soft blue.

She took her cane while Amy hefted their carpetbags, and they helped Mary from the train. The crowds thinned around them, and they stood uncertainly under the wide ceiling of Waverly Station, the thick stink of coal smoke wafting around them.

A woman in a silk dress bumped into Cassandra and gave her cane a look of disgust before hurrying on to take the arm of a man in a fine black suit.

Cassandra's knuckles whitened as she gripped her cane and scanned the station. Henry would be there. He *would* be.

Amy shifted her carpetbag. "Um, it's been many, *many* years since I visited Scotland, but I've heard the Old Town is not the place to be seen these days. Perhaps—"

"Cassandra!"

The sound washed over her like the warmth of the June sun. She turned to see Henry hurrying toward her, Jairus and Domin just behind. They looked worn and a little rumpled and absolutely wonderful.

Henry caught her, embraced her fiercely, and she buried her face in his shoulder, breathing in his familiar scent, reveling in the comfort of his arms. It was improper to carry on so in public, but so was everything else about this journey. She held him like she would never let go.

"You're a beautiful sight," he whispered, "And you didn't change your mind."

"Of course not! Did you?"

He laughed and pulled back so he could look into her eyes. "Never. I love you. I'm only concerned about the danger to you."

"It's no greater than the danger I'm already in," she lied.

"And now I can always protect you," Henry said, taking her hand and looking at her with such fervent admiration that warmth crept up Cassandra's neck and flushed over her cheeks.

She glanced over, suddenly conscious of the friends around her. Mary looked vaguely annoyed by their affectionate display, Amy stifled a smile, and Jairus grinned openly. Domin stood a little farther back, stoic as ever, though he was paler than before. Both Jairus and Domin were dressed in plain, inconspicuous suits like Henry's, with hats pulled low. Though, Cassandra would swear Henry's hair was a bit longer and wilder now. No doubt a trick of her eyes, since Titania's hold on him kept him frozen in time.

Amy took a step toward Domin but stopped short, concern reflected in her eyes. "And how was Scotland this last month?"

"Rainy," Jairus said. "But the hunting was good."

Henry gave Jairus a stern look, and Cassandra sensed they were keeping something from the women. She would press to discover the secret when they weren't in public.

Jairus cleared his throat. "Well, we cleared an impish group of trows out of an old house, and I almost caught a mermaid."

"She almost caught you," Henry said. "And you would not have liked the results."

Jairus laughed. "Yeah, I'm in no position to settle down right now. I'll leave that to you."

Cassandra's face warmed again at the reminder, and Henry looked back at her with a quick smile.

"And the Grigori?" Amy whispered.

Henry's smile fell. "At least some of them are in Scotland, but we don't know why. They've mostly been in the ancient, wild parts of the land—old forests and such—but we've tracked them to Edinburgh as well."

"Then maybe we shouldn't stand about the train station talking about any of this," Amy said.

Henry nodded, taking Cassandra's carpetbag and then her hand and leading the group out of Waverley Station. His gait was quick, and his gaze darted about. Cassandra kept a firm grip on him and her cane so she wouldn't trip. If he didn't want to be noticed, then she didn't want to create a scene.

Henry traced his thumb over Cassandra's knuckles absentmindedly as they walked. It was only a light touch, but it felt so intimate, almost scandalous. Yet, they were soon to be married. She let the warm sensation course through her.

When they were a distance from the station and the crowds had dwindled, Henry spoke to her again.

"We're staying in New Town, in a hotel on Princes Street. It's much more comfortable than Old Town. There's a stunning view of the castle, and a park I think you'll love. Edinburgh is very lively. There are many prominent physicians here, too. I've managed to hear a couple of lectures. We're near the Assembly Hall, you see. I think Amy could manage to have us admitted for music or dancing. A short honeymoon—"

He stopped, forcing the rest of their party to halt as well, though they hung back to admire the grand architecture of New Town, giving Henry and Cassandra a semblance of privacy.

Henry took off his hat and ran his fingers through his wavy hair. "I know we talked about marrying tonight, on Christmas Eve..."

"Oh." Cassandra's chest tightened. "I suppose it's not possible to find someone to perform the ceremony this late? And not on Christmas Day, either?"

Henry's face softened. "Legally, here in Scotland, we only need to declare our intentions before two witnesses to be married. And the Scots aren't much for Christmas celebrations —the church here discourages the festivities."

"Then what?" Cassandra gripped Henry's hand.

"I don't want you to feel cheated of anything. I want the wedding to feel...real. Official. And to have an authority who can vouch for you if anything happens to me."

"I...I suppose that is wise," Cassandra said.

"You're unhappy."

She clutched his hand more tightly. "I'm *afraid*. We've arranged all this, with so many things working against our happiness. I fear that if we let anything delay us, they may keep us apart forever."

He shifted his fingers, lacing them with hers. "Then we won't wait. I found a solicitor who's willing to perform the marriage, and his home is nearby. Domin believes the man's Sabbath-born, so the Fay won't easily influence him if they ever do come asking questions. But I don't want you to feel rushed."

Cassandra shivered at the reminder of their most dangerous enemies. "I don't. I don't feel rushed, or want to wait, I mean. I trust your judgment in the solicitor."

Henry's eyes sparkled with teasing mischief. "What a good little wife."

Cassandra smirked. "No, I intend to be a very troublesome one, always bothering you to take more care."

He laughed and pulled her in. Their eyes met, and Cassandra's cheeks heated. Henry's gaze drifted down to her lips, and Cassandra leaned closer, thinking only of the thrill of feeling Henry's kiss again.

He cleared his throat. "Yes, uh, we'd best go see that solicitor."

She laughed nervously, dizzy from his closeness. "Lead the way."

Henry called for the others. They detoured to leave the women's baggage at the hotel on Princes Street. While Henry made arrangements with the porter, Cassandra admired the gaslight chandeliers and tall windows of the hotel.

Her attention fell on Amy and Domin standing a short distance from the others. Cassandra couldn't hear what they said, but Amy leaned into Domin, all softness and concern. Domin didn't move away, but he didn't bend toward Amy either—only stood as still as stone and whispered something to her, pain on his face.

Cassandra looked away. It felt like eavesdropping, witnessing some measure of whatever ache and longing lay between them. Domin had sacrificed himself—his well-being— to save Amy's life. They cared for each other. But over centuries of knowing each other, and of living and changing, there would develop obstacles not easily overcome. Cassandra's life was complicated enough, and she was only twenty. Still, she wished she could see all her friends as happy as she was.

Henry returned, touching her shoulder, his fingers trailing down to her elbow. "Are you ready?"

He sounded tentative, as though half-expecting her to turn proper and say no, though his eyes shone with longing.

She took his hand and smiled. "I'm ready."

He grinned in return and kissed her fingers.

Escorted by their friends, they walked a short distance to a narrower but respectable lane.

"Rose Street," Henry whispered to Cassandra.

She smiled. Definitely auspicious.

Henry knocked at one of the tall, narrow houses, and a butler admitted them to an entrance hall illuminated by gaslight. The butler bid them wait while he announced their arrival.

Cassandra kept her tight grip on Henry as if half-expecting one of the Fay to appear and whisk him away from her. The house was quiet except for the ticking of a clock, voices from out on the street, and the occasional shuffle of her friends' boots on the thin rug. It was such a strange beginning to a wedding that Cassandra wondered if the butler would come to shoo them away—tell them it had all been a mistake. Yet in the adjoining sitting room, Cassandra caught sight of a small evergreen tree hung with sweet gifts for Christmas. That little reminder of home and the season filled her with a warm, almost floating sense of hope. She squeezed Henry's hand, and he smiled down at her, no hesitation in his eyes.

The butler reappeared and beckoned them upstairs. Cassandra left her cane by the door, leaning on Henry instead and tracing her free hand up the smooth banister to keep her balance. She was not going to fall now.

They stepped into a well-appointed office. Its sole occupant was an elderly man sitting behind the large desk, only a few tufts of white hair still clinging to his shining pate. He stared for a moment, then smiled.

"Ah, yes, I recall now. You require a marriage, performed without delay. No, no need to explain or look abashed. I've seen enough in my years to know sometimes it's better not to ask prying questions."

Cassandra let out a slow breath. She was grateful he did not make the situation awkward. Or more awkward than it was.

The man pulled out a tome and dusted it off.

"Your names and residences?"

"Henry Stewart. Lately of Edinburgh."

"For at least twenty-one days?" the solicitor asked, giving him a sharp look.

"I've had lodgings here for over a month now," Henry said, putting an arm around Cassandra's waist.

Cassandra found her voice. "I'm Cassandra Weaver of...of London."

"Very well." He wrote the names and scanned their friends. "You have your witnesses I see. More than you need. Are there any prior marriages or impediments of kinship to prevent your legal marriage?"

"None," Henry said firmly.

Cassandra gave a jittery nod of agreement. At least he didn't ask if anyone would object to the marriage.

"Then, do you, Henry Stewart, take Cassandra Weaver to be your wife?"

"I do." He pulled her closer to his side so her skirts swayed around his leg.

"And do you, Cassandra Weaver, take Henry Stewart to be your husband?"

"I do," she said, proud of how level and clear the words came out when everything inside her felt warm and trembly.

The solicitor scribbled a notation and closed the book. "It's done then. According to the laws of Scotland, you are husband and wife."

Cassandra stared at him. She understood that an irregular marriage was less formal and wouldn't evoke religion, but was it really that simple? She glanced at Henry, who also looked uncertain.

The solicitor smiled and gave them an encouraging nod. "Go on. You may kiss your bride."

Cassandra flushed and smiled at Henry. He kissed her gently, his lips lingering, promising many more kisses to come. She pulled him closer and returned the kiss.

Jairus gave a whoop, and Henry and Cassandra broke apart, both chuckling. Henry's cheeks reddened, though probably not to match the heat flooding Cassandra's face.

The solicitor cleared his throat good-naturedly. "If you wish to have the marriage registered and obtain a certificate, you must simply declare to a sheriff that you have an unregistered marriage and pay a small fine."

Henry nodded his thanks, and Cassandra mimicked him, but of course, they would not want that. The fewer people who knew, the safer they would be.

And yet, they *were* married. With those few words, their lives were changed. At least, whatever else the Fay might do, they could not say that Henry did not belong to Cassandra, nor she to him. She felt the change even in the way Henry held her hand as he guided her back out of the house, an extra protectiveness in his grip. An extra sense of rightness and belonging.

"Congratulations," Jairus said, once they were back on the street. He dodged a group of boisterous young men no doubt headed for a night at their club. "I suppose I'll have to find a better time to ask for a dance with the bride."

Henry gave him a quelling look, and Jairus laughed.

"It was lovely after all," Amy said quietly. Her poor handkerchief made another appearance to dab at her eyes.

Cassandra stifled a bubbly giggle and embraced Amy and then Mary as well. "I'm so glad you could both be here."

In lieu of her sisters, at least her closest friends could be by her side for one of the most important days of her life. She clung to them, afraid to let the moment slip away.

Domin drew a sharp breath and whispered, "The Grigori! Heading this way."

Chapter Three

Henry grabbed Cassandra and pulled her into the shadows of an adjacent building. Cassandra clung to him. Could their enemies not have given her one evening's peace? But no, that was the whole reason for this hurried, secret wedding.

Domin blocked Amy and Mary from the view of passersby as they scrambled out of sight. The barrel of Jairus's pistol flashed in the light from a nearby gas lamp.

A man in a frock coat and top hat approached slowly, his empty hands raised. The tailoring of his suit spoke of wealth and London. Cassandra didn't recognize the man, but she guessed from Henry's disgusted expression that they'd crossed paths before.

"Stop right there." Jairus leveled his pistol at the Grigori's heart.

The Grigori wet his lips and looked over his shoulder. "Thank goodness I found you! I've been tracking you. Trying to warn you."

Jairus snorted and cocked his pistol.

The man waved his hands. "It's true! Rushford is going too far this time. His plan...it's enough to cripple the Fay. Maybe destroy them. But it will destroy us as well."

"Destroy the Grigori?" Henry asked, stepping forward to keep himself between Cassandra and the man.

"No, *all* of us. All of Britain. Maybe beyond if—"

A gunshot rang out, echoing off the stone buildings. The Grigori made a gurgling noise and sank to the ground, blood flowing down the front of his shirt and coat. Cassandra gasped and covered her mouth. Had Jairus shot the man?

But Jairus turned his gun on someone across the way and fired. The person fled.

"What..." Henry looked back at Cassandra, her shock echoed in his expression.

"After him!" Jairus called.

He took off at a run, Domin on his heels.

Henry kissed Cassandra once, fiercely, and pressed a set of keys into her hand. He breathed, "I'll hurry back to you."

And then he was gone with Domin and Jairus.

"Well!" Amy exclaimed. Her indignation faded as she glanced at the dead man. "We probably should not be found here."

Cassandra nodded her agreement. She gently grabbed Mary, who stared in wide-eyed horror at the body, and hurried away. Only when they put the scene behind them did Cassandra's hands begin to tremble. What had happened? A warning and a murder. What did it mean? A flash of her dream returned to her, of the dying tree spreading its shadow over Britain. She shook the image off and quickened her step.

It wasn't difficult to find the hotel on Princes Street again and determine which room belonged to whom: one clean and prepared for Amy and Mary, one occupied by Domin and

Jairus's belongings, and one that was Henry's. Henry's and Cassandra's. If Henry returned safely from his pursuit. Her pulse beat fast in her throat.

"I don't like the idea of anyone being alone after that," Amy said to Cassandra. "We should help you with your dress, at least, since we didn't bring a maid."

"Thank you," Cassandra said quietly.

She led Amy and Mary into the room and bolted the door behind them.

"Do you believe what that man said?" Mary whispered, looking down at her hands as if afraid they might vanish.

Cassandra looked between Mary and Amy, both Fay. "Surely there's nothing that can destroy *all* the Fay."

Amy frowned. "There are ancient stories of very powerful magics, but anything that would destroy Faerie magic would also..."

"Destroy the human world?" Cassandra asked quietly.

They stood in silence for a long moment.

Amy huffed. "What a thought! And on today of all days. It is a lovely dress." She circled Cassandra with an approving nod. "It is a lovely dress, and it was a lovely wedding. If only..." She loosened the buttons at the back of the bodice. "If only..." She jerked the lacings of Cassandra's corset free, making Cassandra's breath hitch. "If only I had even a fraction of my mother's power!"

Cassandra scrambled to catch the front of the dress before it slipped down. "You wouldn't want to use your mother's power the way she does, though."

Amy dropped into a chair and put her head in her hands. "I am so tired of being helpless. Of watching the people I care about suffer."

Cassandra and Mary shared a worried look.

Cassandra stepped out of the dress and set it aside, pulling a nightgown over her thin linen chemise. Then she knelt by her friend. "You've done so much for us—all of us. We're not entirely helpless. The odds are simply—"

"They saw Jane Tudor here in Scotland. That was what Henry didn't want Mr. Hale to mention at the train station. But Domin thought I—we—should know. Jane was hunting the white stag. The one Mary's sister connected to the Fisher King."

"Why?" Mary whispered.

"I don't know." Amy looked resigned, then her eyes flashed with anger. "But we do know Jane still serves the Dark Lady, and she still hates Henry. More than ever. She's bent on vengeance against all of us. People are murdered in the street in front of us. And Domin won't admit it, but he's suffering." Amy's voice caught. "He's not as strong as he was. I'm afraid... so afraid he's dying. Slowly. Painfully."

"Oh." Cassandra clasped Amy's hands, trying to provide what small comfort she could.

But comforting words felt cheap in the face of such heavy news. Cassandra gazed out the window toward the blackness of the park, the city's gas lamps offering faint illumination of the castle looming over the city. The night was so oppressively wide and deep, threatening to swallow those faint beacons that dared oppose its reign.

She glanced at Mary, who balled her hands into fists. Her face had gone linen-white, but determination lit her eyes.

Cassandra straightened. "I suppose, then, we should all have a good rest. It has been a long journey, and we will need to be fresh for whatever comes next. We have to be ready to fight for the people we care about."

Amy stood and lifted her chin. "You are right, of course.

Come, Mary." She turned for the door, then hesitated. "Sleep well. And...congratulations."

Cassandra offered her friends a weak smile, but as soon as she was alone, she bolted the door again and hurried to the window, peering out as though she might see what dangers Henry faced. As though she might help him somehow. Should she have gone with him? No, she would have slowed the pursuit. But, contrary to her advice to Amy, she was not going to sleep. Not until Henry was safely returned to her. To keep her mind busy, she unpinned her hair and unpacked her carpetbag to retrieve her brush. She arranged her clothes in the closet beside Henry's, pausing to breathe in his familiar scent.

In less than an hour—though it felt much longer—male voices echoed in the corridor, and a soft tap sounded on the door.

"Yes?" Cassandra asked, just to be cautious.

"We've returned," Henry whispered.

She unbolted the door, and Henry slipped into the room and locked them inside. He turned to her and stopped short, and she realized she stood before him in only her nightgown, her hair loose around her shoulders. She and Henry had been on more familiar terms than most newly married couples, having both stayed at Amy's house in London, but never anything this intimate or informal. Henry stared, seemingly dumbstruck.

A warm flush tingled over Cassandra's face and spread down her neck. She did not know what a wife was meant do to in these circumstances—in any circumstances. "Ah, um, the Grigori, then?"

Henry let out a ragged sigh and tossed his hat and coat onto a chair. "Whoever shot our would-be informant escaped. Likely another of the Grigori trying to silence him. He boarded a train, and it was away before any of us could catch up with it. Probably headed back to London." He ran his fingers through his hair. "I'm sorry. I hoped we could at least pretend for a short while... But I'm afraid the honeymoon I hoped to offer you, such as it was, will have to be cut short. I don't know if that man was telling the truth, but we can't ignore what he said."

Cassandra stood beside him. At least she could offer some comfort. Some hope. She gently smoothed his ruffled hair back into some semblance of order, twisting one of the messy curls around her finger. "Of course, we can't ignore them entirely. I don't mind about missing the Assembly Hall or...or those other things. We can enjoy our time together in London, too."

Henry opened his mouth to protest, but Cassandra placed a fingertip over his lips, then stroked his jaw. He closed his eyes.

"We can't ignore the Grigori entirely," she whispered. "Not until we've stopped them. But maybe we can ignore them for tonight?"

Henry's posture of frustration and despair fell away. He opened his eyes and clasped her hand, his touch gentle, warm, a little unsteady. Kissed each of her fingertips and then her palm, sending a thrill through her.

"Yes, I think we *can* ignore them for tonight," he said, his voice low. "For tonight, it's only us. If you're certain?"

She drew a shaky breath and stared into his eyes, so full of love and concern. She placed her hand on his chest. His heart beat fast under her fingertips.

"I am afraid sometimes when I think about the Fay and the Grigori," she said. "I believe what I've said, though. We can't let fear rule our lives. I want to be yours for whatever time we have. For forever. I love you."

"I love you," he whispered. "I'll keep you beside me and protect you from whatever storms come our way."

"We'll face them together."

Warmth flooded through her as she said it, dissolving the last of her fears. This—her and her Henry together—was right. She defied the Fay and anyone else who tried to tear them apart.

She ran her hand up to Henry's neck and pulled him closer, closing her eyes. He kissed her tentatively on her forehead. Her cheek. The corner of her mouth. Finally finding her lips. She returned the kiss, and he deepened it, slow and certain as if they truly had forever together. Then he wrapped his arms around her and lifted her, swinging her around as he kissed her, and in his arms, she felt like she could fly away and leave every worry behind.

Six Months Later

Chapter Four

Spirits rode abroad on St. John's Eve, but the people of London didn't know it. Mary knew, though. She peeked through the curtain of Amy's drawing room at the dark square. Amy's house was the only one where a cross made of fennel hung above the door and a fire burned in the hearth through the midsummer night.

Mary shivered despite the warmth and pulled the curtain shut. Her heart hammered, though she told herself that no malevolent spirits were likely to notice her there. People rarely paid her heed, and she had helped ward Amy's house against their enemies. But Mary felt alone, exposed, since most of her friends had gone out hunting the Grigori. The occultists had been snatching bodies, and Henry was convinced they were going to try some forsaken ritual on that night when the dark things of the world began to awaken with the summer past its zenith.

Soft footsteps made her jump, and she whirled to see Lucien standing in the doorway. Between his soft brown skin and the dark cloak he wore with the hood pulled up, he blended well into the shadows. He held out a cloak for Mary.

"Are you certain about this?" he whispered.

Mary glanced once more at the curtained window. Images of Fay monsters flitted through her imagination, but she stared at the fire to banish them.

"You think the Fay will hunt for changelings tonight?" she asked.

"They like children born on auspicious days like today. They hope they will have more power for the Fay to steal and manipulate."

Mary took the cloak. "Then we have to try to stop them."

She understood why Henry and the others focused on the Grigori—the cultists terrified her, with their determination to control and possibly destroy magic. But Mary could do nothing against the Grigori, not compared to her other friends, and she had seen the changeling children bound in the Faerie realm. At least maybe she could help one child remain free.

Mary pulled the hood low, hoping her pale face didn't stand out more starkly against the dark fabric, and followed Lucien out the back door and through the garden.

He helped her over the garden wall, his grip firm on her hand, and the warmth of his touch lingering long after he released her.

"Are you sure *you* want to do this?" Mary asked as they snuck through the foggy night. "It's dangerous, and the others may be angry."

Lucien shoved his hands in the pocket of his trousers. "I don't think Amy will throw me out, and I don't think any Fay are looking for me at this moment. Anyway, it's a risk worth taking if we can save anyone."

Mary nodded and hurried to keep step with Lucien. He was

only a little taller than her, but despite his mistreatment at the hands of the Fay, he walked with a confident swagger. Maybe it was the terrible ability the Fay had given him—silver words that charmed anyone not immune to magic—but it reminded her of the Unseelie elf Fitzhugh. Lucien's father. Not that she would ever mention the resemblance.

Perhaps it was thinking of Fitzhugh, but a creeping feeling prickled over her skin. Like someone watched her. She glanced over her shoulder. No, it was not in her mind. The fog swirled behind them as though someone had just been there. And too many footsteps echoed off the buildings.

"We're being followed," she whispered.

Lucien slowed and looked behind them. "Where?"

"I don't know, but I hear someone."

Lucien straightened and called out, "Show yourself."

The power in his words sent a shiver through Mary. She was immune to magic as a Faerie changeling, but she could still feel the force of his command. Whoever followed them would have to obey. Unless it was the Fay.

"You could just ask nicely," drawled a voice from the fog.

Jairus stepped into view, his broad-brimmed hat pulled low, hiding the scars marring the right side of his face after the Grigori had shot him the previous year. His hand casually brushed the pistol at his hip—the one loaded with silver bullets—and he carried a shotgun full of iron pellets holstered on his back. He gave Mary a friendly nod.

Mary sighed. As a priest—although a very unconventional one—Jairus could withstand Faerie magic. But he should have been hunting the Grigori with the others.

"What are you doing here?" Lucien asked.

Jairus glanced over his shoulder, frowning at the fog. "The Grigori slipped through our fingers again, and restless spirits are roaming the city tonight. God told me I ought to pay them some heed." He glanced back at them. "But that doesn't answer why you're out here in the dark. If the Fay find you—"

"We're going to find them first," Lucian said.

Jairus looked confused for a moment, then his expression softened. "Ah, this is about your argument with Stewart over the changelings. But how are you going to find one kid in this huge city?"

Lucien met Jairus's gaze with a defiant glare. "I've been investigating. Sneaking out—"

Jairus raised an eyebrow at that.

Lucien hurried on. "Only during the day. And I've been... talking with people. They've told me about a strange lady asking questions about pregnant women. She's looking for illegitimate children who might have aristocratic fathers."

Jairus grunted. "The Fay and their obsession with bloodlines. I guess I'm too American to make any sense of it."

Lucien shrugged. "Sometimes it's about changelings who might have magical abilities—that should make sense even to an American. But as for royal bloodlines...there's something else there. Something the Lords and Ladies are planning, but I've never discovered what."

"Well, there's no sign of the Grigori tonight. Which way to this mysterious lady of yours?"

Lucien pointed toward the East End. "Where else? Where there's plenty of misery, of course."

Jairus studied the fog, seeing things Mary could only guess at, then he nodded. "Let's go."

Mary shivered and looked around, partly wishing she could see what Jairus saw, and mostly glad she couldn't. She stayed safely tucked between Lucien and Jairus as they walked toward the poor neighborhoods of the East End. She'd justified going with Lucien in case he needed help. She had her crossbow, of course, and she could run for help. But with Jairus there, she felt silly. Unnecessary. She had learned she could be brave when needed, but she was always in the shadows of Cassandra and Amy—they were shining figures she didn't know how to hold even a glimmer next to.

They approached one of the workhouses. Mary shuddered thinking of the poor families living behind those thick, dark walls.

"Now there's a place of misery," Jairus muttered. "But I thought it was for poor families. How would the Fay know which child had the sort of bloodlines they're looking for? Or if a child was expected to be born this night?"

"They might glamour the master into telling them," Lucien said, but he sounded unsure.

"What about the Foundling Hospital?" Mary asked.

Both of them looked at her in confusion, and she realized that, having lived in the Faerie realm and America, respectively, neither knew as much about England as she did.

"It's where mothers can leave illegitimate children," she said. "People usually apply to deliver their babies to the Foundling Hospital. But the desperate sometimes leave their babies and hope the hospital will take them."

"A perfect opportunity for the Fay to take them instead," Lucien said.

Jairus nodded, looking grim.

They made their way west to the Foundling Hospital in the fashionable Bloomsbury neighborhood. The imposing brick building sat well back in the grounds, the courtyard in front of it guarded by a wall and three solid gatehouses. Yet through all those barriers, Mary glimpsed green, a little refuge in the city for those not wanted elsewhere.

"Keep out of sight," Jairus whispered.

They pressed themselves against the front wall in the shadow of one of the gatehouses.

Mary's feet tingled from standing in the damp chill, and she began to think they were wasting their time, when a hooded figure cut through the fog. It held a squalling baby to its chest. Mary shifted, ready to intercept the desperate mother and offer to take the baby before the Fay had the opportunity, but Jairus put a hand out.

"Wait," he whispered. "Look at him."

Mary looked again. The figure—male—walked hesitantly, looking over his shoulder as if frightened, and he trailed water behind him.

"He has Faerie magic," Lucien whispered.

"Seelie or Unseelie?" Jairus asked.

Lucien's forehead wrinkled. "Seelie, I think."

"They steal babies, too," Mary said darkly.

Jairus nodded. "We surround him quickly so he doesn't have time to hurt the baby."

Mary nodded and clutched her crossbow.

Jairus whispered, "One...two...three!"

They leapt out and formed a ring around the young man— hardly more than a boy. He clutched the baby protectively, his eyes wide. His cloak and suit, several decades out of fashion, were dry, but water puddled around his feet.

Jairus flashed his gun. "I have iron shot here. Return the infant or I'll have to use it on you."

"Return it?" the young man asked, blue eyes wide in a pale face. "Are you mad? It will die. That's why I brought it here."

"Wait," Lucien told Jairus. He peered at the young man and the infant. "The baby is Fay. We're too late."

The young man cradled the infant. "They left this baby

after they stole the human one. The mother was going to toss it into the river. I couldn't watch it die like so many other hopeless souls."

Mary lowered her crossbow.

"You're a changeling!" Lucien said. "Does your Lady know you're doing this?"

"Quiet!" the young man said, checking over his shoulder. "I don't have a *Lady*. Not all Fay are the same, you realize. But you —you're Unseelie." He backed away from Lucien.

"We're changelings, too," Mary said. "We want to help others like us. What's your name?"

The young man shifted and wet his lips. "I'm...I'm Richard. And if you want to help the changelings, watch over those of royal blood. They are well guarded, but not always well enough. As your current monarchs learned to their sorrow this spring."

Mary's forehead wrinkled, then she gasped. "The Crown Prince lost a child in April."

"The Fay didn't manage to seize it," Richard said, "which we should be grateful for, but the child lost its life. Those with royal blood are in more danger now than ever."

"Why?" Jairus asked.

"I wish I knew, but I do hear rumors. Some of the Ladies have plans to change the balance of our worlds. And they need changelings. Human changelings—royal if possible." He gave a start at a sound from the fog. "But this is not my world. Perhaps you can care for this child better."

He held out the bundled child, so tiny in its dirty blanket. Mary accepted the infant—some poor Faerie child like her, cast off into a world that did not want it.

With that, Richard retreated. The water he'd been standing in followed him like an eager puppy trailing around his feet. Mary blinked in surprise. What kind of power was that?

"Well, that was encouraging," Jairus drawled.

The Faerie baby gave a weak whimper and brought its fist to its mouth. Already, the iron of the human world would be hurting it.

"What do we do with this child?" she asked. "We can't take care of it."

Jairus gestured at the Foundling Hospital. "That water changeling had the right idea. Let's leave it on the steps of the hospital. Surely, they wouldn't let it die."

Mary was not so certain. Lucien was watching her, caught her hesitation.

He smiled. "I'll persuade them not to. We can't help every cast-off child in London, but we'll make certain this one grows up with food in its belly and a safe place to sleep."

Mary nodded, glad to see Lucien finding positive uses for his silver-tongued gift. She glanced back once to where Richard had vanished, and a gust of wind from the Thames blew over her, cold and foul smelling. She tugged her hood back up and hurried after her friends.

Chapter Five

Henry paced Amy's drawing room as Jairus recounted his conversation with the water changeling. Domin listened silently, but Henry could not be still. He should have been there, trying to wring more information out of this changeling, Richard. No, he couldn't have been there. They'd been tracking the Grigori...

But the Grigori had evaded them, as slippery as a trout. The cultists had stolen another body, though. A young woman this time. Freshly dead. Henry couldn't imagine what they were doing, and he wished he didn't have to find out. He ran his fingers through his hair.

"Lucien did manage to convince the Foundling Hospital to take the child," Jairus said. He lowered his voice. "It's frightening enough that the Fay can manipulate people's emotions. Seeing someone do it who can lie as well... Don't the Fay think through the magic they give to humans?"

Henry stopped, watching the second hand tick around the face of Amy's enchanted clock. Its spell kept them safe, but precious seconds slipped away while their enemies did —what?

"The Fay know that giving Faerie magic to humans can be unpredictable," Domin said.

Henry rubbed the scars on his wrist. "That's why they rule their changelings with such cruelty."

Changelings like the child stolen while he hunted the Grigori. He gritted his teeth. He almost sympathized with the Grigori's desire to eliminate the Fay. The Fay's cruelty was terrible but also predictable. What the Grigori were doing scared Henry more because he didn't understand it. Not just the body snatching. Visiting old woods. Questioning people whose families had lived in the area for generations—and killing some of them so no one could discover what the Grigori had learned. Henry and his friends were no closer to uncovering whatever scheme their informant had warned could destroy all of Britain.

"You at least should have told us what you were doing," Henry said to Jairus. "It could have been a trap."

Jairus shrugged. "We weren't having any luck with the Grigori, and God told me I should pay attention to what Lucien and Miss Leland were up to. Good thing, too. That soggy changeling warned us the Fay are planning something— something to do with changelings. Especially those of royal blood."

"Jane and I," Henry grumbled.

"There aren't any others?" Jairus asked.

Henry glanced at Domin.

"There have been in the past," Domin said. "It's possible some still live, though they would be lying low."

Henry ran his hands through his hair. "This could be a misdirection. Changelings can lie."

"But he did seem to want to help the abandoned child," Jairus said. "And he said he didn't follow any of the Ladies."

"No, it must be one of the Lords," Henry said. "Probably the Lord of the Thames."

"Is he friendly?" Jairus asked. "It would be nice to have an ally among the Fay."

"I wouldn't say he's friendly." Domin looked thoughtful. "But he's pragmatic. It might be worth investigating what interest he's taken in human affairs."

Domin and Jairus fell into a discussion about the water Fays' usual disinterest in land dwellers. Henry listened distractedly, but he ended up studying Domin's face. A greyish cast underlay his friend's brown skin, and fine lines showed beside his eyes. Domin didn't complain—he never complained—but Henry suspected his pain was constant and exhausting. How long could they keep doing this?

Discussing Faerie politics wasn't going to help them. He leaned against the wall and shut his eyes, sensing the cords of magic binding him to the Fay. Woven through those were the tendrils of power connecting him to the energy of the land—magic he possessed because of his royal bloodlines. Whatever the Fay wanted with royal changelings, it had to have something to do with that connection.

Henry mentally felt his way along the threads of power coursing through him. The connection to the land sang a quiet harmony—very faint in the city, but always a part of him. The Faerie magic, though, was a constant irritant, like a splinter in his fingertip. He couldn't just pull the splinter free because the magics had grown and twisted together. Without magic to sustain him, he would crumble to dust. If it came down to a confrontation with Titania, he would do it—hurting her as much as possible in the process—but that would leave Cassandra all alone—

"Uh, Stewart?" Jairus's voice broke through his concentration.

Henry blinked and looked around to find that he had painted the walls and floor with frost that sparkled in the summer sunlight flowing through the curtains. That was what happened when he touched the Faerie magic: it wiggled out of his control.

"Apologies," Henry said.

He stalked out into the corridor and took a deep breath. His worries raced between the Fay and the Grigori until a headache pulsed behind his eyes.

He found Cassandra in the dining room, picking at a late breakfast. She'd been out hunting the Grigori with them, and she'd looked so tired, he'd been careful not to wake her early. His wife. The thought still took his breath away. Cassandra was his, and he was hers. Whatever else the Fay had taken from him —might still take from him—they couldn't take the happiness of these few months away.

She looked up and grinned, her eyes brightening, and he managed a smile in return.

"Good morning," she said, standing to greet him with a kiss.

He pulled her close, marveling at the miracle of being able to hold her, feeling her warm and soft in his arms. As if sensing his unease, she returned a tight embrace.

"What were they doing?" she asked, reaching up to stroke his hair and almost making him forget what she was talking about.

He sighed. "They thought it was wise to go out hunting for Fay who might steal the unbaptized on St. John's Eve."

She pulled back to look at him. "Did they succeed?"

His shoulders sagged. "No. They were too late." Another defeat. All of their enemies were a step ahead of them.

"Oh, dear. If only..." She trailed off and bit her lip.

"If only the rest of us had helped?" Henry asked bitterly.

"Lucien did mention his concern."

"But we knew the Grigori were in London, and if they're planning something so dangerous it could harm our world..." Cold zinged along Henry's arms as his frustration built. Cassandra shivered, but she leaned in, not away from him. He tried to calm his temper. "We were so close to catching them this time. And it's not safe to divide like that—especially not for Lucien to go out. If the Dark Lady discovered he was here—"

"I know. But we did what we thought best—each of us did. We can't let the Grigori hurt anyone else. Or the Fay harm anyone, either." Her uncertainty echoed his own.

He sighed and guided her so they could both sit at the table. He laced his fingers with hers, running his thumb over the warm ridge of her knuckle. "I'm afraid," he admitted, knowing he could say to her what he wouldn't dare say to anyone else. "I'm afraid I'm making the wrong choices, and people will suffer for it."

Cassandra met his gaze, her hazel eyes intense. "It's not you causing the suffering."

"Not anymore. But I want—I need—to do more than simply not cause suffering. I've used my abilities to hurt people. Now, I need to use them to make up for some of those hurts."

Cassandra squeezed his hand. "You will. I mean, I think you already have, and I think you'll do even more."

"I don't know how much time we have." Henry turned his hand over. Beyond the scars lacing his wrists swirled a blue tattoo—the mark binding Henry, Domin, and Titania with Domin's oath to protect Henry.

"It's fading," Cassandra said quietly. "He's not doing well, is he?"

Henry shook his head. "The blade will keep eating away at his magic—Faerie and then daemon. I don't know what will happen to him when his magic is gone. Spring-heeled Jack is still alive, but he didn't have the blade trapped in him."

"And Titania must know as well," Cassandra said quietly.

Henry frowned at his wrist. "Yes, hers will be fading, too. She'll know Domin and I are both vulnerable. I'm only surprised she hasn't acted yet. Perhaps because she still fears Domin, but it won't be long before she seeks to take advantage of the situation. I don't know what I'll do. Fitzhugh thought I could be strong enough to break away from her. He thought I could protect the changelings." Henry shook his head.

"I think he's correct," Cassandra said. "I think you're stronger than you know."

Henry kissed her hand. "I hope you're right."

Not just for his sake, or even for Cassandra's. On the Twilight Path, he had promised the restless spirits he would try to undo some of the harm the Fay had caused—and that he had caused for the Fay. Freeing the changelings would accomplish that, but if Henry couldn't free himself, he didn't see how he could help anyone else. Henry thought often of the Ghillie Dubh in Scotland—not an especially powerful Fay, but able to stay free from the courts and protect his land. What strength did he have that Henry lacked?

"The problem is we're running in too many directions," Cassandra said, interrupting his thoughts. "We believed the Grigori would try something on St. John's Eve because it's a powerful night for magic, and they've been acquiring ritual objects. The ram's tallow candles and the...the corpses."

"Yes," Henry said. The grave robbing had him especially concerned. They might be experimenting on corpses, but there were especially dark rituals that used parts of the human body.

"But maybe they weren't prepared, or it wasn't the right night. The next powerful day is in August, isn't it? Lammas—a day of harvest." She shivered when she said it.

"It is." Henry sighed. "So little time to discover what they plan to do."

"Do we actually have to know their plan to stop it?"

Henry looked at her. "What do you mean?"

"Of course, ideally we would know exactly what they wanted to accomplish, but if we suspect they'll try a ritual in August, we only have to be ready to intercept them."

"I suppose that's true."

"Then, in the meantime, we can spend a little time trying to discover what the Fay are planning."

Henry considered that. If the informant murdered in Edinburgh was correct, the Grigori's plans threatened to upend their world. He could not ignore that. But they could not afford to ignore the water Fay's warning. It would do them no good to save the world from the Grigori only to lose it to the Fay. Henry didn't like the idea of dividing their forces, but maybe they could divide their time.

"Let's talk to the others, but I think you might be right," Henry said. "How did I get lucky enough to have such a clever wife?"

Cassandra beamed at him. "Maybe by being so clever yourself."

Henry gripped her hand. He hoped he could be everything

she saw in him—or even a part of it—before it was too late for any of them.

Chapter Six

Amy tried to focus on her friends' argument about the Fay and the Grigori, but she almost couldn't hear what they said past the emotions they flung along with their words.

"You should just ignore them." Telesm's mouth curled at one corner. "They'll fight each other, maybe solve both your problems at once."

Lucien jabbed a finger at Telesm. "You might be able to ignore the depravities the Fay commit against changelings, but I never will."

"Whoa, there." Jairus held his hands out. "We're not ignoring the Fay. But the Grigori are killing people. When I think of that old woman they murdered in Glamorgan..." He shuddered.

Amy shivered in sympathy, the others' anger and frustration washing over her in waves of heat and ice. Beneath it all, she felt the thing none of them spoke: a cold slithering whose unwelcome touch sent goose bumps over Amy's shoulders and worked its way into her heart, making her pulse race and her knuckles turn white where she gripped the edge of the chair.

Domin cast her a concerned look. She took a deep breath and released her grip on her chair. The coils loosened around her heart. She closed her eyes, trying to shut out all the feelings.

Amy should not have been able to sense her friends' emotions—they were all immune to Faerie magic. At least, she should not have felt them so strongly, not more than a whiff like distant smoke in the air. But this was thick, choking, filling her throat and burning her eyes. Ever since she had thrown the full force of her emotions at the Leannan to confuse and overwhelm the Faerie monster, Amy was more...open. She didn't think she pressed her emotions on others unawares, but theirs flowed into her, unbidden and uncontrolled. Was this how Domin had always felt?

She glanced at him, but he watched the others now, willing to let them argue. Too tired to join the argument.

A warning prickled over Amy's scalp as if she were being watched. But her friends were focused on their discussion, and the curtains were tightly shut against the afternoon sun.

Amy focused on the pendulum on her clock. The spell created by Amy, Mary, and Lucien together now wove its way through the gears of the clock and poured around the house with every click—the beating heart of the living spell. As long as the hands moved, Amy's house was a refuge where neither the Fay nor the Grigori could touch them—not directly. At least, that's what she hoped.

"We're not forgetting them," Henry said. "But we need a different strategy. Right now, we're chasing the Grigori, left to witness their...their inhumanity but helpless to stop it. I want to get ahead of them. The next date they're likely to try a ritual is Lammas, the first of August."

Jairus nodded. "So, we cut them off. But even if we don't need to know what ritual they're performing, we do need to know where."

Amy's shoulders itched. As if a hand hovered close, about to brush the back of her neck.

"Old woods," Domin said. "Whatever they're after, that's the common thread."

He glanced at Telesm, who shrugged. "There are many ancient and dangerous creatures in old forests and trees."

"In Scotland, I had nightmares of a rotting tree reaching over England," Cassandra said.

Domin studied her. "Could you tell where it was located?"

She shook her head, her lips pursed in frustration.

Ding, ding, ding, the clock's bells chimed a mad ringing not associated with the hour.

Amy started and covered her ears. The sound echoed inside her skull.

"The wards!" Telesm's eyes flashed with excitement.

Everyone jumped to their feet, and Domin swished the curtains back to peer outside.

"What's out there?" Cassandra asked.

Domin shook his head. "I see nothing out of the ordinary."

"Is the spell defective?" Mary whispered.

"I don't think so," Amy said, rubbing her ear. "I believe it's been trying to warn me. I felt...something wrong. I didn't know what it was."

Domin pulled the curtains shut, making sure they were tight. "Whatever it was, it's gone. The spell served its purpose."

Amy cocked her head, listening. Domin was right. The unease had melted away, leaving only wisps of fear and alarm in the room.

She nodded, and her friends warily returned to their seats.

"Well," Jairus drawled. "It's clear we have to act."

Henry looked to Lucien, who sat upright and defiant in his chair like a martyr about to face the Inquisition.

"How did you know the Fay were looking for more changelings to steal?" Henry asked.

Lucien lifted his chin. "I've been lurking around the bad parts of the city, listening. Someone had to pay attention to the Fay."

Henry took a slow breath, giving Lucien a look of displeasure that spoke volumes. "And what exactly did you hear?"

"The Fay have been haunting workhouses, foundling hospitals, midwives in the East End. They're looking for changelings—for auspicious ones, I'd say."

"Are they usually so active in hunting for changelings?" Cassandra asked.

Domin shook his head. "They're more likely to wait for a promising child to cross their paths. This must relate to what the changeling Richard said. They need human changelings for something."

Silence fell over the group.

"I'm going to the workhouses," Henry said.

Everyone looked at him.

"What?" Amy asked.

"As a surgeon-in-training. I have enough experience to be helpful to the sick there, and I might be able to discover if the Fay have been there, and what they're looking for."

Amy didn't say it, but she thought everyone should stay in the house where it was safe. She didn't like the idea of any of them going out alone. Everyone else nodded their agreement, though, so she kept her thoughts to herself.

Jairus talked with Henry and Cassandra about his ideas for

tracking the Fay as they left the room, and Telesm demanded Mary and Lucien follow him for some sort of changeling magic lesson. That left Amy alone with Domin.

Her heart fluttered. Silly. It wasn't like she hadn't known Domin for years—centuries—and she'd certainly been alone with him many times before.

Domin frowned and parted the curtains a crack. The fog had burned away, and it would be a lovely summer day, but the sunny world beyond the window pane seemed far removed, something to be admired but not touched.

Amy came to stand behind him. He shifted slightly and glanced down to acknowledge her. She stood stiffly, too aware of all the unsaid things that had hung between them over the last months. Domin had said he didn't want to live in a world without her. Or, she was fairly certain that was what he'd said. She had been so close to death. Close enough to feel its breath on her skin. Domin had given up his own opportunity at healing to bring her back. And now...

He spoke politely to Amy—was kind to her—but he acted as though nothing had changed.

She ached at it. At being near him constantly, but not any closer than before. Not after that moment. He might be content, but she could not be. She was happy to have him around, happy to be his friend again, but she had been so certain that they might be something more.

"Domin." She put a hand on his arm.

He turned to her, his watchful gaze softening as it fell on her face, and they stared at each other for a long moment.

"Amy." He spoke her name gently. Intimately. There was a longing there. She knew she wasn't imagining it. It was raw. Mingled with uncertainty.

"Are you concerned about the Grigori?" he asked. "We failed to find them this time, but—"

Domin should have been able to sense her emotions. Should have known what she felt wasn't worry. And she should not have been able to feel these raw, unfiltered sensations from him.

"I'm concerned about you," she said, her voice low. "About us."

She'd said it all wrong, but from the surprised and guarded expression that crossed Domin's face, he understood more than she meant him to.

"Amy," he said again, though this time he sounded tired. "You know that... Have you ever met a daemon—a full-blooded daemon?"

She hesitated, trying to remember. "I don't think I have."

He nodded. "They've become very rare. They're always a little more spirit than matter—it's why I can, or could, change my appearance—but if the bloodline they're bound to weakens or dies out, they fade." He stared at his hands.

"You think you're going to fade away!" Amy grabbed his hands, solid but perhaps colder than they used to be. "No. You're bound to Henry, and he's still here. None of us are going to vanish."

He gripped her hands back, looking sadly at their interlocked fingers. "We don't know. Henry may succeed in freeing himself from Titania. He may choose to age. Or she may take revenge on him. I would do what I could to stop her..."

"She's still frightened of you," Amy said. "And Telesm may find a way to remove the fragment. I know...I know you have seen many difficult years. But you needn't assume the worst."

He smiled a little. "Amy, I'm here to protect all of you. That means I have to think of the worst. To be prepared."

"That sounds exhausting," she said quietly.

He sighed, his shoulders sagging. "It is."

Amy squeezed his hands and then released them. She didn't want to add to his burdens with questions he perhaps wasn't ready to answer yet. Or, with questions she didn't want to hear the answers to.

She left him to his post and went to the garden door. She swung it open, took a quick peek to be sure the neighbors weren't about, and then sat beside the little statue of a dog Telesm created to keep watch over the garden. Its twin stood by the front door. They were supposed to be guardians—a last resort if the warding spell failed to deter any of their enemies. The statue was cold, unmoving, giving no indication that some magic lived inside of it.

She looked instead at the roses in full bloom, their sweet scent wafting across the garden and discouraging Unseelie visitors. A bumble bee hummed by, making its clumsy way to the flowers. Amy gently stroked its fuzzy back and let its simple joy for life and its task course through her. Then it fumbled on to the next flower. She rested her hand tentatively on the dog's head and felt nothing but the chill of carved stone under her fingers.

"You dislike your guardian." Telesm's voice made her jump.

"I don't dislike it," Amy said, looking to Telesm warily. Domin's half-brother didn't care for her. Didn't trust her.

"But you don't like it, either."

"I don't want to seem ungrateful," she said.

"But you are ungrateful, so tell me why."

Amy sighed. "It's not very...intimidating."

In fact, its cocked ears and grinning mouth were dishearteningly adorable.

Telesm folded his arms. "What shape did you expect it to take?"

"I don't know, but you have stone lions at your cottage, and I have a lap dog."

"Wards give you what you need, not what you want. Your magic influenced the shape it took."

Amy glared at him.

Telesm raised an eyebrow. "And perhaps you shouldn't underestimate it."

She looked again at the stone dog, then shrugged off the reassurance. "How can you be so unconcerned about the Fay? You trust your magic so much?" Of all of them, fear touched him the least.

He shrugged. "In part, yes. I am arrogant, as you know. I don't consider it a fault when it's based in fact. But more than that…"

Amy watched him, curious. Telesm was not one to have a friendly chat with anyone.

"We had a saying in Persia: 'This too shall pass.'"

"I've heard it," Amy said. "You imagine if you wait long enough, our problems will just…go away?"

"Yes. Because they will. Given time, everything 'just goes away.' Pain. Happiness. It's all fleeting. It's not worth all this trouble."

The bumble bee buzzed past again—content in its ceaseless work to collect pollen for a summer that would soon be gone.

"Then what do you consider worth the trouble?" Amy asked.

"The trouble of worrying and becoming involved with obnoxious people and being inconvenienced at every turn? Nothing. Nothing is worth the trouble."

He turned to go, but understanding jolted Amy like a shock of electricity. "You're lying."

Telesm turned and raised an eyebrow. "Pardon me?"

"She's worth the trouble. The girl the basilisk turned to stone."

Telesm's face darkened. "You don't know of what you speak."

Thoughts flooded Amy's mind—thoughts and feelings and memories that weren't her own. She had to speak them or burst. "Ankhira. Her name is Ankhira. When I touched her back at your cottage, I saw...she cared about you, and you about her. You never told her, but she knows."

Telesm stared, his eyes unfocused. "She cannot know that, because I let that moment pass, too. It slipped away, and I can't bring it back, like trying to snatch a grain of sand from the wind." He regarded her then with narrow eyes. "And if she cannot know that, then neither can you."

He turned his back to Amy and stormed off into the house. She stared after him. He was right. She should not know what the girl felt in her stone sleep. Should not have a glimpse into someone else's dreams and memories. But she did. When she fought the Leannan, she had tapped into some buried human part of herself that felt like no Fay knew how to feel. She had awakened something powerful and frightening. And now, she didn't know what to do with it.

Chapter Seven

While Henry visited workhouses, Cassandra busied herself with studying. She'd bought every book on ancient lore she could find in London's shops, so Amy's library now housed a respectable collection. She wrinkled her nose at the dusty scent of one particularly old volume. One of these had to offer a clue about the Grigori's next ritual. But Telesm was correct: the catalog of terrifying creatures who dwelt in ancient woods was long. She had to narrow it down to those who might offer the Grigori what they wanted: access to magic.

Cassandra flipped pages awkwardly with her weak right hand while holding the pen in her left, scratching occasional notes on Amy's creamy stationery.

She had only begun her list when Amy brought her a letter. "Delivered by the evening post."

Cassandra took it, recognizing her mother's handwriting. Her stomach tightened as it always did when she corresponded with her family. She missed her sisters—especially Georgina—but she had to keep them away from the Fay. Keeping the two parts of her life separate sometimes felt like it was tearing her into pieces, too.

She opened the letter and read it, then let out a little groan.

Amy gave her a curious look. "Is all well?"

"They're coming to town for a visit."

"You enjoy seeing your sisters."

"But I don't enjoy keeping secrets from them."

"Ah," Amy said. "I'm sorry."

Cassandra nodded and folded the letter away. "They hope we'll be attending the ball hosted by Mrs. Greaves. It seems so... trivial. When we don't know what the Grigori or the Fay are planning, I mean."

Amy smiled a little. "Some might accuse me of being overly trivial, but I think attending a ball could be refreshing. Henry can take you, and at least you'll be able to dance. Everyone has been so serious lately, but what good is it doing us? We might even learn something by mingling in society. If Mrs. Greaves has not sent an invitation, I will encourage her to do so."

"But is it safe?" Cassandra asked.

Amy frowned over that. "If we stay together, we'll be safe."

Cassandra nodded, though doubt wormed its way around her stomach. Still, after all her sisters had seen last autumn, it might be better to encounter them in a formal setting like a ball than to bring them into Amy's home and try to make excuses for all that was strange there. Amy had convinced them the events of the Wild Hunt had been some unexplained occurrence—possibly supernatural—but Georgina already looked too knowing. She guessed that Cassandra wasn't sharing everything, and she was curious. Worse, Cassandra thought Georgina had looked hurt when she insisted there was nothing left to know. Cassandra wanted to be able to share everything with her sister, but sharing in this case would put her in more danger—if Georgina even believed her.

The front door banged open below, and a cold wind roared through the house to rustle Cassandra's papers.

"Henry!" Amy scolded.

"Apologies," he called and appeared a moment later in the library doorway, his expression dark.

"What did you learn?" Amy asked.

"That workhouses are only marginally better than the Fay regarding how they treat children." His shoulders sagged. "But nothing helpful, I'm afraid."

Cassandra stood to embrace him, but he stepped back.

"I'm sorry," he said. "I need to scrub my hands. And possibly burn these clothes."

"Bravo!" Amy said. "That waistcoat does not flatter your eye color."

Henry gave her a withering look. "Because the workhouses were filthy."

Amy's joviality faded. "I've heard they are terrible places."

"Nothing you heard could have done justice to how terrible they are. The masters profit off the work of the poor who have no way to better themselves or escape. The only reason I can imagine the Fay having an interest in the children there is because they are already half broken. If I didn't fear hurting the innocent, I would burn the workhouses to the ground and, and—"

"And set them all free?" Lucien asked from behind him.

Henry sighed. "Yes. And set them all free. But the workhouses and the Faerie changelings: what can we do for so many? Where would they go? The Faerie changelings...most would die without magic to sustain them."

Lucien folded his arms and stared at Henry. Henry just

shook his head and stormed down to the kitchen, no doubt in search of boiling water.

"We'll find a way," Cassandra said, trying to soothe the hurt and frustration lining Lucien's forehead.

"I'm tired of waiting!" Lucien stomped off in the opposite direction.

"Oh, dear," Amy said.

But Cassandra understood. She was tired of waiting, too. Amy was right. Leaving the house—even for something trivial like a ball—would be good for all of them.

When Cassandra made her way at the end of the day to the garret room she shared with Henry, she was still concerned. But there was something soothing about stepping into her own little room, her home with Henry. The potted rose he had given her grew in the window, stretching for the light. All of Amy's house felt welcoming, but this room was Cassandra and Henry's alone—the only place that belonged just to them, where they could relax and be only themselves—not changeling or human, not royal or common, and not hunted by anyone. A place where they could pretend to have the life of freedom they craved.

Henry, now wearing a different suit, smiled wearily at her.

"You had a terrible day," Cassandra said.

Henry embraced her. "Yes. Made worse because I can do nothing about it. I'm not even a proper surgeon, and no way to become one when I don't exist in this world, for all intents and purposes."

Cassandra squeezed him tighter. "You exist. And you will find a way to help."

"If I could break free from the Fay's hold, I might be able to teach other changelings to do the same. I couldn't help all of them, but even just some, one at a time..."

Cassandra gripped his hands. "Yes, it adds up. You will find a way. I know it."

Henry kissed her and met her eyes. "Something is troubling you. The Fay's plan for the changelings?"

She sighed and sat on the edge of their bed. "No. Well, yes. But not just that. I had a letter from my family. They are arriving in London in the next two days."

Henry sat beside her and took her hand in a comforting grip. "London is not so dangerous as it once was."

"But they are not foolish—especially not Georgina. And it is dangerous for her to notice too much."

Henry gave a little start.

"What?" Cassandra asked.

"It struck me—I once thought that way of you. When we first met, I wanted to tell you more, but I was afraid to draw you into this world."

"I hope you don't regret it now!"

"Not at all. Though, it was not I who drew you in. I can't say I'm sorry that you are here, of course—it is the greatest happiness I know—but I'm not sure how I would feel if I had been the one who brought you into it. Selfish, I suppose."

"Would it be selfish if I told my sisters more?"

He smiled. "Your motivations would be much different than mine. No, I think whatever you do will be to help them."

"But intentions are not enough," Cassandra said. "Not when it endangers them, perhaps either way. And I feel like it's my fault."

Henry tightened his grip on her hand. "Never think this is your fault! It is the Fay who are doing this to us."

She sighed and traced the scars on his wrist, the thick white marks warm under her fingers, reminders of pain that would never fully heal. Pain inflicted by the Fay.

"Would you tell them, if they were your sisters?"

He tilted his head. "I suppose in a way they are, aren't they? They don't know it, but they're my family now, too."

"I hope someday they can know that," Cassandra said. Though even if they never did—even if Sophie thought Cassandra had chosen to foolishly pine away and remain nothing but a spinster companion to Amy—Cassandra could not regret her choice. Could not regret the happiness of belonging completely to Henry.

"I'll protect them either way, you know," Henry said. Then he sighed. "As well as I can. I wish I could do more. I wish you didn't have to be afraid for them, for us. If I could only master my abilities... I hope you never have reason to regret—"

Cassandra silenced him with a kiss. When she broke away, he smiled.

"I don't remember what I was saying," Henry said, "which I suppose was your intent."

"If I'm not allowed to blame myself, then neither are you. We take it one day at a time. We'll see my sisters at the ball. We'll try not to involve them any more than necessary."

But if they asked questions, Cassandra didn't want to lie to them. She was afraid to speak to Georgina. Afraid of what things might have to be unsaid—or said.

Chapter Eight

On the night of the ball, Cassandra dressed in the blue gown
Amy had purchased for her in the autumn when they were
tracking the Wild Hunt. Amy had insisted on a few
modifications to update its style, but for Cassandra, those
changes did not disguise the reminder of the fury of the Wild
Hunt or her sorrow over the young artists killed by the
Leannan. With all of their efforts—Jairus scarred, Domin's
energy slowly draining away—they had only managed to push
off the threat for a while. Now, Cassandra's family were in
London again, and again, danger lurked in the fog and the
hidden alleyways.

Amy's complaisant lady's maid, who enjoyed her salary well
enough not to question the couple living in the attic, finished
Cassandra's hair and left with a quick curtsey.

Cassandra studied her reflection, then picked up Georgina's
little rose brooch and added it to her dress.

"You look perfect," Henry said, smiling at her as he fastened
his cufflinks.

"So do you," she said, straightening his collar. Then she balled her fists. "I have to remember not to do such things in company tonight. Especially not in front of my family."

He took her hand and kissed it. "I'm sorry. I know this is difficult. On the bright side, since they don't know we are married, we can still dance and not be considered unfashionable."

She smiled at this offering. She would enjoy dancing with Henry, but when she thought of the deception they had to practice, her stomach knotted until she felt ill. She did not regret her decision, but there were times the worry ate at her, stealing her appetite and making her especially tired of late.

Henry escorted her downstairs, where they found Amy, Domin, and Jairus dressed for the evening. Mary lingered behind them in her regular dress, with a few oil stains on the sleeve.

"Aren't you going with us?" Cassandra asked Mary.

Mary ducked her head. "I thought I might stay here with Lucien. He can't go out, and we've been experimenting on using our magic together, with Telesm's help."

Cassandra and Amy exchanged a quick glance. Mary and Lucien spent a great deal of time together. At first, Cassandra wasn't sure she trusted Lucien—especially not after he had tricked them to go into the Unseelie Kingdom after Mary's human sister. But now, Cassandra had seen nothing but positive things from Lucien, and she worried a great deal about what would happen if the Dark Lady realized he had absconded and tried to reclaim him. Henry had taught Lucien how to fight back a little, but there was only so much any of them could do against the terrible Lords and Ladies of the Fay.

Telesm wouldn't attend a ball, which he saw as beneath

him, so Mary and Lucien would have some extra protection, and they were safer in the warded house than outside of it.

"I hope you plan to dance tonight," Amy said to Domin, her voice light, but a vulnerability in her eyes.

Domin hesitated for a moment. Maybe thinking about his injury. He could not change shape, after all, and some of Society would frown to see his darker skin, despite the fine clothing Amy had procured for him. He had once told Cassandra that he preferred not to pretend to be someone else, even when it was less convenient, but she wondered if he now missed the convenience of being able to hide. She knew he missed the strength that had come with his abilities, saw it in his constant worry about the safety of Telesm's wards and the way he tried to force himself to stay awake even when he now needed more sleep like the rest of them.

But Domin gave Amy a quick bow of the head. "I will if you would like me to."

Amy pinked at that.

"I suppose that leaves me as the only gentleman without a lady to escort," Jairus said as if suddenly realizing the odd numbers.

"Extra gentlemen are always welcome at a ball," Amy reminded him, prodding his shoulder with her fan.

Jairus ran his hand over the scars pockmarking the side of his face. "Of course."

Cassandra wanted to assure Jairus that he was just as charming as ever, but she couldn't deny some people would look on his scars askance. She knew it well. She picked up her cane.

They walked through the streets, careful to keep their clothes clean as they made their way through the smoky fog to the house where the ball was held. Music and light spilled down the stairs in a welcome. For a moment, it reminded Cassandra of a fairy story—not a *real* fairy story, but the kind she had once dreamed about, with magic and dancing and happiness at the end of it. She feared that her own fairy story might not have such a nice ending, though at least she already had her prince. She looked up at Henry with a smile, and he grinned back at her, his smile brighter than any magic she could dream of.

The London crowds were smaller in the summer, but when they entered the house, the flow of people in bustled ballgowns and dark suits whisked them into the ballroom, where couples spun about the floor in a polka. For a moment, the light and heat and the whirling people made Cassandra dizzy. But then Henry caught her arm, and all was well again.

"Cassie!" Georgina hurried up to her, Sophie and their mother close behind.

Henry stepped back, allowing Cassandra to embrace her sister. Cassandra squeezed Georgina, then noted how much older she looked already. A little silver cross glinted at her throat. When had Georgie started wearing a cross?

"You look well," Georgina said. "Oh, you're wearing the brooch I painted for you. I can't imagine it's very fashionable." She studied Cassandra carefully. Maybe too carefully. Was she suspicious?

Cassandra pushed her worries aside and spoke clearly so Georgina could read her lips. "I'm not so concerned with what's fashionable. The brooch reminds me of you. It is so good to see you again. I've missed you."

Georgina's smile bloomed and faded as quickly as a daylily. "I've missed you, too. You...you could come home, you know."

Cassandra's chest tightened. "Oh, I would like to, but...but I'm needed here."

Georgina smiled tightly. "Of course." She glanced at Henry standing a respectful distance away. "I suppose I understand."

Cassandra wanted to object—she wasn't trading them for Henry or for anyone else. They wouldn't be safe with her at home, and she couldn't protect them unless she was there with her friends, fighting the Grigori and the Fay. "There's more to it than you know. London can be...unsettling, and my friends here need my...my support."

Georgina's expression softened. "I believe that after what we saw last autumn. We left so suddenly, and your letters didn't mention... I hope you can tell me more of what happened. It was all so strange."

Cassandra fumbled after an excuse, but she was saved by her mother and Sophie approaching. Sophie smiled weakly at her sister, her gaze darting between Cassandra and Henry speculatively.

Her mother fixed an almost predatory smile on Henry. "Mr. Stewart. How lovely to see you again. I'll be very disappointed if I don't see you dancing with our Cassandra tonight. Isn't she looking lovely? One hardly notices the cane."

Spots of shame burned on Cassandra's cheeks. She wished she could tell her mother she was already Henry's, and no longer her mother's problem. Mrs. Weaver didn't have to worry anymore about her crippled daughter because her crippled daughter had found someone who didn't see her as broken or a burden. He saw her for her. More than that, Cassandra no longer saw herself that way, either.

"She looks perfect," Henry said. "I look forward to many dances with her. And how are you and your daughters?"

"Oh, we are enjoying a lovely time in London. This is a much more pleasant season than the last time we visited."

Yes, their last visit, when the Wild Hunt harassed the city

and the Grigori attacked Georgina's art teacher right in front of her.

"Indeed," Henry said.

"And your studies?" Mrs. Weaver asked. "They progress well, I hope."

"Uh, yes," Henry said.

"Mr. Stewart," Robert Ashby's voice cut through their conversation. "I was hoping to—Oh!"

Sophie flushed and turned to see Robert. His focus turned wholly on Sophie, whatever he wanted to ask Henry forgotten. Cassandra's stomach tightened. His interest in Sophie seemed sincere, and he had tried to help them in the autumn, but Cassandra had seen him there with the Grigori, seen him with his black cloak in that dungeon helping to summon a demon. And he fled before the Dark Lady as she cut down his father. Was he safe for her sister?

"Sir Robert." Her mother's interest practically dripped from her tongue now, especially as it rolled over Robert's title.

He flinched a little when she said it—so tiny a reaction that Cassandra might have missed it if she hadn't been watching. He had not adjusted to his father's title. And hopefully, that meant he would never step into his father's role as a betrayer of her family.

"It is good to see you," Sophie said shyly.

The worry in his eyes dissolved for a moment when he looked at Sophie, seeing her only with admiration.

"We have missed you in Drixton," Mrs. Weaver added. "Will you be opening the house back up soon?"

"Oh, yes, I... It brings back unpleasant memories. I'm not certain when I will return, I'm afraid. But..." His attention turned completely to Sophie again. "But I am so glad to see you here. Miss Weaver, if I might ask for a dance?"

"Of course," Sophie said, her face glowing with happiness.

Cassandra winced inwardly. She wanted Sophie to be happy. Happy and safe. Of course, Cassandra had chosen a course that was not safe, but she did that with her eyes open. Sophie did not know, and Cassandra didn't know how to warn her, or if she would even listen.

Robert cast a quick glance at Henry. "Stewart, if I can have a word later?"

Henry gave him a sharp, searching look. "Yes, naturally."

As Robert led Sophie away, Georgina watched them a little wistfully. Georgina was nervous to come to a ball, Cassandra knew, because her near-deafness made it difficult to track the music and the conversation. But she had loved dancing before the fever stole so much from her, and at least she should have that much happiness.

Cassandra caught Henry's eye and made a subtle head motion toward her sister.

He smiled his understanding and approached Georgina so she would be able to read his lips. "Miss Georgina, would you like to dance?"

Georgina gave a start, her eyes wide. She glanced at Cassandra, as if for permission, and Cassandra smiled at her.

Georgina grinned. "I would love to. Thank you, Mr. Stewart."

He guided her into the dancing.

Cassandra stood awkwardly next to her mother.

"How is Lady St. Clair?" her mother asked.

"Very well," Cassandra said. "She is here, of course. Probably dancing."

And she saw Amy out there on the floor, dancing with Domin.

Her mother looked perplexed. "Who is that she is dancing with?"

Cassandra thought of Telesm's boasting and smiled. "I hear he is related to a Persian prince."

"Ooo." Her mother looked suitably impressed by that. Any prince was quite worthy, after all, and England did not hold a monopoly on them.

Cassandra relaxed at her mother's complacency. She was not in danger of being whisked away from Henry and her friends as long as her mother approved of Amy. Her mother cared for her; Cassandra knew that. Her pressure for Cassandra to conform, to marry comfortably, were what she saw as best for Cassandra's future. After all, there were seven girls to provide for, and though Cassandra's father had made his fortune, it spread thin between so many daughters.

"How are my other sisters?" Cassandra asked.

"Oh, they are doing quite well in their lessons. Lottie is learning to read, and Lillian's embroidery is lovely. Jane is almost ready to be out."

Cassandra heard the unspoken concern: Jane had to wait until at least some of her older sisters were married before she made her debut. With Sophie jilted once—and then apparently forgotten by Robert Ashby until that night—and Cassandra and Georgina regarded by many as less desirable, it must be frustrating for her younger sisters. Yet Society had its pitfalls, and Cassandra couldn't help thinking that Jane might be better off waiting longer. At least until the Grigori were less of a threat.

"And how is Anne?" Cassandra asked.

A worry line creased Mrs. Weaver's brow. "She seems healthy enough. Sometimes I think she's, well, she's a little different from you other girls. She's often staring off at things, and she's beginning to speak, but saying such odd words."

Prickles crawled over Cassandra's skin. Domin had said her youngest sister would be gifted. Powerful in some way that the Fay wanted to either control or to destroy. What abilities were developing in her?

"What kind of words does she say?" Cassandra asked cautiously.

Her mother wrinkled her forehead. "I don't always understand clearly. I've heard her say 'oak' and 'stag' and 'fairy' and what I think is...well, some darker words that children have no place knowing."

Cassandra wanted to press but sensed her mother would consider whatever Anne said inappropriate and not share it. "What does Nancy say about her?"

Her mother's face softened slightly. "Nancy says Anne is fine and not to fret about it. She's very protective of the child, and she was so good with all of you."

"I'm certain Anne is well, then, if Nancy says it." Nancy knew all about the Fay, after all, having been a midwife to them once. "Perhaps Anne just overheard her older sisters reading fairy stories or something similar."

Mrs. Weaver smiled slightly. "Yes, perhaps you are correct."

"I'm sorry I haven't been there to see Anne growing up. And my other sisters as well."

"Well, we would welcome you to visit them while we are here. I'm certain they would like to hear of your time with Lady St. Clair."

Cassandra blinked. "You mean they are here in London? All of them?"

"Yes, of course," Mrs. Weaver said. "With your father and I both coming to London, we thought it would be good for your younger sisters to begin to get a little polish, even if they can't be out yet. And Nancy came along to help, so of course we couldn't leave the littlest girls."

Cassandra's stomach swam at the idea. Her entire family, all of her sisters, here in London. Though, it might not be any more dangerous than being in Drixton, near the Old Woods. And she could ask Nancy about Anne.

Her mother straightened. "Oh, I see Mrs. Brockhurst. Excuse me while I go ask after her daughter who was doing poorly."

She left Cassandra to muse over what she'd said. There had to be a way to bring Domin to see Anne. But would he still be able to discern as much about her? That was probably linked to his Faerie abilities and not his daemon ones—and his magic was fading.

Jairus strolled over to where she stood, giving her a friendly nod. His gaze found Georgina dancing with Henry, and he smiled a little. Georgina glanced their way at one point in the dance, and her cheeks pinked when she saw Jairus watching her.

Cassandra cast him a sly smile. "You should ask her to dance."

Jairus gave a guilty start. "Who, uh, your sister? She's grown up, hasn't she?"

Cassandra smiled to herself. "She has. She's a young lady now. And she likes to dance. So do you, I believe."

"Well, I do, but I've seen the looks some ladies have given me. I may not be such a desirable dancing partner anymore."

"I don't think my sister would say that. You know, since she lost her hearing, she's not as comfortable dancing, but she still enjoys it. Especially when she can dance with someone she knows."

Jairus looked interested in that appeal to his sense of

chivalry. "Oh, well, if she wouldn't object, it has been a while since I've danced."

When Henry and Georgina finished their dance, Henry brought Georgina back to Cassandra.

"Miss Georgina," Jairus said, catching her eye. "May I have the next dance?"

Georgina's gaze brushed over Jairus's scar but seemed to barely register it. She flushed with pleasure and looked to Cassandra for approval.

In Society's eyes, Cassandra would not have been a proper escort since they didn't know she was married, but she felt suitable enough to watch over her sister, and apparently Georgina felt the same.

Cassandra gave her a reassuring nod.

"I would love to," Georgina said, lowering her eyes.

Jairus offered an arm and led Georgina to dance.

Cassandra caught Henry's arm, pulling him closer, forgetting for a moment that they should not be so near in public.

"What happened?" Henry whispered.

"All of my sisters are here in London. I think we should try to see Anne. My mother says she's been saying strange things."

Henry's eyes flashed with concern, but before he could ask more, Robert approached him, apparently having taken his leave of Sophie.

"Stewart, I need to talk to you."

Henry stepped back from Cassandra, putting on his more polite mask. "Very well, what is it?"

"I've been trying to track down the Grigori—to help you, to atone for what my father did."

Henry's expression went stony, but he nodded for Robert to go on.

Robert cleared his throat. "I've met one of them who had a warning for me—one that he would like to pass on to you."

"How can you trust him?" Henry asked, leaving unspoken the rest of the question: How can we trust you?

Robert looked down. "I suppose you can't completely. Not yet. Not until he proves himself. But can't you at least listen to what he has to say?"

Henry sighed. "I suppose we can do that much. You'll have to help us get in touch with him."

"That won't be difficult. He's here, in the card room."

"One of the Grigori is here?" Henry took a step back and balled his hand like he might land a fist in Robert's face. Or cast some magic on him.

"He's been attending social events, hoping to catch you for a private word, away from the other Grigori. He said something about Edinburgh." Robert wrinkled his forehead at that. "He said he tried to approach your home, but something held him back."

"Which means he intends us harm!" Henry's words drew curious looks from those nearby.

Cassandra grabbed Henry's arm. "Let's catch Domin and Amy's attention. Either this is a trap and we need to leave, or this is our chance to learn what the Grigori are planning."

Henry let out a slow breath. "Yes, you are right, of course, my wise...friend."

He looked for a moment like he might kiss Cassandra, but that would be the scandal of the summer. Instead, he caught Domin's eye and motioned him and Amy over.

Chapter Nine

Henry quickly explained Robert's proposal. Amy studied the young man, who flushed under her gaze. She felt his shame and his guilt, but no deceit. Mainly an anxiousness to prove himself.

"I don't think Robert is trying to deceive us, at least," Amy said.

"Are there any other Grigori here?" Domin asked Robert.

Robert shook his head. "This man... He's afraid of the others."

After what they'd seen in Edinburgh, Amy could believe it.

"Very well," Domin said. "We'll meet him in the garden."

Robert hurried off.

"Is this a bad idea?" Henry asked.

Domin's lips quirked. "Maybe your recklessness is influencing me. Amy can sense if the man is telling the truth, but I don't want either of the ladies too close to the Grigori. And I want Hale."

Amy spotted Jairus on the dance floor with Georgina. But their set was almost finished. She tried to catch Jairus's eye, but his focus was entirely on Georgina. Oh dear. That could create a complication.

When the set finished, Henry hurried up and whispered a word in Jairus's ear. Jairus's soft expression turned to concern, and he left Georgina with a lingering bow over her hand. The girl watched him go and could not fail to see her sister leaving the room as well. Curiosity mingled with hurt and frustration in Georgina Weaver, and Amy didn't need her Faerie abilities to read them. Yes, definitely a complication.

The cool of the garden felt delightful after the sticky heat of the ballroom. Amy positioned herself behind Domin and Henry, with Cassandra taking a seat near a boxwood hedge.

It wasn't long before Robert approached with a middle-aged gentleman bearing an aristocratic hooked nose. Jairus strolled up casually behind them, his hands in his pockets so his pistol handle glinted from under his coat.

The Grigori stopped and glanced between Henry, Domin, and Amy. He had no protections against Faerie magic, and his emotions were so strong Amy could taste them. He held himself with pride—held it like a shield—but behind it, he quavered with fear. Amy braced herself against his feelings. They made her want to grab at everything she could find to keep herself safe.

"Thank you for agreeing to meet with me," the man said in a nasal voice. "I think we can be of benefit to each other."

"I'm not interested in a partnership," Henry said. "Sir Robert said you had a message for me."

The man clammed up, glaring at Henry. Amy wished she could give Henry a subtle kick. He was not a diplomat.

Amy studied the Grigori, trying to worm her way around his feelings to get to the truth beneath them.

"You mean to use us," Amy said. "How are you any different from the rest of the Grigori?"

She didn't have to push hard. He was so frightened, he wanted to tell them.

The man's eyes glazed slightly. "I just want answers. Understanding. There are things in this world that seem impossible, and I want to unravel them."

"You want to unravel us," Amy said.

"If I must. I don't like secrets! And I am not used to things being denied to me."

Henry looked like he had something to say about that, but Amy put a hand on his arm.

"Then how are you different from the other Grigori?" she asked.

His eyes grew more distant. "They have no scruples. And I think Rushford has gone mad." His words came faster. "He's meddled with dark powers in the past, and now he speaks of one that will change everything. A witch. One so destructive that they locked her soul away long ago so she could never rise and summon the darkness that follows her. He thinks she'll give him power, but I think he's wrong. I, and a few other of the Grigori, think she will destroy us."

"A witch?" Henry asked. "Do you know her name?"

The man shook his head. "Rushford will not speak her name. But he plans to bring her back."

"The bodies!" Henry said.

"Yes, they are to give her a new home. Her and her children. He says she is mightier even than the Leannan and full of dark magic, but I believe some things should not be meddled with."

"He's been searching in old woods," Henry said. "Does he know where to find her?"

"I think he does now," the man said. "That's why I decided

to risk contacting you. He traveled west recently with some of his most loyal followers. They returned looking triumphant. But he will not tell us yet where they found her."

"They're waiting for Lammas," Henry said.

"Yes." The Grigori pulled out a handkerchief and mopped his brow. "That is the day this world ends."

A chill raced over Amy at that. His fear was so visceral, that it nearly doubled her over, and she pushed away her connection to him, wanting to run to somewhere full of sunlight that shadows never touched.

The man blinked, coming out of Amy's hold over him. "I... You did something to me! I did not want to give you that information without something in return."

"Yes, you did," Amy whispered. "You're so frightened of this witch that you wanted to tell us, even if we did not offer anything in return."

"You're right to be frightened," Henry said. "And here is what I'll give you in return: Leave. Leave the Grigori. Leave England, even."

"I want to understand," the man said, practically begging.

"Trust me," Jairus said from behind him. "There are things we're better off not knowing. Things that will haunt you forever if you look on them. Accept what you have, and be grateful you weren't given more than you bargained for."

The man furrowed his brow at that, but he cast one more searching look at Amy, then hurried off.

The rest of them gathered together.

"Did you all hear?" Henry asked.

Everyone nodded.

"We need to return home and include Telesm in this discussion," Domin said. "Miss Leland and Lucien as well."

Cassandra looked regretfully back at the house, but she

didn't make any objection. Not in the face of what the Grigori threatened. They hurried through the night, Cassandra not even returning to bid her sisters farewell.

Back in the bright lights of her house, it was hard for Amy to believe what the man told them. An end to their world? Perhaps it was a ruse. Rushford was egotistical and conniving, but Amy did not think him insane.

Yet Telesm looked very serious as he listened to their account.

"Do you believe this man?" Telesm asked.

"I remember him," Cassandra added. "He was the Grigori who objected to torturing us back on Michaelmas. I think he's not as power-mad as the rest of them."

"He believed what he said was true," Amy admitted. "But this talk of a witch whose soul was trapped? That sounds like an immortal creature—a Fay—yet the few true witches were humans who found a way to bind themselves to some deep magic."

"What about Faerie changelings?" Mary asked softly.

Domin looked to her. "What do you mean?"

"In Drixton, some people thought I was a witch. I even thought I might be one."

"A Faerie changeling might have any number of powers," Henry said. "Maybe it's possible for one to become a witch. But I didn't understand what he meant about darkness following her. And her children?"

"Carmun," Domin said softly. "It must be the Carmun. She is the only witch powerful enough to threaten the Fay."

Amy shivered. "I have heard whispers about a terrible evil associated with that name."

"Yes," Domin said. "It was supposed to have been before any of our lifetimes. She was a Faerie changeling who made forbidden alliances to gain power. It was said that her sons were pestilence, famine, and darkness, and they followed in her wake, nearly consuming Ireland."

Jairus straightened at that, his brow furrowed. "The horsemen," he muttered. "But what became of this Carmun?"

Domin shrugged. "It's hard to know exactly what happened that far in the past. But the stories say the Fay chose four heroes, one female and three males, to stand against the Carmun and her twisted 'sons.' They banished the plagues and darkness and bound her in an oak grove."

"She's not dead, then?" Amy asked.

"They could not kill her. Like certain other Faerie creatures, she had learned to walk in both worlds, so the best they could do was banish her."

"And if Rushford raises her?" Jairus asked.

"She would wreak vengeance against the Fay, but she would also return plague and famine to the human world, a sickness that would overtake the land."

"She'll destroy both our worlds," Henry said.

Domin looked weary. "If there's even a possibility that Rushford is seeking the Carmun, we have to stop him before all else and whatever the cost."

"But where?" Cassandra asked. "It's the same problem we had before. To the west, but there are still many old woods in that direction."

Telesm rattled off several phrases in what Cassandra had to assume was ancient Persian. "They'll kill us all. We need a map."

He hurried out and returned with a large and somewhat yellowed and tattered map of the British Isles.

"The Carmun was originally imprisoned in Wexford on the coast of Ireland, but the oak grove there was destroyed," Telesm said, tapping his finger on the map.

"Does that mean the Carmun is dead after all?" Cassandra asked hopefully.

"Or already released?" Amy added with a shiver.

"No." Telesm whisked his hand over the map. "The oaks would have transferred her keeping to others of their kind. Probably Scotland or Wales, but we can't rule out parts of England with ancient groves."

Domin nodded. "There are many old woods in those places, and we know the Grigori have been searching them. But that leaves too much of Britain."

"It's west, not north," Henry said, placing a hand over Scotland.

They stood in silence, staring at the rest of the map. They had less than a month to discover which ancient grove held the Carmun.

"We should go see Cassandra's sister Anne," Henry said. "If she is a seer, as Domin suspected, she may provide some hints."

"Well, we can't all go," Amy said. "That would look quite odd. But they'll expect me to accompany Cassandra. And Henry's presence won't surprise them."

"Domin should come," Henry said. "He might be able to tell us more about the child."

"No, I won't," Domin said sharply, his face drawn. His voice softened. "I'm not able to sense things like I once did, and they would find my presence strange. Take Hale. He can offer extra protection, and the family knows him better. Trusts him."

Jairus shifted uncomfortably, but he didn't object. None of them did. Amy lowered her eyes to the tattered edge of the map. They all knew Domin's powers were fading. Was it possible that little Anne would suggest help for Domin? Not if there wasn't any. Telesm was Domin's best hope, searching for something that would heal him.

The others ate a cold and quiet supper and went to rest until the time came to visit Anne and hope the toddler could somehow provide answers.

Amy, however, couldn't relax. She should have been afraid of the Carmun. She *was* afraid of the Carmun. But the thing that wormed through her stomach was her worry for Domin.

It was well after midnight when Amy's clock began a raucous chime. Amy started up from where she had been trying to relax on the sofa with one of Cassandra's books of lore. The warning of the wards pressed against her head. She risked a peek through the crack in the curtains, but the fog hung densely over the square.

Domin hurried down the stairs from wherever he had been resting. His hair was disheveled, something Amy had never seen before. "Who's out there?"

Amy moved close to him. "I can't see. It's too dark."

Unnaturally dark.

"Probably Unseelie." Domin peered outside, his green eyes clouded with worry.

"You're not certain?" Amy asked.

Domin saw with something deeper than sight, able to look directly into one's heart, if not their mind. Or, he had been able to.

He was silent for a long time. "I can tell they're Fay. And they mean us harm."

The wards had made that clear enough. Though Amy hadn't known they were Fay. Somehow, that was less frightening to her than human enemies. The Fay had to obey certain laws, while humans could choose not to.

Something moved in the darkness, and Amy caught a glimmer of red. "Is that Jane on her stag?"

After a long moment, the unnatural darkness faded, and the crickets began their song again.

"They were only testing," Domin said. "Wanting to see how well protected we are."

"Who do you suppose they're after?" Amy asked. "Henry? Lucien?"

"Either is possible. They might see us as a nest of hornets they would like to eliminate all at once. If it was Jane, she's bent on revenge against all of us." He glanced at Amy. "But we will not be easily attacked here, and now they are aware."

Amy nodded, relieved, though they could not stay in the house all the time.

"Do you think they know about the Carmun?" Amy asked.

"I'm certain the Fay know the Grigori are planning something. I think if they knew it was the Carmun, they would have acted by now, and it would not be subtle."

Amy shivered. "That changeling, Richard, said the Fay were trying to change the balance of the world. Could it be something to counteract the Carmun? Or even the Grigori?"

Domin went still, his face thoughtful. "Yes, that's possible. I wonder if the Lord of the Thames would tell us anything. Perhaps I will try to find him while you visit the Weavers."

Domin turned to leave. To sleep again? He slept more now than he used to.

Amy followed Domin into the corridor and put a hand on his arm. "Any word from Telesm on a cure?"

Domin lowered his gaze. "He has had no success with a healing potion. But it doesn't matter."

"Doesn't matter!"

Amy caught Domin's hand and turned it over, revealing the blue tattoo fading against his brown skin. She traced the swirling lines, losing herself for a moment in the feeling of his warm skin beneath her fingertips. Her cheeks warmed, and she looked up to see that Domin had closed his eyes, his lips slightly parted. She stepped closer, and he opened his eyes. His gaze locked on hers, then traced her face down to her lips.

He sighed and clenched his hand into a fist. "It doesn't matter." His voice was low, husky. "I didn't want my Fay magic. I don't like what I once did with it."

"Yes, you made mistakes once. But your Fay magic is part of who you are." She tapped the tattoo. "And those of us who care about you care about all of you."

Domin stared for a long moment at the tattoo—at Amy's fingers resting on his skin. Then he sighed.

"Amy, I... Thank you for your concern, but we need to focus on the Carmun."

He pulled away gently and returned up the stairs. Amy watched him go, her throat too tight to call him back to her.

Chapter Ten

Cassandra had to steel herself for the visit to her family, to avoid betraying herself and Henry to any of them. As they left Amy's house with Jairus and Amy, Cassandra took Henry's arm in a tight grip, and her gaze went to the fading tattoo, a reminder that they were all more vulnerable now. Furthermore, if Titania knew about Cassandra, she would leverage that against Henry as well. Cassandra would not be a pawn for the Fay.

They walked to the house Cassandra's family had let for their visit. A quick word with the footman, and they found themselves in a comfortable sitting room appointed with blue furnishings and gold draperies.

Georgina greeted them first. Her face brightened when she saw Cassandra, and then she noticed Jairus. A slight flush reddened her cheeks, and her eyes darted between him and Amy, obviously doing the calculations: two ladies, two gentlemen. A crease of worry settled on her brow for a moment, but then she shook it off and greeted Cassandra with an embrace.

"I'm so glad we're here and able to visit more often," Georgina said. She looked up at the others, her eyes resting on Jairus. "That all of you are here."

Did Jairus flush a little under her interested gaze? Cassandra couldn't be certain, but she managed to hide her smile. Then to erase it completely when she remembered that Jairus lived a dangerous life that Georgina knew nothing about.

Sophie came in just after Georgina. Her welcome for Cassandra was more polite but still sincere. She could barely look at Henry, though, no doubt remembering how he had crossed words with her when she berated Cassandra.

"Mother is out, and she'll be sorry she missed you," Sophie said. "Won't you all sit?"

"I was hoping to visit the rest of our sisters as well," Cassandra said.

Sophie hesitated, no doubt wondering if this was proper.

Cassandra smiled. "It will be good practice for them before they enter Society, and in front of those who are friends and won't think less of any of us if their manners fail."

Cassandra sensed Amy tensing, ready to push if Sophie refused, but she didn't need it.

Sophie smiled. "Certainly, you're right. It will be an opportunity for the older girls."

"Bring the younger ones, too, if you please," Cassandra said. "It won't hurt anything, and I miss seeing them."

Sophie nodded once and went to fetch their sisters.

"What have you been painting?" Cassandra asked Georgina.

Georgina's eyes brightened. "I have several ideas for my next project. Let me show you!"

Georgina fetched a sketchbook stashed beside the sofa. Cassandra sat next to her, and they flipped through Georgina's drawings. Many of the scenes were typical: the London street, figures strolling through Hyde Park. One that looked like a loose sketch of Jairus Hale. But several of the drawings had a different feel that reminded Cassandra of the picture Georgina had painted on the walls of her room while under the Faerie enchantment. One showed a dark cloud engulfing a village. Another showed a dying figure before a crumbling lakeside castle. If the gift of sight ran in their family, Georgina had dark visions.

"Where is this?" Cassandra asked, pointing to the castle.

"It's not a real place, I don't think, only something from my imagination," Georgina said, but her eyes looked troubled.

"And where did you get the inspiration for this one?" Cassandra prodded gently, seeing an image of a twisted male figure like some kind of wraith.

"It's rather gothic, isn't it?" Georgina fidgeted with her silver cross necklace. "I'm not sure where the idea came from. I think maybe a dream. I have rather vivid dreams at times." She looked troubled for a moment, then shook it off and smiled. "I know Mother wouldn't approve of those, so I don't intend to paint them. But it helps clear my mind to sketch them."

Cassandra nodded, trying to look only politely interested, but the pictures in Georgina's sketchbook seemed almost alive on the page, and she once again remembered her dream of the dying tree's shadow reaching for all of them.

Finally, Sophie returned with their younger sisters. The two older girls, Jane and Lillian, composed themselves like the proper ladies in training that they were, but the younger two, Lottie and Anne, shepherded by Nancy, gawked openly at the visitors. They would rarely leave the nursery. Especially Anne.

Amy watched the little girl with deep interest. Cassandra didn't know what the Fay could see in her youngest sister, but she was grateful that Jairus's christening protected the child for now.

Nancy set the child down, and she stood a bit unsteadily, a finger stuck in her mouth as she stared at the guests. Then she smiled and pointed to Amy.

"Fairy! Pretty!"

Amy grinned and knelt, holding out her hands in an invitation for the girl to toddle over to her.

"Oh, goodness," Sophie said. "She's only beginning to talk and says the strangest things. Don't let her pester you."

"Not at all," Amy said with a smile for the little girl clinging to her fingers. "I didn't have any children in my brief marriage, and I quite like them. They're so...uncomplicated. Especially when they are someone else's," she added with a twinkle in her eyes.

A flash of sadness showed in Amy's eyes as she watched Anne, but then she smiled again. Of course, Amy would likely never have children because she was Fay—especially if she chose not to pursue a relationship with a human, as seemed likely based on the looks that passed between her and Domin. Henry might not be able to have children either—not while Titania held him. Cassandra felt a twist of sorrow, but she pushed it aside. She would enjoy whatever good she could snatch from life and not allow any regrets.

Cassandra knelt beside Amy. Her youngest sister was entranced by Amy, though, probably seeing glimmers of her magic. Henry moved to stand behind Cassandra, and Anne looked up to him. Her smile faded, and she frowned somberly at Henry. It sent cold prickles over Cassandra's skin.

"King," Anne proclaimed.

Then she turned her attention back to Amy, who made funny faces at her.

Cassandra exchanged a glance with Henry. Anne saw his royal blood. What would she be able to discern when she was older? What could she tell them now, with her limited vocabulary and understanding?

Nancy watched the whole exchange with a worried frown. They needed to talk to her about what she had observed of Anne.

Jairus seemed to sense the need for a distraction. He sauntered over to the sofa where the other girls sat, flashed one of his winning grins, and drawled out a greeting. Even with his face scarred, the girls tittered at his attention. No, perhaps more because of the scar. Cassandra smiled to herself. Jairus proceeded to do a series of sleight-of-hand tricks with a coin, which distracted even Sophie. Georgina's face shone as she laughed at his tricks.

Cassandra motioned Nancy closer and whispered, "Anne sees things, doesn't she?"

"Far too much."

"Mother mentioned she speaks of dark things. What are they?"

Nancy's eyes clouded. "It frightens me. She speaks of plague. Death. Darkness. Blight. No child should know of those things."

Cassandra looked to Anne with concern. She seemed quite happy, making faces with Amy, but she would have a burden to bear if she saw the darkness of the world—darkness beyond her small circle—even at such a young age. But she saw no way to protect her from it. All they could do was try to quench the darkness so she did not have to dream of it.

"We'll take her words as a warning," Henry promised Nancy, keeping his voice low. "We'll make certain they do not become reality."

Nancy pressed her lips together—doubting Henry?—but she nodded. "I hope you can."

The child's words seemed to confirm the Grigori's warning about the Carmun. But they needed to know more than the Carmun's threat. They had to know where to find her.

Henry spotted a globe on one of the side tables and brought it down to Anne's level. He spun it to catch her attention. She looked away from Amy, entranced by the whirl of the globe. Henry traced a finger on it, forcing it to slow, then turned it so the little island of Britain faced Anne. He held it out to her, saying nothing, waiting to see what she would do.

Anne stared at the globe and then at Henry, seeming confused.

"Show us the darkness," Cassandra whispered to her little sister.

Anne's face clouded. She looked once more to Cassandra and then to Amy, who gave her a little nod.

Anne stuck out the tip of her tongue and pointed to Wales. West, as the Grigori had warned them. But Wales was huge and mostly unsettled. Too much for them to search in less than a month.

"We need an atlas—a map of Wales," Cassandra whispered.

Nancy frowned, but she left and returned shortly with an atlas open to Wales.

Once again, Anne hesitated. Then, her face puckered, and she jabbed a chubby finger at a place slightly inland from the swoop of Wales's west coast. "Witch."

Cassandra drew a sharp breath and looked to Henry. The Carmun.

Nancy scowled and picked up Anne, cradling her close. "That can't be good for the child."

"I'm sorry, Nancy," Cassandra whispered. "But she has told us something very important."

Nancy looked between Henry and Amy, then her shoulders slumped a little. "I just want to keep her safe."

"So do we," Henry assured her.

Georgina noticed them with the atlas. "What are you looking at?"

"We're planning a journey," Amy said quickly. "With the railroad now reaching Aberystwyth, I believe we should travel there."

Clever, Cassandra thought, the way Amy danced around the truth. Cassandra would have to help deceive her sisters once again.

"Aber what?" Georgina asked. "I think my lip reading has failed me."

Amy smiled kindly. "No, it hasn't. A-ber-ist-with. It's on the coast in Wales."

"Oh, Wales, that would explain it!" Georgina gave Cassandra a look half longing and half reproachful. "Certainly, there are beaches in England that are easier to pronounce—and closer to visit!"

Amy closed the atlas. "No doubt, but Aberystwyth is likely to be the next big thing. We'll be some of the first to see it."

Georgina frowned. "But Cassandra needn't go too. While we are here in London, she can stay with us and rejoin you after your journey."

Henry looked like he might agree, but Cassandra wouldn't stay behind while her friends were in danger—while her family was in danger. She had to help protect them.

Cassandra stood and drew her sister aside so the others wouldn't overhear.

"I am sorry," Cassandra whispered. "But Amy needs me."

Georgina balled her fists. "And we don't? It's like you've... you've traded us for your friends now."

Cassandra rested a hand on Georgina's arm. "No one could ever replace you." If only she could explain that she was trying to help all of them.

Georgina let out a slow breath, the hurt showing in her eyes. "I miss you, Cassie. The others don't understand like you do. And I hoped to see more of you while we were here."

"Oh, Georgie." Cassandra's heart ached. She took her sister's hand. "I would like that, too. This trip should be short, and then I can see more of you."

"I wouldn't mind becoming better acquainted with your friends." She glanced to where Jairus spun tall tales to entertain the rest of her sisters. "Then we could all visit or go to parks and balls."

Cassandra's stomach tightened, but she forced a smile. "Perhaps sometime."

Georgie drew back, clearly hurt by her vague response. Cassandra tried to think of some excuse to cover her hesitation, but Georgina turned her back, effectively silencing Cassandra.

Cassandra feigned a good temper while they finished their visit with her sisters, but all of them were quiet on the walk home. Cassandra clutched Henry's arm. Hot tears caught on her eyelashes, but she blinked them away. There had to be some way she could keep her sister safe without losing her. Perhaps she *would* have to tell her more. But she was not going to involve her in the hunt for an undying witch powerful enough to threaten even the Faerie Lords and Ladies.

Domin waited for them at Amy's house, his face even more serious than usual.

"No luck?" Amy asked him.

"I could not gain admittance to the Lord of the Thames's

realm. He owes me nothing, so I didn't necessarily expect a warm greeting, but he seems to have cut himself off from everything."

"That changeling looked like he might have come from the river," Jairus said.

Domin shrugged one shoulder. "If needed, we might find a way to Thames's realm through the water, but I don't know if it's worth the time."

"It was a long shot," Jairus said. "But we found some news at the Weavers."

"Anne Weaver is a seer," Amy said. "The power rolls off of her. We'll have to protect her as she gets older—old enough to be seduced by the Fay, though she should be safe in her innocence for now."

"And what does she see?" Domin asked.

Henry ran his hand through his hair. "Plague. Darkness. Very cheery things for a child. Of course, she can't tell us more, even if she understands it herself, which I doubt at her age. But she pointed to the west coast of Wales in the atlas and said, 'witch.'"

Domin nodded grimly. "The Carmun is in Wales, then. We must go as well."

"Even with this hint, Wales is not a small place," Amy said. "So much of it is difficult to access."

"Then it is good that we have almost two weeks until Lammas."

Chapter Eleven

It would be easy to get lost in Wales. In Aberystwyth, Amy had used the beach and the tower of the castle to stay oriented. Out among the mountains and ancient woods, where they could go days without seeing another soul, Amy lost all sense of direction. She couldn't help remembering tales of the medieval Welsh hero-prince Owain Glyndŵr who had harassed his English overlords from this wilderness until he simply vanished as if swallowed by the mists.

And now she and her friends ventured into those same mists, chasing rumors and shadows. A forest of sessile oaks towered over them. Moss clambered over the ground and up tree trunks, filling the air with its green scent. Amy closed her eyes and listened to the ancient trees. As a child of the Lady of the Woods, she should have felt more at home here than almost anywhere she had been. The gnarled oaks had their own breath, their own pulse. It was ever so slow, the long sleep of ancient giants. And so peaceful.

Yet Amy sensed discontent beneath the long rest. That

discontent was what had brought her friends to these woods, along with hints from shepherds who described men in fine London clothing traveling this direction. But it was easy for the Grigori to get lost in these woods as well. Like looking for a single acorn in a forest of trees. And Lammas was only a few hours away. Only the pervasive sense of wrongness gave them an idea of where to search.

"The feeling is getting stronger," Henry whispered. "There's something dark here—something the land doesn't want."

"I feel it, too," Jairus said. He kept a hand on his pistol, though it would do little good against the depth of darkness Amy sensed, like a sickness leeching into the air and the water.

She glanced at Domin, but he said nothing. How could he not sense it? Even Cassandra and Mary looked uneasy, holding their crossbows in tight grips.

"It's almost dusk," Domin said. "Almost Lammas. We're running out of time to find the Grigori."

"I believe the Carmun's resting place is close," Henry said. "The Grigori probably are as well."

"We need to flank them," Jairus said.

Amy glanced around at her friends. "I don't like the idea of splitting up."

Jairus sighed. "I don't either, but we have to find the Grigori, and we have too much ground to cover."

Henry nodded. "We go in groups of two: Cassandra and I, Jairus and Miss Leland, and Domin and Amy. That way, no one's alone, and each group has someone who can orient themselves to whatever darkness we're feeling."

His words hit Amy. That was her—the one who could sense the darkness. Not Domin as it should have been.

Jairus directed them in their search areas.

"We can see which way is west by the sunset," he said. "We'll sweep toward the south."

They nodded their agreement and crept off in their separate directions. Amy clung close to Domin, needing the reassurance of his presence. The ill feeling gathered around her, making her stomach turn and her head feel light.

The feeling closed in as they walked deeper into the woods. Amy stumbled, and Domin took her arm, helping her stay on her feet. The oaks grew larger, so wide that Amy would not have been able to wrap her arms around them, and then so enormous that Amy could have stepped into the decaying hearts of the oldest trees.

Domin paused and put his hand on the massive trunk of one of the trees. Amy gave him a curious look.

He smiled slightly, almost embarrassed. "It's not often I come across a living thing that's older than I am."

Amy grinned. "Well, you look much better than the tree."

He chuckled, then grew serious. "I hope...I hope I haven't come to my end quite yet."

Amy grabbed his hand. "No. Of course you haven't."

He squeezed her hand, held it a moment, then he sighed and let go, leaving Amy wanting to reach for him.

"The spirit of this place is unsettled," he said.

Amy nodded, glad he could feel that much but concerned that he didn't feel more. Amy touched another tree. Much of the wood was rotten, the bark helping to hold it together. It would not last much longer. Something small would crack it to the core. Amy shivered and pulled her hand away.

"The trees are suffering," she said. "Something dark has touched them. A shadow lays over these woods."

Domin nodded. "Which way?"

Amy considered. Normally, shadows moved away from the

light, but this one was more like a whirlpool of shadow, drawing darkness closer to it, the shadows deepening and thickening.

She pointed. "That way."

They walked deeper into the woods. But they weren't alone. Footsteps shuffled through the thick carpet of leaves and moss. From the east. Not their friends.

Domin grabbed Amy's hand and pulled her into the hollow cavity of one of the ancient oaks. It was like stepping into a cocoon, the thick wood of the oak tree sheltering them in its embrace. Voices sounded in the woods, and Domin stepped closer, protecting Amy from whomever approached. The warmth of his body pressed against hers was utterly distracting, and for a moment, she forgot all about anyone who was chasing them.

Domin leaned down so his lips brushed her ear, and he whispered, "We'll follow them."

The warmth of his breath against her skin made her shiver. She looked up to meet Domin's eyes. His pupils were wide in the dark, reflecting her image. They stood like that, so close, her face tilted up to his in the shelter of the oak. Domin studied her eyes, her face, her lips. He put a tentative hand on her arm.

And his feelings washed over her. His attraction to her. Traces of guilt. Longing. Confusion. She reached up to touch his face, and he closed his eyes. But could he feel what she felt, too? Not as his Fay abilities faded. She realized with a jolt that he had not intended to let her feel his emotions. His control was melting along with his Fay magic. She had seen something she was perhaps not meant to see of him, and she didn't know what to do with that. Except to try to protect it.

She longed to kiss him, but not when he was confused or uncertain. Instead, she stepped into his arms, embracing him. He hesitated for a moment, then returned the embrace, holding her tightly. Amy could hear the steady thrum of his heart. She could also feel the dissonance from the sliver of iron lodged near it, the enemy slowly, silently sapping away his magic and his vitality. She wished she could pull it free and save him, but it was beyond her power.

"Come," she breathed. "They have passed."

He nodded, his cheek brushing hers, and released her. But he kept a hand on her back as they peered out and then followed the Grigori deeper into the ancient forest. Into the shadows and the sense of a malevolent presence causing the trees to wither under the force of its anger and resentment. Amy sensed their pain, their silent cries for help. Domin looked only vaguely uneasy, the dwindling remnant of his Faerie power not fully able to grasp the twisted agony around them.

Amy followed the sensation as it became more pressing, making it difficult to breathe. Domin steadied her, and they continued on. Domin kept one ear cocked, perhaps tracing the approach of their friends from other angles. Certainly, he would know where Henry was, at least. They were not facing the full force of the Grigori and their supernatural ally alone.

A blow slammed into her side—a sharp lance of pain. She gasped and fumbled at her torso to find a long iron bolt jammed into her ribs.

Somewhere, sounding far away, Domin snarled and lashed out at their attacker. Thumps and grunts punctuated their fight.

Amy jerked the bolt from her side. The iron stung her hands, spread cold down her arms and into her heart. The long weapon was almost elegant in its sleek design. Humans were so good at creating. Why did they have to use that spark to cause pain?

She turned dully to see Domin engaged with three men. If

only he could change shape, they would not have troubled him. One of the men raised a gun. Loaded with iron like Jairus's?

Amy swung the bolt around and jabbed it down into the man's back. He collapsed with a gurgling shriek. Amy pulled the bolt free and turned away, not wanting to see the damage she had done.

But the other two humans faltered, and Domin took the opportunity to strike both of them, bringing the first man to his knees and then smashing the second's head into the first's. They both collapsed to the forest floor.

Amy dropped the iron bolt, and immediately the warmth of the forest washed through her, stitching her injuries.

"Amy!" Domin caught her. "How badly did they injure you? Is the iron out?"

She nodded against his chest. "I'm recovering already. Quickly! What about our friends?"

Domin's eyes focused on something far distant. "Henry is unharmed, at least. We need to stop Rushford."

He grabbed her hand and pulled her forward, toward the center of the darkness.

But the darkness was changing shape—changing its nature —even as they approached. The sun had set, and Amy recalled that in ancient times, the new day began when the sun dipped below the horizon. Lammas had begun. The hungry thing sleeping in the darkness stirred, raising its head like a dragon whose hoard had been disturbed. The trees shuddered in silent pain as a pulse of magic washed over the woods in a fetid breath.

"We're too late," Amy groaned.

Chapter Twelve

Domin's enraged shout echoed through the forest, and Henry hesitated, his steps uncertain on the thick leaf mold of the forest floor.

Cassandra grabbed his hand and squeezed. He met her sympathetic gaze, and she gestured him forward. Henry gritted his teeth. She was right. Domin would tell them to focus on the Grigori. Domin could manage a fight, and it would provide a distraction.

With Cassandra holding Henry's arm for support on the uneven ground, they crept nearer—near enough to hear the low murmur of voices chanting something oozing with wrongness like writhing worms.

Henry pulled Cassandra behind the trunk of one of the massive oaks. A carpet of moss crept over the bark, brown and prickly where it should have been cool and soft under his hand. The darkness of the place seeped in around the edges of Henry's thoughts like half-remembered snatches of nightmares, some dark thing reaching claws for him and his feet too heavy and slow to escape it.

He drew a long breath and leaned out to peer into the dusky forest.

Ahead, the Grigori gathered around another oak, one so massive the half a dozen or so men could not have embraced it had they all joined hands. The oak's trunk had split and decayed, its center rotted out until its knobs and hollows resembled a host of withered faces. Some of the tree's gnarled branches reached feebly for the last rays of the setting sun. The rest contorted around the rotting wood in its heart so that the secret snarled in its roots would never be released. But the Grigori were calling forth that ancient secret, and the oak was too old and too tired to hold the darkness when it stirred.

Several cadavers—three men and a woman—lay on the ground around the tree, the rigid bodies arrayed in robes. The Grigori likewise wore dark robes, the hoods casting their faces into shadow as they chanted. Rushford was obvious because he stood in front of the others, nearly touching the old oak.

Cassandra readied her small crossbow. Henry wished for Jairus's shotgun. The iron of the weapon interfered with his magic, but the magic in these woods was sluggish. Blighted. He motioned for Cassandra to stay quiet and drew his rowan stake. Ice crackled along the stake into a sharp point when he summoned it, but it was laced through with dark threads of decay. At least if he attacked, he would disrupt the ritual and draw Jairus's attention—and Domin's, if his friend had subdued his foes.

He charged for Rushford, calling a cold wind from the Welsh mountains to lash at the cultists. The Grigori flinched from the icy blast that tore back their hoods, but Rushford drew his shotgun. Time seemed to slow as the double barrel rose up, up, up. The sounds of the forest faded until all Henry heard was the pounding of his feet, the wind rushing past his ears. Rushford braced the gun against his shoulder. Henry parried the barrel with his ice dirk. The ice shattered when it impacted the gun.

The boom of the errant shotgun blast tore through the quiet, ringing in Henry's ears.

Henry swung the stake at Rushford, smashing his nose. Rushford shouted, and blood poured from his face. Henry raised the stake again. Two of the Grigori grabbed Henry's arms. He kicked out, connecting with a knee, and one of the robed men collapsed.

Another Grigori leveled a pistol at Henry's face.

He froze.

"Don't kill him," Rushford said, holding a handkerchief to his nose and looking at Henry in disdain. "The witch might like him."

"You don't know what you're doing, Rushford!" Henry shouted, more to alert his friends than to warn Rushford.

He willed Cassandra to stay hidden. She had her crossbow, but that was meant for Fay, not humans with guns.

Rushford smiled coldly. "On the contrary, I know exactly what I'm doing. And the sun has set. You're too late to stop us."

He turned back to the oak and repeated his chant, his voice rising to a shout.

Quiet fell over the forest.

With a groan, the oak cracked to its roots, the sound louder than the blast of a gun. The ground shook, nearly knocking Henry and his captors off their feet. Cold washed over Henry—much more biting than any he could control. The edges of his vision went black, and his stomach writhed as though some living things fought inside of him.

Rushford stood before the splintering tree, a sharp grin cutting across his face as he watched the last life seep from the oak.

"Carmun!" Rushford called. "Come forth into a new world."

The last remnants of the ancient oak crumbled into fragments of rotting heartwood and bark. The dust formed a loose figure hanging in the air.

The forest went silent—a kind of silence Henry had never known. The birds no longer sang, the breeze stilled in the leaves, but beneath that, the heartbeats of squirrels and mice, the quiet murmur of life that ran through trees and grass and lichen, all froze, as if hoping their small sparks of warmth would go unnoticed by the dark thing gathering form in their midst.

The shape it took was that of a woman, or a mockery of one. A collection of shadows deeper than the gathering night pulled together like tendons and bones, all angles and edges, radiating a cold desire for destruction—no, for oblivion. Henry had never sensed such pure, unfocused malevolence, and it rushed through him like frigid water pouring through his veins.

He had to be free of it or his blood would turn to ice. He twisted desperately, and the Grigori dropped his arms, mesmerized by the Carmun.

Henry backed away, but the Grigori paid him no heed. After all, what harm could he do to their plans now? He didn't know how to stop what the Grigori had started. His hope had been to intervene before the men found the Carmun's resting place.

Beside the shadow figure of the woman, three smaller figures took form, equal to the first in cold and darkness. All of Henry's instincts—even his connections to the energy of the forest—screamed at him to flee.

He rushed for Cassandra, and she caught his hand, squeezed so hard it ached. Yet he welcomed the ache as a reminder of life—that all in the world was not this being of hatred looming above them.

Rushford stepped forward. "Carmun, we have awakened you to seek your revenge on the Fay." He gestured to the corpses on the ground. "We have brought vessels for you and your sons. We ask for a place in your kingdom."

"Yes, my son," her voice hissed. A voice bitter and sharp like spikes of ice in Henry's ears. "Your offering is acceptable. We will all have our revenge."

The figure reached out a limb glimmering with blackness. She bypassed the stolen corpses and instead touched Rushford. He froze.

One of the smaller shadow figures dissolved and coiled around Rushford.

Rushford shrieked, a desperate, animal cry. He tried to claw the shadows away, but even as he flailed, the darkness spread over him like frost stained with old blood, seeping into him, pitting his skin with shade and decay.

The screaming stopped. What was left of Rushford stood before the Carmun, head bowed, limbs loose as a broken marionette. Shadows dripped from him, puddling on the ground at his feet. Everything the shadows touched withered.

"Run!" Domin called, his voice loud enough to carry across the clearing.

A single shot rang out, and a bullet slashed through the Carmun and into a tree behind her. Jairus, no doubt.

The wisps of icy shadow trailed the bullet, infecting everything they touched. Where the bullet hit the tree, blight spread across the bark, withering and cracking it.

A few of the Grigori stood still, perhaps transfixed or simply too stunned to move, but the rest fled.

Cassandra tugged at Henry, and they hurried away, Cassandra limping over the uneven ground.

The ache of the land at the Carmun's touch pounded inside Henry like an endless scream in his mind. He couldn't tell everything the darkness would do—not yet—but he could feel the sickness spreading into the land. Into its magic. It made him ill, creeping through him like a cold fog in his head, in his bones. His magic turned fuzzy and distant. Only Cassandra's hold on him kept him moving forward.

Jairus and Mary found them. Jairus had his gun at the ready, covering their escape. Henry wanted to be able to fight as well, but he couldn't. All he could do was flee from that creeping wrongness that seeped into the world behind him.

He stopped short at the sight in front of them: a dark fog rising from the ground and swirling into a funnel of wispy darkness. A cold malevolence radiated from it.

The others didn't note it, kept hurrying toward it.

"Wait!" Henry called, forgetting to keep his voice down.

His friends stopped, looking at him in surprise.

Voices from somewhere behind them warned him he had given their position away. But somehow, that didn't matter. None of it seemed as terrible as that darkness lying in wait for his wife and his friends.

"Don't move," Henry said, dropping his voice. "Don't you see it?"

Jairus, Cassandra, and Mary exchanged uneasy glances.

"See what?" Cassandra whispered.

They didn't. They truly didn't see it. That frightened Henry as much as the darkness. Because he knew what he saw, perhaps because it went deeper than seeing: he felt the wrongness of it deep in his bones and in his blood.

"There's something there, in front of you," Henry said quietly, as though he could avoid disturbing the...thing. "I think it's one of the Carmun's, uh, sons. It's hungry."

Cassandra sidled closer to Henry, and Mary stepped behind them, her eyes wide. Jairus raised his gun, looking for a target, but Henry doubted even Jairus's iron would be enough to stop it. This magic was older and deeper than any power of the Fay, perhaps reaching back before light had ever touched the face of the earth.

They backed away, but the twisting black form followed, hovering in their way.

"Why can't we see it?" Jairus asked. "I feel it now— something *wrong*—but I can't see anything."

"I don't know," Henry said. "I suspect it has something to do with my connection to the land. I just know none of us should touch it. Go back the way we came!"

They turned, but the thing swirled, agitated, reaching toward them like the fingers of a misty hand until it encircled them.

"Stop!" Henry pulled Cassandra behind him as the mists closed the gap. "We're trapped."

Cassandra put an arm around Mary, keeping her close. Their eyes were wide, faces pale. They sensed the thing, even if they couldn't see it.

The darkness circled like a whirlpool, near enough that Henry could smell the icy coldness of it. Jairus's eyes widened, and he fired into the space in front of them, but the whisps twirled aside and reformed.

The darkness paused as if tasting this new threat.

"Did I get it?" Jairus asked.

The darkness began its circling again.

"No," Henry said.

It was up to him, and all he had was magic that felt leaden and weak. He pulled on it anyway, summoning a blast of icy wind. It tore leaves from the trees, but it did not affect the dark mist. He tried again, pulling at the Faerie magic woven through him. It hurt, burned to use the foreign power, but he used the pain to stay focused and pushed a bolt of pure magic at the darkness.

The black mist flinched, sprawling back. Henry smiled grimly. It could be hurt.

A coil of darkness darted forward, twining around Henry's leg.

Cold plunged over him like a fall into freezing water, knocking his breath away.

Henry Stuart. I see you. Child of this land, I will free you from the Fay. I will make you and your magic my own.

The darkness spoke with the voice of the Carmun. And he was trapped. Trapped just as Rushford had been.

The cold pricked Henry's skin like hundreds of needles. He couldn't move, couldn't breathe, could barely think. Darkness clouded his vision, seeped into his lungs with each struggling breath. He was going to die. Worse, he was going to become a puppet creature just like Rushford. Desperately, he felt for the Faerie magic woven through his body and pulled at it. The pain crackled over his nerves, locking his jaw, but he drew it to him until spots flashed over his vision. He shoved the energy at the creature.

The darkness screamed in his mind, and the shadowy thing recoiled, hovering before him like a wraith. No longer trapping his friends.

Henry gasped a lungful of air. "Run!"

Jairus grabbed Mary and Cassandra's arms as Cassandra sputtered a protest.

Then Domin was at Henry's side. He carried a burning torch made of an oak branch, wielding the flame at the darkness. The heat of it scorched Henry's still-cold skin.

Henry wasn't certain if Domin could see the darkness, but he must have been able to sense it. He whirled the torch faster than Henry could follow, parrying the tendrils of darkness as though fencing with them. The darkness coiled into a tight spiral, like a snake ready to strike, Domin holding it off with the meager light of the torch.

Warmth worked its way through Henry's body. Darkness had to yield to light.

Henry snatched the torch from Domin and called on the fire, fed it with Faerie magic and all of his memories of the summer sun and the comfort of warm hearths in the winter. The flame roared up, dancing in every color and gleaming with magic.

Henry swiped the shadow creature. The fire sliced through it. A scream echoed in Henry's mind, and the darkness retreated.

The flame died down to a flicker of orange light. Henry swayed, almost dropping the torch. His arms felt numb and shaky, his hands disobedient, as though they belonged to someone else.

Cassandra was at Henry's side again in an instant. He grasped her hand, grateful for her warmth after so much cold.

Domin took the torch. "We need to leave this place. Now."

They all followed him, dashing through the ancient trees.

Henry pulled Cassandra along with him, focused on keeping both of them on their feet. They all stayed in the circle of light cast by the torch. Behind them, in the darkness, something terrible and inhuman howled, an enraged hunter's cry, the sound snapping at their heels like the hounds of Annwn as they fled.

Chapter Thirteen

Cassandra woke from another nightmare. She'd hardly slept since they returned from Wales, remembering Rushford's screams and the desperate way Henry had looked when the darkness circled them. They tried to track the Carmun and the Grigori, but both had disappeared, leaving behind only a blighted track of woods. So, they were in London again, tracing any hints of the Carmun. Something with that much power would not stay hidden long. Carriages rumbled by at all hours, and gas lamps blazed against the darkness, but Cassandra knew the Carmun was out there, and that she wasn't finished yet.

Cassandra's stomach churned. Henry slept beside her, his forehead wrinkled, perhaps at his own nightmares. She wanted to soothe his worries away, but he hadn't been sleeping well either, and she didn't want to disturb him. She slipped out of bed and grabbed her dressing gown. Maybe she could find something in the kitchen to calm her stomach, if not her mind.

The exhaustion was catching up with Cassandra. She felt

dizzy, and she kept a firm grip on the smooth polished banister as she made her way down the stairs.

A dark figure stepped out of the shadows when she reached the ground floor. She gasped and looked for something to defend herself.

"It's only me," Domin said. "Checking the wards on the house. Something is out there."

"The Carmun?"

"No. Nothing quite that powerful."

"Oh." Cassandra placed a hand on her jumpy stomach. "The wards are secure, then?"

"Yes. Nothing that means us harm should be able to get past them. I would like to verify with Telesm, but I think that will stop the Carmun's influence as well. At least for now."

"For now?"

"As she grows stronger, I don't know what will stop her. Maybe some of Telesm's weapons, though he hesitates to bring them into the world because of the power they contain. But this is...the Carmun is something different. Once, even the Fay almost fell before her, and they are not as strong as they were in ancient times when there was less iron and more magic in the world."

"They will work together against her again, won't they?"

"Possibly, but we may not like the way they do that."

"Oh. True." The Fay had sent the Wild Hunt through London to stop the Grigori the previous year, and that had not been to the humans' advantage. Cassandra looked toward the door. "But, what's out there, then?"

"Something Fay. I think." Domin's teeth flashed in a snarl. "My senses are changing, and I...I'm not certain I can be as useful as I once was."

"You're the only one who knew something was out there,"

Cassandra said. How strange it was to have to reassure Domin about anything. "If they're Fay, and they don't trigger the wards, could they be an ally?"

"Perhaps. But they must have their own agenda as well." Domin frowned and stared at the door.

Cassandra imagined some Fay on the other side doing the same. She laughed, and Domin gave her a quizzical look.

"The Fay must be as uncertain as you are. You are both watching and waiting for the other. It would be safe to open the door, would it not?"

Domin smiled a little. "Most likely. Stay behind me, though."

Cassandra nodded and followed Domin to the front door. He opened it a crack, and Cassandra tried to peer past him, but he blocked her view. After a moment, he swung the door wider. Cassandra peeked out to see the dark figure of a horse standing alone in the empty, moonless square.

"Pooka?" Domin called.

Cassandra gave a start. The last time they had encountered the pooka, she had been an uneasy ally.

The horse limped forward. Stumbled. Its form slowly shifted into that of a human woman with long, black hair and a strange, angular face. She collapsed to the dusty street.

"Domin," the pooka called with a raspy breath. "So much iron. Even the air is poison."

Domin rushed down the steps. "May I touch you without harm?"

The pooka looked up at him, her sharp face pale and full of hollows in the darkness. "So, it is true. Your strength wans as well. No need to fear me, though. I could not harm you even if I wished it now."

Domin nodded and helped the pooka to her feet. He guided her toward the house.

She pulled back. "I sense protections on the house."

"Only against those that mean us harm."

"But it is not your home. You cannot invite me inside."

"Should I wake Amy?" Cassandra called.

"No." The pooka shook her head, her long, lank hair falling forward to curtain her face. "I am no tame creature to dwell indoors."

"Why did you come?" Domin asked.

"I was the only one who could fight past. The witch's powers are like my own. Except she does not respect the cycles, the times of life and death. All will blister and blacken before her."

"She has attacked Mab's kingdom?" Domin asked.

"Laid siege to it. Her darkness eats away at it. She'll poison all of our island. Blight and plague fester in it even now, and she sows seeds of hatred and terror across the kingdoms, Fay and human."

Cassandra covered her mouth. There was no escaping the Carmun, then.

"Did Mab send you for help?" Domin asked.

The pooka chuckled, a low noise almost like a cough. "There is no help. She sent me as a herald to the other courts with a warning: Our end is come."

Cassandra shivered and wrapped her arms around herself.

"Mab has always been theatrical," Domin said. "Do you wish to rest? There is a garden behind the house."

"There is no rest for me in this place of iron. How do you bear it?"

"I am only part Fay," Domin said quietly.

"I have delivered my message. I will continue on. But many other Fay will flee this direction. Not all of them will be friendly. And even the iron of London will not keep the witch back forever."

"I know." Domin released the pooka's arm, and she transformed back into a horse. With a flick of her tail, she turned and hobbled away from the square.

Domin walked heavily back to the door and shut it, blocking out the chill of the night.

"She is attacking the Fay first," Domin said, probably as much to himself as to Cassandra.

"Even the Fay do not deserve that," Cassandra said. And she thought of the innocent among them—especially the changelings.

"No, they do not. And our worlds are connected like muscle and bone. One cannot do without the other. I'm afraid we will see many Fay refugees invading London before this is through."

Just when Cassandra thought her sisters might be safe in the city. A wave of sticky heat swept over her, and she leaned against the wall, fighting the urge to be sick.

"Are you unwell?" Domin asked.

"Oh, perhaps a little. I had come down to get something to eat or drink. I feel a bit faint."

Domin offered an arm in the darkness. She imagined her family's shock if they knew she was in a dark corridor with a man not her husband, but Domin was her friend and Henry's, and she trusted him completely. She lived by different rules now that her family wouldn't know or understand. She trusted these rules, trusted herself to do what was right, but it made her feel quite adrift, more cut off than ever from the human world. And yet, she also felt brave, like she was stepping forward into some new future that she and Henry—and their friends—would forge together.

She took Domin's arm. They took only a few steps before he stopped suddenly and studied her, his face shadowed in the dim moonlight in the corridor.

"Does Henry know?" he asked.

"That I'm going to the kitchen? I didn't want to bother him."

"Not that—oh. Hmm. *You* don't know."

It was hard to tell in the dim light, but Domin might have been embarrassed. Awkward, certainly.

Cassandra wrinkled her forehead. What was he talking about? He couldn't sense her feelings anymore, and even if he could, there was nothing untoward in them, only concern about the future. Another wave of dizziness came over her. Was she ill? More ill than she knew? Was she dying? If so, she was glad of whatever time she had with Henry, though she wished she could stay by his side through whatever challenges came his way.

"Is it... How much time do I have left?" Cassandra asked.

Domin was silent for a moment, then, to her shock, he chuckled. "You're not dying. From what I understand of it, your illness should pass in a matter of months."

"Of months, but..." Cassandra gasped. "Do you mean I'm..."

She dropped Domin's arm and leaned back against the wall, pressing her hands to her belly. Of course, as she counted days, the timing, it was possible. "But I thought we couldn't, I mean..."

So much for tossing aside the rules of the human world. Her face burned. She could not discuss this with Domin. Amy, perhaps, but not Domin. This was terribly, terribly awkward.

Yet Domin was Domin, as unruffled as ever. "It seemed unlikely, but Henry is not actually Fay, and you certainly are not. In fact, Tam Lin had a child with a mortal as well, so perhaps the outcome should have been expected."

Cassandra wanted to laugh and also to die of embarrassment right there on Amy's fine imported rug in the corridor. No, it was a rather common outcome, all things considered, but she would *not* discuss that aspect of her life with Domin. As her mind settled with the idea, a new cold gripped her, sending another wave of nausea through her stomach.

"But what will this mean for...for our child?"

Domin drew a long breath. "It is dangerous for the child. Doubly dangerous for you, now. The Fay would use both of you against Henry, and they will want the child for its bloodline. Perhaps especially as they scramble for something to help them against the Carmun."

Cassandra wrapped her arms protectively around herself. The Fay would not have her or her child. "Will the child have magic?"

"Not unless the Fay claim it. Henry's magic isn't inheritable as natural Fay magic would be."

That meant the child would live a normal lifespan, as she would. As long as they could protect it. Would that be more difficult for Henry? Especially now?

"What a terrifying time to bring a child into the world," Cassandra whispered.

"I suppose it usually is frightening." Domin considered her. "Yet new life also means new hope."

"But how do we keep it safe?"

"We keep you safe," Domin said matter-of-factly. "Once

he's born, Hale can christen him, and he has the same protection as other children."

Warmth spread over Cassandra, dispelling the chill that had settled in her limbs. "It's a boy?"

"Oh," Domin caught himself as if he hadn't meant to share that. "Yes, it is."

Of course, Domin would know that as he sensed the new life within her. Especially because...because he would be sworn to protect the child, as he was sworn to protect Henry. Cassandra suddenly realized how much rested on this child for the Fay, for Domin, for her and Henry. Oh, and for her family, whom she would have to hide it from.

"I think...I think I must ask you to fetch me that bread before I am sick on the floor. And then, Henry and I have a great deal to talk about."

Chapter Fourteen

Henry woke slowly, exhausted from nightmares of the Carmun, her darkness hunting him through never-ending woods with roots that tangled his feet. And when she caught up with him, her face became Titania's, her expression twisted in sick glee at capturing him again. Fitzhugh had made it clear that Titania still had plans for Henry, and despite his best efforts to hold her off, he feared that someday she would claim him. He might die fighting back against her, but he could never be in her thrall again. Lucien, he knew, felt the same. They tried to hone their magic, but they were turning the weapons against the ones who forged them, and Henry feared they could not triumph that way.

Yet Cassandra was curled up next to him, her face peaceful in sleep, the rise and fall of her chest steady and slow. Whatever else happened, he had this—this moment, this brief happiness. His only real fear was what would become of her if he died. The Fay were patient, and perhaps Titania would not claim him back until Cassandra had lived out her life, but he did not think that would be the case. Despite his agelessness, Cassandra would likely outlive him, and he could provide little for her future comfort. His hope lay in Amy or others of their friends continuing to protect her. Yet it was like salt in his mouth, the thought that he could not be the one to always keep her safe.

She stirred and murmured in her sleep, and he crept out of bed to let her rest.

On his way to the dining room, Lucien caught his arm.

"I need your help," Lucien said.

Henry's heart sank at Lucien's expression. He'd been left mostly to himself as they tracked the Carmun—enough time to get himself into some trouble.

"It's about the changelings," Lucien added.

Henry took a deep breath. He was glad someone had been thinking about them. "Tell me."

"I think I need to show you instead." Lucien motioned for Henry to follow him to the garden behind the house.

A young boy stood there holding an apple like it was a treasure, his clothes stained to an even shade of grey from London's dirty streets. His cheeks were hollow, his eyes wide, his ragged shirt loose on his body. He looked five or six, but he was probably a couple of years older, small because of poor health. And not just in the way of a normal human child living in the filthy streets of London: he was clearly Fay.

Henry knelt to look the changeling in the eye. "What's your name?"

"Will," the boy mumbled.

"I found him by the workhouse," Lucien said. "He was going to turn himself in."

Henry winced at the thought of any more children going to those terrible places. "You don't have a family?" he asked gently.

The boy looked down in shame.

"I don't have a family either," Henry said quickly. "Or I didn't have a proper family. They're all gone. But I have a different kind of family now. The workhouse is probably not the best place to find that, though."

The boy gave him an agonized look edged with frustration. "I'm just so 'ungry! My belly aches until I can't sleep, and I can't work because my 'ead don't feel right."

"I'm sorry," Henry said. He pointed to the small fountain in Amy's garden. "Go wash up and you can eat your apple, and then we'll get you more to eat."

"What do I have to do for it?" the boy asked. Not wary or angry. Just resigned.

"Nothing," Henry said quickly. "You don't have to do anything. Once we know you a little better, we'll find you something you like to do."

The boy didn't look like he believed Henry, but he seemed too weary and hungry to care. It made Henry ill. The boy shuddered when he dipped his fingers in the cold water of the fountain. Henry stood beside him and touched the water, calling the warmth of the summer sun to heat it.

The boy looked at Henry, confused, but then hurried to scrub some of the dirt from his hands and face, setting his apple down only long enough to wash and then snatching it up again.

Lucien gestured for Will to follow him to the house, and the boy gave Henry a nervous look and followed after.

"What do you think you're doing?" Telesm asked, standing on the back steps of the house and blocking Lucien and Will's entrance.

"Saving this child," Henry said, moving to stand behind them.

Telesm gestured to Will. "You're bringing an unknown Fay into our sanctuary. Did you know that the pooka passed this way last night? She warned of danger: danger from the Carmun and danger from the Fay fleeing the witch."

Henry paused at the news, but then he looked down at the boy. "He's a changeling, like you. Certainly, you don't see him as a threat?"

"Oh, are you saying I'm not threatening?" Telesm folded his arms.

"You are not a child," Henry said. He waved toward the carved dog by the door. "Do you not trust your own abilities?"

"I do not trust anything, not with the Carmun loose."

Henry flinched at that. Not that he thought this child represented a threat—Will showed no reaction to Telesm's wards, and the stone dog did not stir. But they did have bigger problems than one child. Still, he would not turn the child away, not when he was already here.

Lucien stepped up to Telesm. "There's nothing I can do about whatever is happening out there with the Grigori and their witch, but I can help this child and every changeling who comes across my path. I suppose this is proof that it's the human changelings who have compassion—even on the Fay."

Telesm rolled his eyes. "You are a dramatic young man, human."

"Amy would not leave this child outside," Henry said, "and it is her home."

"Oh, yes, Amy." Telesm's lips curled up. "We all trust Amy now."

"We do," Henry said.

Telesm huffed and moved aside so Henry could bring the child indoors.

Will stopped inside and gawked at Amy's high ceilings. He shifted his feet, his filthy shoes leaving prints on the rug.

"What can we do for him?" Lucien whispered to Henry.

"First, a bath. There's so much soot in the air and on him, and some of it might have traces of iron."

Lucien looked taken aback by that. "The Fay are so fragile in our world, aren't they?"

"In some ways. Human technology hurts them. Hurts the land." That was something Henry could feel, but Lucien never would. His gift was different. "Yet as people forget what they once knew, they are less prepared to protect themselves from the Fay. The innocent will suffer the most."

"Then someone needs to protect them, don't they?" Lucien asked, giving Henry a meaningful look.

Never did Henry think Lucien and Fitzhugh would agree on anything, but they both nagged him about the idea of him becoming a Faerie Lord able to protect the changelings. They were father and son, after all, though Henry doubted Lucien would ever feel any affection for the father he believed had deserted him. And maybe Lucien was correct. When Henry thought of what he would do to anyone who tried to separate him from Cassandra, he did not understand how Fitzhugh had let Lucien's mother go, especially since he seemed to have truly cared for her. Perhaps the Unseelie magic had poisoned him until he could not care properly anymore. Yet Fitzhugh still cared somewhat about Lucien and the memory of Nanette, Lucien's mother. Not enough to defy the Dark Lady—not even if he could—but enough that he had not betrayed Lucien's hiding place. It might be because of Fitzhugh that Lucien was still alive, convincing the Dark Lady to overlook him or save him for some future need.

Henry led Will and Lucien to the kitchen. The cook—an elderly lady good at ignoring the odd goings-on in the household—took one look at them and went off into her pantry. Henry poured water from the stove into the tin tub and tested the temperature. Lukewarm.

The boy looked hesitantly at Henry, then he dipped his fingers in the water. In a moment, steam rose from the tub.

A chill went through Henry, and he exchanged a look with Lucien. Was this boy a royal changeling, too? No, he was Fay, not human. His magical nature was manifesting itself through heat.

"Are you good at warming up water?" Henry asked.

"I saw you do it, too," the boy accused. He lowered his head. "My ma said I have a devil, and that's why my touch burns. She run me off."

Henry ached for the boy. "I'm sorry. She was wrong. You don't have a devil—only an ability to do magic. And, that woman was not your mother."

He would never doubt that some human parents of changelings were true parents to their children, as Mary Leland's had been to her, but any woman who would throw an innocent young child out into the street with a harsh word was no mother.

"Who are you?" the boy asked. "What is this place?"

"This is a place where magic is safe. Eventually, we can teach you to use your magic, if you'd like. You don't have to stay here, but if you do, you'll be protected." Henry hoped that remained true. "In the meantime, scrub yourself off. It might make you feel less ill. Lucien will see if he can find any clothes for you, and then we'll have breakfast."

"Yes, sir," Will said, the first flickers of hope in his eyes.

Lucien hurried up to search through the old trunks of clothes for something that might fit Will. Henry realized he hadn't had his breakfast, and went to remedy that before he had to introduce Will to everyone else. There was a limit to how many changelings they could cram into one house.

Cassandra was in the dining room, a plate with several rolls in front of her.

"No ham this morning?" Henry asked, ready to cut some for her from the sideboard.

She went a shade paler. "No, the rolls are just what I need. My stomach is a little unsettled."

Henry wrinkled his forehead. "You're ill? You should have said something. Tell me the symptoms."

Cassandra looked almost frightened for a moment, and Henry's chest tightened. Had she been hiding a serious illness? Would he lose her so soon after all? His magic protected him from sickness, but Cassandra had almost died of a fever once, and she might be more susceptible.

She looked almost guilty. "Well..."

"Please tell me," Henry said. "I'm still studying. Perhaps I can find some treatment."

"That might not be possible, but I will tell you and see what you think." Despite her serious words and pale skin, her eyes twinkled.

"Yes, I'll do anything," Henry said, clutching her hand. He felt her pulse. It beat fast. Was she nervous? Or was this part of the illness?

"It started with feeling tired. Lightheaded sometimes. And then the sickness came. Many foods smell abhorrent to me, and I struggle to keep my breakfast down. Yet if I don't eat, I feel worse."

"Any sign of fever?" Henry asked, gently touching her forehead, her cheeks. They were slightly flushed. Yet he struggled to think of a fever that caused these symptoms.

"And then..." Cassandra glanced down and plucked at her napkin, her cheeks burning brighter. "There is no sign of my monthlies."

Henry stared at her, struggling to make sense of what she said. It almost sounded as though... "But that's not possible."

"Well, in the normal way of things, I'd say it is possible," Cassandra said, still flushing, but also with laughter in her eyes. "Even likely."

Henry flushed at that, too, and laughed. "But...the Faerie magic..."

He stopped. He didn't know for certain that being afflicted with Faerie magic was the same as being Fay. And he had been fighting the magic. Fighting the hold they had on him. "If this is true... If you are certain..."

She pressed her lips together. "I wasn't certain—didn't even suspect—but Domin caught my arm when I was feeling faint, and he said...he said it is certain." She looked to him, her eyes bright with raw vulnerability. "He said it is a boy."

Henry sucked in his breath. All of his feelings ran round in his head, in his chest. A boy. A child. His and Cassandra's. It felt like a miracle, a defiance of the Fay. A triumph for human life.

He embraced Cassandra, gently, nestling his face in her hair.

"A boy. Our child," he whispered, then worry slipped in. "Oh..."

She pulled back and looked at him. "Yes. There are the Fay to consider. Domin said they will want the child."

All that warmth and happiness in Henry's chest crystallized into something hot and sharp and fierce. He held Cassandra tighter. "They won't know. I will never allow them to touch you. Or our child."

He would destroy them all, burn Elfland, before he let that happen.

And he remembered Will and all the other changelings who had no one to protect them. He held Cassandra tighter, afraid he wasn't enough to keep any of them safe.

Chapter Fifteen

Mary watched as Will tentatively explored Amy's small garden. A ghost of a smile crossed his face when a butterfly flitted past. He watched it all with such raw wonder that Mary ached for him. She was a Faerie changeling, too, rejected by the Fay, and the human world had not been kind to her strangeness, but at least her human parents had cared for her and made certain there was safety and beauty in her life.

Lucien came to sit beside Mary, his knee just brushing hers. It sent her stomach flip-flopping in a way that was strange but not unpleasant.

"How is he today?" Lucien whispered, bending close so the child could not hear.

Mary enjoyed the warmth that his nearness brought, leaned into it. "I think he's looking a bit better already. When he's stronger, he might like to live with my father and sister in the country. I'm glad you brought him here."

The corner of Lucien's mouth lifted. "I knew it would do

him some good. After all, you helped me to see hope again." He cleared his throat. "You and your friends."

Mary's cheeks warmed. "You've helped me, too. I see now that there's something we can do. Even if we're just..."

"Just changelings?" Lucien asked. "Don't forget, Telesm is a changeling, too."

Mary made a face. "Yes, but he's so...so sour. I'd almost rather not have his help."

Lucien laughed, and Mary grinned at him.

"Well," drawled Fitzhugh's voice from the garden wall. "Isn't this...domestic."

Lucien's face went hard, and Mary's breath caught. Fitzhugh pulled himself up to sit atop the wall, his posture relaxed, and he observed them with a smirk.

Will gasped and scampered back to Mary and Lucien like a frightened puppy. Fitzhugh's smirk deepened.

"One of these days, the Fay are going to realize Amy's running a changeling hotel here," Fitzhugh said, leaping down from the wall to land as gracefully as a tiger in the garden.

The back door burst open, and Amy stuck her head out. "Is anything amiss? I have a sudden headache as if..." Her gaze fell on Fitzhugh. "Oh, you. Of course."

Fitzhugh chuckled. "Yes, me. You see, I can sense your wards, but they're not forcing me away. I'm not such an enemy to you."

"Well, I'm not inviting you inside," Amy said.

Fitzhugh shrugged and walked closer, hesitating at the rose bushes. "As you like. We can have an al fresco discussion. A picnic, if you wish."

"Just tell me what you want," Amy said.

"I'd like to speak to all of your friends about a little incident in Wales."

The color left Amy's cheeks. "Very well."

A few minutes later, the others trailed out, Domin leading them, followed by Jairus and Henry, with Cassandra hanging in the back. The last couple of days, Mary thought Henry seemed especially protective of his wife. Perhaps it was knowing that the Carmun was out there. Mary quickly looked away from them, reminding herself that Fitzhugh could not know about Henry and Cassandra's marriage.

But Fitzhugh watched Cassandra where she stood, her arms folded defiantly. And protectively, Mary thought, like she was trying to be sure Fitzhugh could not sense anything from her. Fitzhugh looked thoughtful for a moment, but then he turned his attention to Henry.

"You have not been behaving yourself," Fitzhugh said, wagging a finger at him.

"What do you mean?" Henry asked warily.

Fitzhugh rolled his eyes. "Wales? The Carmun? What else would I mean?"

Mary looked back and forth between them. She was not always good at understanding people, but she sensed a tension there she did not understand. Fitzhugh was playing some game, and it was sure to be dangerous.

"What do you know of the Carmun?" Domin asked, breaking the silence.

"Likely no more than you do, unfortunately. I know she is a formidable enemy of the Fay, and that someone—the Grigori, I assume—has set her free."

"You have no information that we need, then," Domin said.

"Oh, I don't know if that is true," Fitzhugh said. "There is so much you don't know."

"You wish to barter knowledge?" Domin asked warily.

"In fact, I do not." Fitzhugh's gaze cut to Lucien for a

moment, then he looked to Henry. "I gather you are still not free of the Lady of the Woods."

Henry only folded his arms in response.

Fitzhugh rubbed his forehead. "It pains me to have to say this, but you are selling yourself short, Henry Stewart. And we need our resources at their best. The Fay are...I can only say 'panicked' in truthfulness. The witch and her so-called sons threaten all of our realms."

"We're ready to fight her," Jairus said, hand on his pistol.

Fitzhugh laughed. "Oh, priest, do you think you can defeat her with bullets? No, her power is deeper and deadlier. A blight spreads over the land, consuming crops and whatever life it touches. And it's not alone. There has been an outbreak of disease across England. Smallpox. Typhus."

"Famine and pestilence," Jairus muttered.

Fitzhugh raised an eyebrow. "Indeed."

"How *do* we fight her, then?" Amy asked.

"I don't know what you'll do, my dear," Fitzhugh said. "And I'm under a geas not to speak of my Lady's plans."

Henry huffed. "If you're not here to help, you may as well go."

"I have two pieces of information to aid you, in fact," Fitzhugh said. "I'm probably your most generous benefactor."

Henry rolled his eyes.

"The first thing is specifically for you, dear Henry. A hint, since I doubt your ability to put the pieces together on your own. Despite Jane's obvious limitations after the Wild Hunt debacle, my Lady hasn't thrown her off. There's a reason for that—a purpose. And Titania will be calling on you to counter her. The Lady of the Woods is weakening, you know. She was before, but the Carmun is especially poisonous to her glades and glens. You might be her one hope against my Lady and

Jane. Of course, that's if you decide you don't want to forge your own path."

"More royal blood nonsense," Henry said. "Either tell us what you want to say, or else stop teasing us."

"Alas, I am bound in how much I can reveal," Fitzhugh said. "But I did bring another piece of information to prove my goodwill."

"Well?" Henry asked.

"This information is for your changeling friend Mary Leland."

Mary's eyes widened. She thought Fitzhugh had forgotten about her as he usually did. She stared at him in horrified fascination.

Fitzhugh smiled at her like a wolf. "Maude."

Mary blinked. "What?"

"It is a name that has value to you, though you don't yet realize it. Names have power, and if someone has lost their name, then they, too, are lost."

Mary's forehead wrinkled. "Maude? Who is that? One of the changelings?" Another possibility jumped to her mind. "My mother?"

Fitzhugh ignored her question. "And now, I have done what I can for you all." He hesitated, his normally mocking smile fading to a more serious expression. "Despite what you may think of me, I do not enjoy suffering for its own sake. I only use what tools I must to seek justice." His gaze drifted to Lucien for a moment, but then he looked to Henry again. "And survival. I hope when we next meet, it will be in more pleasant circumstances."

He gave Cassandra one last speculative look, then he climbed nimbly over the wall and was gone.

Chapter Sixteen

Cassandra felt ill. Fitzhugh knew. She was certain he knew. The only question was how he would use it against them.

Henry took her elbow. Squeezed it hard. They shared a worried look. They hadn't told their friends yet about the baby —it seemed too dangerous to speak the words out loud—but soon they wouldn't be able to keep it a secret.

"How do we stop her?" Jairus asked.

Cassandra wasn't certain if he meant Titania or the Carmun. Maybe it didn't matter which.

Domin scanned the adjoining rooftops, where several crows lurked. "Inside."

They all hurried in, out of the way of prying eyes and ears. Mary escorted the frightened young changeling in with them.

"We can track where the outbreaks are happening," Henry said, as soon as the doors shut behind them.

"Fitzhugh made it sound like they're all over the country," Amy said.

"There must be a pattern," Henry said. "There is with any

outbreak. Though, we saw what she did to Rushford. She has help. Her...her children."

"And we still don't know how to hurt them," Jairus said.

They stood in silence.

"In the stories, it was three male Fay and one female one who stood against her and her three sons last time," Cassandra said.

"The Fay are not as strong as they once were." Domin sounded weary. "And we don't know if she has the same number of 'sons' as last time. She might be limited to three again, but we can't be certain."

"We probably don't have that many Fay allies anyway," Amy groaned.

"Changelings!" Lucien said.

Cassandra gave a start and glanced at Henry, who shared her confusion.

"You could have changeling allies," Lucien went on. "Plenty of them. The Fay might even give them their freedom in exchange for help if the Carmun is that dangerous a foe."

Domin considered Lucien. "Possibly. But most changelings are children, and their abilities are untested. Unless we were certain of how they would help—that they *could* help—I would not risk their lives."

"That's still the question." Jairus sounded impatient. "We don't know what weapon to use against them."

"I wonder..." Cassandra trailed off. None of the stories she'd found said how the Fay had stopped the Carmun in the past. The information seemed to be lost to time. "What if Anne could tell us something? She was babbling about the blight."

"She's not easy to make sense of," Henry said cautiously.

"Do we have any better source of information?" Cassandra asked.

Henry sighed and shook his head.

Cassandra looked at the others. They all nodded or shrugged their consent.

"Who should talk to her?" Amy asked.

"I think..." Cassandra surveyed their faces. "All of us. If the answer is changelings, or Fay, or something else we haven't thought of, the more of us who are there, the better chance Anne has to tell us something we can make sense of."

Lucien looked uncomfortable. Cassandra could sympathize. He had been staying out of sight when he snuck out of the house, not going to visit young ladies. But this was probably safer than his usual excursions to the East End.

Amy straightened and said, "Excellent. Then let's prepare to bring a rather large party for a morning visit."

In less than an hour, they were all dressed and headed for the Weaver's lodgings. Cassandra took Henry's arm, and Amy walked close to Domin, taking the lead. Mary and Lucien hung back uncertainly, and Jairus walked in the rear, his gaze alert, challenging anyone who came too close.

They reached the house, and the startled footman admitted their large group to the sitting room. Cassandra tried to sit, but the footman brought a tray with steaming drinks, and the strong, almost burnt scent made Cassandra's stomach turn, so she stood and moved away.

Georgina hurried in to greet them. She made her curtseys and then embraced Cassandra. "I'm glad you're back so soon. And how was Aber...uh, Wales." She cast a cold look at Amy.

Cassandra winced at her sister's rudeness. At least she could lie in response to the question. "It was lovely. But I'm glad to be back and able to visit again."

"Mother and Sophie are out. They've gone to visit the Ashbys." Georgina rolled her eyes. "Again."

"I'm sorry to have missed them," Cassandra said. And she was, but it wasn't pressing to their visit today.

"I would love to see your youngest sister again," Amy said, a magical nudge to her words. "Children are so delightful."

Georgina hesitated. Domin had suspected that she had some resistance to magic, and she was stubborn in addition. But there was no reason to deny Amy's request, unusual as it was.

"Nancy can bring her down, can't she?" Cassandra asked. Nancy might have some advice about how to quell Cassandra's churning stomach, if Cassandra dared to tell Nancy of her situation.

Georgina rang for a maid and instructed her to send for Nancy and Anne. Then Georgina lifted one of the cups, offering it to her guests.

"Coffee?" she asked. "Mother has taken a liking to it."

The scent wafted around Cassandra, and her stomach lurched in protest. Henry gave her a worried look, but she shook her head. He couldn't show too much concern in front of Georgina. Oh, how Cassandra hated lying to her.

Another wave of the scent hit her, and she realized she needed some fresh air. Quickly. She mumbled an excuse about Nancy and hurried for the corridor.

Alone for the moment, she took long, slow breaths. She hoped that the others were covering for her behavior. She hoped she could make it through the visit without revealing too much. Her mouth watered unpleasantly, and her stomach gave another twist.

Cassandra lurched into an adjourning room and grabbed a vase, losing all the breakfast she'd managed to keep down. She leaned her forehead against the wall and blinked back tears. What a dreadfully awkward situation.

"Cassie?" Georgina asked from behind her. "I came to…

Oh! You're unwell! You needn't have come to visit so soon if you needed rest. This is my fault for chiding you for going."

Cassandra managed a weak laugh. "No, this is definitely not your fault."

"But, did you become ill on your journey? You should have told Lady St. Clair."

"I'm... It was just the smell of the coffee. I'll be well again in a few moments." She rested a hand on her churning stomach, and she couldn't help smiling a little.

Georgina studied her for a moment, then her eyes grew wide, and she glanced back toward the room where Henry and the others waited. "Oh, Cassie!"

Cassandra flushed. "What?"

Georgina put a gentle hand on Cassandra's back. "I've always thought it was foolish to demand couples wait so long before getting married. But certainly, Mr. Stewart will make everything right. If you act quickly, no one will know. Few will even suspect. And our parents will help you until Mr. Stewart's career is established. You know they'll be happy."

Cassandra winced, torn between laughing and crying. There was no point in denying what Georgina had already guessed. "Yes, I'm certain they would be. It's not them. It's Henry's, um..."

"I've seen how he looks at you. He'll not leave you helpless. But... Do you mean his family would not approve of you? I know they are supposed to be well-born, but he works for a living, and you offer a dowry. Many families make such a match with benefits on both sides."

Cassandra shook her head.

"It's your limp, then? How can they be so shallow! Especially when Mr. Stewart seems so kind."

Cassandra sank into a chair and buried her face in her

hands. She was glad to see Georgina took a practical turn of mind about a perceived scandal, and thought so well of Henry, but she didn't want her sister to think she had been weak-willed or foolish. That was no reason to endanger her sister, though, to spare Cassandra's reputation. No, the problem was that Georgina looked ready to go to battle for Cassandra, and she did not need her sister marching off against unknown dangers.

Cassandra looked at her sister, careful to speak clearly so she would catch every word. "Oh, Georgie. Henry and I are already married. In secret."

Georgina looked shocked, happy, and then hurt. "And you didn't tell any of us? But you know we'd be happy... It is something with his family, then. Are they that terrible?"

"They're not his family. His family are dead," Cassandra said, trying to decide how much to divulge. "Certain powerful people have taken an interest in him."

Georgina's eyes blazed with anger. "And they don't think you're good enough! Well, he'll have to tell them now, and they'll have to accept it. They can hardly want him to hide his... his own wife!"

"They would not accept me, even if I wanted them to, but it's not even that. Georgina, they are dangerous. You can't imagine. They would use me to control Henry. They might hurt you or our other sisters, even, to make him do things."

"Good heavens!" Georgina sat next to her. "This is all so gothic. What sort of people are they? Criminals? But what could Mr. Stewart possibly do for them? Is he a spy or something of that nature?"

Cassandra ran out of answers there—at least answers that she could safely give. "I'm sorry, Georgie. So sorry. But I can't tell you more. It isn't safe—for you or for him."

Georgina watched her closely. "But Lady St. Clair knows,

doesn't she? Your friends know all about this secret life of yours. Just not your family. Your sister!"

Cassandra sighed. "They know some of it at least. They don't know about the baby yet."

"*Yet.* You're going to tell them. You weren't going to tell me."

"I want to tell you everything—but not until it's safe."

"Is it ever going to be safe, whatever this great secret is?"

"I...I hope so."

Georgina grasped her silver cross necklace. "I would help you, you know. I can keep secrets. I haven't gossiped about those strange events last autumn. I know things are happening that you're not sharing. It's all related somehow, isn't it?"

"Georgie... I love you. That's why I can't tell you more. Not now."

Georgina huffed and strode out of the room.

Chapter Seventeen

Even to Domin's rapidly dulling senses, little Anne glimmered with power. She toddled into the room with her nurse Nancy, as innocent as any young child, but her eyes took in everything —things that most people would never see. If Domin's life was nearing its end, he was glad one of his last acts had been to keep the Fay from stealing this child—for her own sake and for everyone else's.

Anne stopped in the middle of the room and took in the people assembled there. She glanced past Henry and Jairus and paused for a moment at Mary and Lucien. Then her gaze lingered on Domin, either because he was a stranger, unusual with his darker skin—though she had not been so interested in Lucien—or because there was much for her to understand about him. He doubted she was seeing the future—he had little enough future left—but his past was a lengthy tome for a small child.

The girl looked at Nancy and pointed to Domin. "There dragon!"

Domin wrinkled his forehead. Maybe that was the best way the child had to express what Domin was or had been. He had certainly caused pain and chaos in his early years when he served his Faerie mother.

Nancy looked confused as well. She could see some of the power that emanated from the Fay, but she obviously didn't comprehend the child's understanding of Domin. Well, she didn't know his past.

Georgina was still speaking to Cassandra somewhere, so they could be frank.

"Is that what you see, Anne?" Nancy asked.

The girl toddled over to pat Domin's leg. "Nice dragon."

Amy suppressed a smile, and Jairus burst out laughing. "A very nice dragon."

Anne grinned at Jairus and then went to Amy, her eyes adoring. "Pretty fairy. Funny."

Amy smiled and knelt on the floor by the girl, crossing her eyes to make the child laugh.

A very pretty fairy, even when making silly faces. Domin allowed himself to watch Amy for a moment, to enjoy her happiness. She had always been beautiful, even for a Fay. Her magic, after all, came from the woodlands, with all the natural grace of a carpet of bluebells dancing in the spring sunlight and the splendor of autumn leaves cloaking themselves in brilliant colors. But she had once carried some of the woodland's indifference and treachery as well. It had broken Domin's heart, though he had not realized how he had come to admire Amy's determination and liveliness until she betrayed him.

Now, though, she had learned to stand apart from her mother and had blossomed with exquisite beauty, the hope and promise of the first roses of spring. And just when Domin was fading like the lingering wisps of the twilight. When she leaned close to him, all he wanted was to pull her nearer, to discover if her lips were as soft and sweet as they appeared. But he couldn't promise her any kind of a future when he didn't have one to offer. He couldn't break her heart just when she had found it again.

Amy looked up to catch him staring at her. She flushed prettily and glanced down, her long eyelashes hiding her eyes. Domin took a steadying breath and reminded himself why they were there.

He knelt by Anne, on the other side from Amy.

"Has she still been speaking of dark things?" Domin asked Nancy.

The white-haired nurse nodded, her eyes troubled.

Domin met Anne's eyes. "You have bad dreams?"

The little girl sucked on her fingers and gave Amy a questioning look.

Amy rested a hand on the girl's back. "The, uh, nice dragon wants to help."

"Plague," Anne whispered. "Blight."

Domin's heart ached to think a young child had to see such frightening things. "Those are bad dreams indeed. We want to make the bad dreams go away—for you and everyone. But to be rid of darkness, we need light. Do you understand?"

Anne nodded somberly.

"Good," Domin said. "Do you see any light, Anne? Can you tell us where to find it?"

The little girl pouted and looked around the room, focusing on the windows. Domin wondered if she didn't understand. She had years before she truly grew into her powers, and they might be expecting too much now.

But Anne's eyes unfocused as she stared at the light filtering through the glass. She walked unsteadily to Henry. He sat to be closer to the child, and she stared into his eyes. She cocked her head, considering him.

"King," she declared, patting his hand with her chubby one. "Drink."

Henry looked to the others in confusion. "Drink what?"

Anne ignored him. She returned to Domin and patted his chest, just where the piece of iron ate away at his magic and his strength. "Hurt."

Domin drew a slow breath. "Yes. I'm hurt."

"Hurt her," Anne said softly.

Then she reached for Amy, burying her head in the elf's shoulder.

Amy swept the child into a protective embrace. They all shared confused glances.

Domin touched his chest. The iron splinter devoured magic. Would it also hurt the Carmun? Probably. But taking the iron from his chest would likely kill him. Unless...

"Spring-heeled Jack," Domin said.

Before they could speak anymore, Georgina flounced into the room. Domin could not sense emotions like he once did, but she was clearly upset. She noticed Anne clutching Amy and rolled her eyes.

"Oh, I'm sorry Anne is bothering you!"

"Not at all!" Amy offered her a weak smile. "She's a dear."

Cassandra reentered the room, her face pale and drawn with worry. A flare of protective concern washed over Domin—either because he was still able to feel some of what Henry felt, or because his daemon instincts knew he needed to keep their child safe.

Stopping the Carmun would certainly be a part of that. If Domin had to, he would sacrifice himself, allowing someone to cut the iron out of his chest—Telesm wouldn't do it, and neither would Henry, but Jairus might. He wasn't heartless, but he was practical.

Spring-heeled Jack still had a piece of that blade, though. He might be persuaded to give it up, even if by force. He was dangerous to approach, but he had his weaknesses.

As the others made strained small talk until they could politely leave, Domin planned how they could track Spring-heeled Jack.

Chapter Eighteen

Cassandra felt like her heart would burst when she thought about the way Georgina had looked at her throughout their visit. She did not want her sister involved with the Fay. But Georgina suspected things, and she was smart, curious, and resistant to the numbing influence of Amy's magic.

Her friends gathered at Amy's dining room table to discuss the little information they had scavenged from Anne. Even Telesm emerged from his room to join them. Before they launched into more weighty matters, though, Cassandra had to talk to them about Georgina.

She fidgeted with her napkin. Henry looked at her curiously, his worry evident. She attempted a smile, hoping to reassure him that all was well, but based on the increased concern on his face, she failed.

"I have to tell everyone something," she said.

Amy looked up, her face brightening. "Is it about the baby? I was hoping you'd say something so I could congratulate you."

Henry tensed, and Cassandra's face burned. "No, I wasn't...

I mean, eventually I was going to, but...it's so new..." Did everyone know more than she did?

No, by the surprise on the rest of their faces, it was news to everyone else at the table except Domin.

"Oh, dear." Amy went pale. "I'm sorry. I sensed the change, and I thought..."

"Congratulations?" Jairus said, raising his glass with a quirk of his eyebrow. "Even if earlier than you intended sharing, that's happy news."

"You are managing to break from Titania's hold then," Telesm said to Henry. "Though she is going to be angry."

Henry looked ready to say something sharp in response, but Cassandra put a hand on his arm.

"I think Cassandra had something else to tell us," Amy said with an apologetic look at Cassandra. "I'm sorry, but what did you want to speak to us about?"

"It's Georgina, my sister."

The faces that watched hers were full of concern. Especially, she thought, Jairus's.

"Is she unwell?" Jairus asked.

"No, she's quite well, but...she's seen enough strange things that she was beginning to put some of it together. I didn't tell her more—it's not safe, and I have no right—but I thought everyone should know that she's likely to discover at least some of what's happening."

"Are you certain you want your sister involved?" Domin asked. "It is dangerous."

"I know, but I can't stop her from seeing or thinking. You said yourself she is likely Sabbath-born, and she's been dreaming and painting things that she could not have known on her own."

"Are the Fay targeting her, then?" Jairus asked, tensing as

though ready to spring into action.

"I don't know," Cassandra said. "I hope not. But if they do, would it be better if she were prepared?"

"It's your choice," Amy said, "but if this blight is spreading, it might be safer for her to know at least some of the threat."

Silence fell over the table. Cassandra wished they could tell her what to do, but of course, it was her choice. To be fair, it ought to be Georgina's, but she couldn't offer the choice without also offering danger.

"We need to make sense of what Anne told us," Jairus finally said. "We knew from Fitzhugh that the Fay are planning something with the royal changelings. That's what she meant by calling Stewart 'King,' right?"

"Most likely," Domin said.

"And what they're doing is supposed to help against the Carmun?" Amy asked. "But they had this plan in place before they knew she was a threat."

Telesm shrugged. "Their power has been waning for some time. So, they already had a plan to restore their power, give them some advantage over humans. It happens that this plan will also help against the Carmun."

Henry looked down at his hands. "Then we need to know what the Lords and Ladies want with me and the other royal changelings."

They were silent for a long time. Cassandra stared at Henry, feeling ill. Titania would not leave him in peace if he was essential to her plans—and if he could stop the Carmun, then he would not lie low.

"Drink," Jairus said. "The child told you to drink. What does that mean? Is it symbolic, like Domin being a dragon, or is it literal?"

Telesm tapped his fingers on the table. "There are any number of elixirs that might give Henry various powers."

Henry perked up. "The healing elixir. Maybe we're going to find a way to recreate it so we can remove the shard from Domin."

Telesm glowered at this. "No unicorns, remember? And I won't see anyone trying to carve up my brother for a bit of magical weapon. I have other weapons at my cottage that may help against the Carmun—terrible ones. I was hesitant, but perhaps terrible situations call for terrible solutions."

Cassandra was surprised Telesm would consider using the powerful objects he hid from the world. Even he felt the threat of the Carmun.

"We can also try to retrieve the shard of the dagger from Spring-heeled Jack," Domin said. "But that's immaterial to whatever Henry needs to drink."

Henry looked to Telesm. "What elixirs would be most likely to help, then?"

Telesm sighed and scratched his head. "We don't know what the Carmun's weakness is, so I don't know where to start. We can just start pouring potions down your throat until one helps."

Henry grimaced. "I'd rather be a little more precise."

"Let's look at this a different way," Amy said. "The Fay and their obsession with royal changelings. What do they have to do with the Carmun?"

They all looked to Henry.

"Royal blood gives us a link to the land. Can I use that to fight back against the Carmun?"

"You could try, but I don't think it would be enough," Domin said. "If only..." His eyes widened, and he whispered, "The white stag."

Henry leaned forward. "The white stag?"

Domin had gone silent and still.

Cassandra watched him closely. She didn't trust Domin's silence. It likely meant danger for Henry. Yet she could not be possessive of him when it came to fighting the Carmun. She knew that, but her heart rebelled against it.

"But the drink..." Domin mused.

"Tell us, brother!" Telesm snapped.

"Who has the strongest connection to the land?" Domin asked. "Stronger even than a royal changeling? Someone who is likely wounded by the Carmun's presence?"

Telesm shook his head. "I don't know all the creatures of this miserable island."

But Cassandra had been studying them, reading all those books, and the answer washed over her with a thrill. "The Fisher King! And he's the keeper of the Holy Grail."

Jairus leaned forward. "Really? Is that true?"

"I've never met him," Domin said. "But that doesn't mean he's mere legend. We've seen his stag—or at least the stag the Fay associate with him."

"He's real, then," Amy said. "Or, the Lords and Ladies believe he is."

"If he can fight the Carmun, then where is he?" Jairus asked.

Domin shook his head. "He is difficult to find, and he cannot fight directly. He helps to keep the land's magic healthy, though, so he might be able to push back against the blight."

"Who is this king?" Jairus asked. "I've heard of him in stories, but I never understood him."

"He's not easy to understand. But he's a guardian of the land."

Jairus cocked his head. "He's a daemon for Britain? For the whole island?"

Domin looked up at that. "I had not made the connection. It's not usually how daemons work, even the few that are bound to places and not families. But yes, he is a daemon of sorts."

"What does that have to do with royal blood?" Cassandra asked. "I thought daemons were Fay, not human."

"They're neither Fay nor human. Guardian spirits, rather," Domin said slowly. "The Fisher King is a being unique to your island, though. Old rumors claim he has royal human blood. Perhaps he is part daemon as I am and found a way to take all of Britain under his protection. If so, he is very powerful but very old."

"We need to find him," Henry said. "To offer our aid. That's what Anne was telling us."

"The Holy Grail," Jairus mused.

"First," Domin said, "I want to understand more about his role and what the Lords and Ladies want from him." Domin's lips curled back. "Fitzhugh was interested in sharing information with us. I think it might be time to discover what else he knows."

Chapter Nineteen

Henry kept a tight grip on Cassandra's hand as Telesm set up a spell to contact Fitzhugh. Fitzhugh's blood mingled human with Fay, so he could not be summoned as Henry had once summoned the Lady of the Mountains, but they could at least reach out to him through magic.

"I don't like this," Cassandra whispered. "We shouldn't involve Fitzhugh." She rested a hand on her belly, though it did not yet show the child growing within.

Henry pulled her closer. "I don't like bringing Fitzhugh into our plans either, but Domin's correct: we need to know what the Lords and Ladies plan."

"What if we find the white stag? It has appeared often to us, and it might lead us to the Fisher King."

He frowned. "It might, but that could be what Fitzhugh wants—to follow us to the Fisher King."

"Oh." Cassandra frowned. "He's just playing games for the Dark Lady, then."

"I'm not so sure," Henry said. He glanced toward Lucien

and lowered his voice. "Things have changed. You know...you know I would die for you. Kill for you—"

"I don't want you to—"

He caressed her cheek. "Yes, you always ask the best of me. And above all else, I want to be better for you. And when I think of our child, of someone harming either of you... I would do anything to stop them—rend Elfland's magic to tatters. I think, for you—both of you—I could do it, too."

"Henry..." Cassandra looked torn between admiration and fear.

He put a finger on her lips. "Now, think of Fitzhugh. He has long been a selfish creature, but he wasn't always so, according to Amy, and I do think there's a shred of...of humanity left in him. And he recently discovered that he and a woman he cared for, maybe loved, had a child, and that his Lady stole that from him. He's angry at her, and he's dangerous because he knows more than almost anyone about her plans. He'll want revenge, and if there's anything good left in him, he'll want to help us, at least to help Lucien. The question would be if there's enough of his own strength left in him to throw off hers."

Cassandra stared at him with wide eyes.

"So, we're scrying for Fitzhugh?" Amy asked Telesm, ending their private conversation.

"It's not a scrying spell," Telesm said, laying out a basin. "But it uses the same principle. We not only have to find Fitzhugh, we have to whisper to him. It's tricky, but fortunately, I'm very clever."

Amy rolled her eyes.

Telesm smirked. "We need a connection to him, though."

"Well, if I ever had anything of Fitzhugh's, I don't anymore," Amy said.

"Oh, we have something better than some trinket." Telesm looked to Lucien.

Lucien folded his arms. "He is nothing to me. Certainly not my father."

"He hasn't been a father to you in most senses of the word," Telesm said. "But you do share his blood."

"I'm not pricking my finger for him."

Telesm shrugged. "I don't need your actual blood. You just have to hold the bowl and think about him."

Lucien huffed. "In that case, I'd rather give you my blood after all."

He glared defiantly at the rest of them, then he looked to Mary, who gave him a sympathetic nod.

"Oh, very well," Lucien said. "But I won't be the one to speak to him."

"I can do that," Telesm said. "I just need you to fix the reflection on him."

Lucien took the shallow basin as though it were full of spoiled milk instead of water. He let out a long breath and then stared into the basin. Glared at it, really.

"That's good," Telesm said. "Focus on him."

Henry shifted forward, curious, but he could see nothing.

Telesm, though, smiled and leaned closer to the still water. "Douglas Fitzhugh, we desire to speak with you under a flag of truce."

Lucien stared at the basin a moment longer. "He's gone."

"Yes." Telesm took the basin from him. "I believe he heard us. Now we just have to see if he will respond."

"How long—" Cassandra began.

A knock sounded on the rear door.

Amy gave a start. "I believe that's him."

"He was waiting for us to contact him," Henry said.

"Does he actually mean us no harm?" Cassandra asked quietly. "Or is he tricking us?"

Amy sighed, her shoulders sagging. "Either way, we're not inviting him into the house."

She opened the garden door.

"You wanted to see me?" Fitzhugh asked. "You've succeeded in capturing my attention."

"In the garden," Amy said.

Fitzhugh twirled his cane. "It's rude to summon someone's attention and then not allow them in."

"As if we would trust you that much," Amy said.

Fitzhugh smirked. "Wise, my dear. Then you will join me in the garden?"

They filtered outside—all except Lucien—and Jairus came prepared with his shotgun loaded with iron.

"The Grigori learned that trick from you, you realize," Fitzhugh said, eyeing Jairus's weapon.

"I'm well aware," Jairus said through clenched teeth.

He bore the scars from the Grigori's shot against him and Domin.

"Assuming you didn't bring me here just to blast me full of iron, how can I help you this lovely day?" Fitzhugh asked.

"What can you tell us about the Fisher King?" Henry asked.

Fitzhugh smiled. He was excellent at deception, but Henry thought the smile was sincere—perhaps even relieved.

"Oh, you've finally caught on. Yes, the Lords and Ladies have been interested in the Fisher King for some time. He is weakening, you see, and that creates...opportunities."

Domin's eyes narrowed. "What kind of opportunities? What is your Lady planning?"

Fitzhugh only smirked and spun his cane. He was playing games with them. Henry was tempted to turn around and slam the door on Fitzhugh. But he caught Cassandra's thoughtful stare.

"It's like the question game he played with me in the orchard," she said quietly. "He can only answer certain things."

Henry realized she was right. Fitzhugh had to be under a number of geas, so he could not tell them exactly what they needed to know, or even prompt them to ask the right questions, but if they discovered the right way to ask, he might tell them much.

"Does your Lady know how to find the Fisher King?" Cassandra asked.

Fitzhugh smirked and poked some of Amy's roses with his cane, knocking a flutter of white petals to the ground.

"He probably can't say anything about the Fisher King and the Dark Lady," Henry said.

Amy eyed Fitzhugh. "You cannot say what your Lady intends. But do you know what my mother is planning? I believe she is involved in this as well."

Fitzhugh breathed out, barely concealing a satisfied smile. "There I can only speculate, of course."

"Of course," Henry said. But in speculating, Fitzhugh could reveal what his Dark Lady thought.

Fitzhugh studied the silver tip of his cane. "Your mother probably senses the dwindling power of the Fisher King. It hurts her—makes it harder for her to maintain her power."

"The Fisher King gives the Lords and Ladies power, then?" Cassandra asked. "I mean, how does he do that? And why?"

Fitzhugh shrugged. "He doesn't give them power. I don't know him, have never met him, elusive as he is, but I suspect he isn't fond of the Fay."

Cassandra's forehead wrinkled. "Then—"

"He is tied deep into the magic of the land, the ebbs and

flows of life and death, the cycles of the seasons, the energy that flows through all things in the land. In other places, I've heard, these things flow naturally, but at some point in the past, the Fisher King took hold of the magic of this island."

"He would be very powerful, then," Henry said.

"Maybe power was his intention," Fitzhugh said, "but magic that swift and deep is no more tamable than the currents of the sea."

"So, what does he do then?" Amy asked.

"He is a shepherd for the land and its most powerful magic. He is also the keeper of some treasures at least as powerful as those held in Telesm's cottage or the Otherworld, according to lore."

Henry knew two things about the Fisher King from the stories the Fay and humans told: his health was tied to the land, and he guarded the Holy Grail.

Fitzhugh went on. "And if the land and its energies are wounded, he heals them."

"Like with the blight," Cassandra said.

Domin looked thoughtful. "The tale of the Fisher King is almost as old as that of the Carmun. Perhaps he took up his mantle to repair her destruction."

"Perhaps. I care little for lore." Fitzhugh shrugged, looking bored.

"But why doesn't he stop her again?" Jairus asked.

Fitzhugh rolled his eyes. "As I said, he is growing weak. He cannot heal the land if he himself is injured. He may be attempting to hold her back, slowing the sicknesses she spreads, but in the end, his strength will fail, and the Carmun will finish what she began long before our lifetimes."

"Then...what do we do?" Cassandra asked, looking ashen. "You said the Lords and Ladies have a plan?"

"I can only speculate," Fitzhugh said again, and his words seemed to come with great effort. He fought against the geas, picking his way through his words like a person tiptoeing through shards of shattered glass. "But the Seelie Queens may hope to renew the Fisher King's strength by placing someone else on his throne."

"Can they do that?" Amy asked.

Fitzhugh shrugged. "Fay Lords and Ladies can be replaced. Why not the Fisher King?"

"Could they replace him with a Fay?"

"No," Fitzhugh said, and he looked at Henry.

"Then who..." Cassandra followed his gaze and stared at Henry.

Fitzhugh didn't respond directly. Probably could not. But Henry could almost feel Cassandra's horror weighing in that gaze as she came to the same conclusion he did.

"Royal blood gives one a connection to the land," Henry said slowly.

Fitzhugh only smiled.

"The Unseelie Court has Jane," Henry went on, "And the Seelie Court has me. Their obsession with royal bloodlines... But if it were even possible for me to replace the Fisher King," Henry said slowly, "then wouldn't Titania still have a hold over me?"

"Of course," Domin said. "That's what both courts want: to control all the magic—the power and energy—of the land. They could do that and perhaps even defeat the Carmun by controlling the Fisher King."

Amy's eyes went wide, and Cassandra stifled a gasp.

"There, I always knew you weren't *such* fools," Fitzhugh said with a smirk.

"But why the other changelings?" Mary asked, her voice barely audible. "Why are they seeking more now?"

Fitzhugh looked surprised, though Henry couldn't be certain if he was surprised she had spoken or surprised that she had noticed their scheme to claim more changelings. Either way, he did not reply.

Henry couldn't focus on that for the moment. He felt ill. He had no idea how one replaced the Fisher King, but he was certain he didn't want to do it. Didn't want the responsibility and power. Didn't want to leave Cassandra. And their child... "Are you saying if I don't take the Fisher King's mantel, then Jane will? Those are the only options?"

Fitzhugh shrugged. "You could try to keep the Fisher King on the throne, but he has grown weak. The Fay don't know why, but they can feel it, and they will take advantage."

Henry groaned. "Maybe we can restore his health somehow."

The Grail. It was supposed to offer healing. Anne had said, "Drink." But why couldn't the Fisher King drink from the Grail and heal himself? Maybe it didn't work that way.

Amy's eyes brightened. "It doesn't have to be Henry or Jane. Just someone of royal blood."

Fitzhugh gave her a speculative look. "Someone from a *legitimate* bloodline, my dear. You and I may have royal blood, but we never had a claim to the throne."

"I wasn't thinking of me," Amy said primly. "I believe it is time for you to depart."

"You think you can banish me so easily?" Fitzhugh asked.

"I think we cannot trust you with our plans any more than you trust us with yours."

Fitzhugh looked like he wanted to argue. Did he sincerely wish to help? Want to join with them in their planning?

Fitzhugh could be useful if it suited him. But his Dark Lady could force him to reveal all he knew unless they could craft a powerful geas over him—which he was unlikely to agree to.

Finally, Fitzhugh shrugged. "Very well. I will leave you to your scheming. But be aware, many eyes are on you, and many minds are turned toward the problem of the Fisher King."

They watched Fitzhugh leave. Henry thought his light steps seemed forced, his shoulders slightly stooped with worry as he went.

Once he was gone, they hurried for the sanctuary of the house.

"Well?" Domin asked Amy as soon as they were inside again.

"I may know of another changeling who would qualify." Amy's eyes shone.

"Who?" Henry asked. He hadn't heard about any other royal changelings, but then, he had only learned of Jane the previous year.

Amy smiled. "King Edward."

"Edward Tudor?" Henry asked. "Henry VIII's son? I thought he was a faerie changeling—the one traded with Jane."

Domin looked at Amy with admiration, and a smile turned his lips. "No, not Edward Tudor. Edward of the House of York, the Lost Prince."

"The Princes in the Tower!" Cassandra exclaimed. "The ones who disappeared. Edward and Richard. You mean, their uncle didn't murder them?"

"No," Domin looked weary. "Richard III was not such a villain."

"Were you their guardian?" Henry asked. Going from the care of an uncle to the care of the Fay did not seem like a good trade.

"I had other charges during the War of the Roses. But Amy is correct, the Princes in the Tower escaped with the Fay. I have seen them, though it has been many decades."

"Then either one could become the Fisher King, if they are still alive," Cassandra said. "Oh, unless they are terrible like Jane."

"I don't think they would be," Amy said. "I've heard rumors of them dwelling in the court of the Lord of the Thames. After all, his river flows right up to the Tower of London, where they were held. Lord Thames doesn't mingle much with the other Fay, but I have a sense that he is not cruel. He doesn't usually capture changelings. He might be willing to free one of them outright, and if not, he would probably not be worse than my mother—assuming we can't heal the Fisher King."

Domin nodded. "The Lord of the Thames's power is not what it once was, but he maintains his court. There's a chance the princes are still with him."

"Our first choice is to heal the Fisher King," Henry reminded them. "I suspect the Grail may offer us a solution. It seems he cannot just drink from it and heal himself."

Cassandra's eyes lit. "In the stories I've read, he can't heal himself. He needs someone else to do it by asking the correct questions. If we find him, maybe we can find the right question and use the Grail to restore him."

"Some gifts must be offered to us—we cannot take them upon ourselves," Jairus mused.

"Maybe," Telesm said. "But you do need a plan in case he is too grievously wounded, or the Grail does not act as you expect, or even if the Fisher King refuses or is unable to help."

"Then we seek the Lost Princes and the Lord of the Thames," Henry said.

"I tried to speak to him, if you recall," Domin said. "About the changelings. I could not gain admittance."

The challenge in his words went unspoken: could Henry succeed where Domin had failed?

Henry held up his hands. "You don't have water magic. I think I can make it so the Lord of the Thames cannot ignore us. We find the Lost Princes, and then we find the Fisher King."

Jane could not become the Fisher Queen—she was unbalanced, and the Dark Lady would bring suffering to the land. It would not be much better to let Titania control Henry as the Fisher King. And his heart ached to think of being forced away from Cassandra, not there to protect her. Not there to see their child. No, if there was another royal changeling who might take the place of the Fisher King if necessary, Henry had to find him.

Chapter Twenty

It was Jairus's turn to keep watch that night. Domin had gone out to track rumors of Spring-heeled Jack, and he would need to rest when he returned. He needed much more sleep of late. Not that Jairus minded standing guard. He was restless, and it suited him just fine to have something to do. He worried for his friend, though—for, unlikely as it once seemed, a friend was exactly what Domin had become.

Jairus had avoided friendship for years, had wanted to do everything alone. Now, he knew he had been a fool. In fact, at times like this, when the others had turned in early, Jairus felt the weight of loneliness. Maybe it hadn't bothered him before because he thought he deserved it. Maybe a part of him was afraid he still deserved it—deserved to be alone after letting a thirst for gambling creep into his blood and watching his nephew die because of it. But there were times that the voice in the back of his mind spoke to him of peace and forgiveness. He had never touched another card or placed another bet, and he'd spent five years doing everything he could to make up for his mistakes. The weight of that guilt was a heavy thing to carry. How could it ever be enough? He was, as the Fay liked to say, a priest. He believed in forgiveness in a general sort of sense, but somehow, he couldn't believe it for himself.

A movement outside the window caught his eye. A fellow dressed in Roman armor drifted aimlessly past the window. One of London's many ghosts. Jairus wondered what had trapped a soul there for so long, but when he tried to speak to the dead, they didn't pay him any heed. Maybe they couldn't see past whatever sorrow kept them linked to this world.

Maybe they hadn't forgiven themselves. Maybe holding onto their past mistakes was keeping them from the future.

Jairus shook off the unexpected thought and looked heavenward. "Alright. I'll think about that."

He returned to staring out the window while he brooded on the issue. Something moved outside, a human form hurrying toward the house in the darkness. Small, and sneaking, so not Domin. Jairus braced himself for the striking of the clock and its warning spell, but nothing came. This was no enemy then.

A frantic pounding sounded on the door.

Jairus rushed to yank it open.

Georgina Weaver stared at him with frightened eyes. The sight of her fear stirred something deep and protective within him, and he fought the urge to storm into the night, guns drawn, to attack whatever terrified her.

"Mr. Hale!" she gasped. "Is my sister here?"

Jairus studied her carefully. There were shapeshifters in the world, after all. Had Georgina always had such expressive eyes? And those flashes of red in her hair?

"Mr. Hale? Please, I need help."

Jairus couldn't ignore that. He stood back but still didn't offer a verbal invitation.

Georgina pushed past him for the shelter of the house. Not Fay, then, since she could enter uninvited. She had simply grown into a very pretty young lady. And that meant she was in some danger to appear here so late at night, still dressed in a gown for a ball or party. The late hours of London meant it wasn't unreasonable for her to be awake at midnight, but it was unreasonable for her to be alone.

She wrapped her arms around herself. Jairus shucked off his coat and offered it to her, and she took it with a stuttered thanks and lowered eyes.

He shifted so she could read his lips. "What are you doing here at this hour?"

"I know it might have been foolish," Georgina said. "But I saw something, and I didn't think it could wait."

"What was it?"

"A stag. A white stag. But...but it could not have been real, er...normal, I suppose? It was almost glowing, and it seemed to want me to see it. Yet my mother and sister..." She choked a little. "They said it was only an ordinary deer, and then they acted as though it wasn't even there."

"But you're certain of what you saw," Jairus said levelly. She was Sabbath-born, Domin had speculated. Cassandra hesitated to tell her everything, but she had warned them her sister was piecing things together. Georgina Weaver saw things more clearly than was safe for her.

"I'm certain. It just stood there, right out on the street, in front of everyone. Like it was waiting to be noticed." Georgina narrowed her eyes at him. "I know strange things are going on. Things Cassie doesn't want to tell me about. For instance, why you're acting like a footman in Lady St. Clair's house."

Jairus couldn't help smiling. "Well, you're not wrong. There are strange things afoot. That's why I'm keeping watch here while the ladies of the house sleep. In fact, I'd like to see this stag, if I might. Do you think you could show it to me? Uh, would you trust me to accompany you?"

Georgina studied him closely, then she nodded. "Yes, I trust you, Mr. Hale. Mother or Sophie would say it's foolish to trust any man, but I get a feeling around some men—a bad feeling— and you're not like that. You make me feel...safe."

Jairus couldn't help but be warmed by her words. "Normally, I would tell you to listen to your mother and older sister, but time is of the essence if we're going to find that stag again."

"I saw it close by. We were coming home from a dinner party. I snuck back out to warn you. Cassie said there were dangers, but I thought—I sensed—that you needed to know about this."

"I think you were correct," Jairus said. "But you do need to be cautious."

She nodded, but she did not look abashed. If anything, her eyes flashed with excitement. "After last fall, with the...ghosts, or whatever they were, I did some reading in the books Cassie left behind. I started wearing this." She held up the silver cross. "The cross against evil and the silver against ghosts."

This young lady was too adventurous for a life of dinner parties and dances. But Jairus knew it was not his role to encourage her dangerous pursuits. It was, however, his role to protect anyone who needed protecting, and Georgina Weaver could use an escort in this dangerous world—at least for that night.

Jairus followed her out into the square—close enough to keep her safe, but far enough not to intrude on her person. She motioned for him, and they jogged through the evening, occasionally passing other party-goers returning home. The lights blazed in some houses, marking balls or musicales still well underway, but the bright windows left deep shadows in the alleyways and corners.

They reached another, smaller square lined by quiet houses. Georgina scanned the shadows, her expression falling. Then she turned back to Jairus.

"It was here. Right here!"

"I believe you," Jairus said.

He knelt to study the ground. Yes, hoofprints from a deer marked the soft dirt.

"Those are from the white stag, aren't they?" Georgina asked, her voice close to his ear.

He started and looked up at her, her face close and alight with excitement. He was suddenly very aware that he was alone with a pretty girl in the dark.

He cleared his throat and stood, stepping back to a respectful distance. "Yes, there was a deer. And its prints vanish."

"It's not a ghost if it left marks," she said. "But how could it disappear?"

Jairus shrugged one shoulder. "Magic?"

Georgina cocked her head. "I'm not sure if you're teasing me. That stag was beautiful enough to be magical."

"Maybe I'm not teasing. I think the best thing now is to get you safely home, though. Where there is beautiful magic, there is likely to be dark magic as well."

Concern flashed in her eyes. Jairus hated to take away the excitement for her, but she needed to know it wasn't safe to run after magical creatures in the night.

"Very well." She touched the cross at her throat. "I wish I understood more."

Jairus wished she did, too. He didn't want to draw her into danger, but he liked her instincts. And the brightness of her eyes, especially when she looked at him.

"Maybe someday you will," Jairus said. "But be careful what you wish for."

"Sometimes, Mr. Hale, I grow tired of being careful."

His lips quirked in a repressed smile. "In that case, I am glad I'm here to see you safely home."

The defiance in her face softened a little. "So am I, Mr. Hale."

Feeling presumptuous, he offered an arm, and she was quick to take it. Georgina Weaver was too good for an on-the-run monster hunter like him. He knew he had nothing to offer a young lady except a quick smile, protection in the darkness, and maybe a lively dance at a party. But Georgina gripped his arm like she found some comfort in his presence, and that made him feel worthy to offer it to her.

Even after he saw her safely inside—sneaking in through the back door like a maid stealing time with a beau—the warmth of her fingers lingered on his arm.

This was no time for such thoughts, though. Perhaps there never would be for him.

They had the Carmun to worry about, after all. When he returned to Amy's house, he could almost feel the presence of his friends. Worn and bruised, every one of them, and the main fight hadn't even started. The others had paid it little notice, but Jairus hadn't failed to hear in the original story that it took equal forces to stop the Carmun the first time: three men and a woman. He usually figured out how to fight the monsters he faced by listening to their stories. Their weaknesses always showed up there, sometimes hidden between the fear and magic of the old tales.

And the Carmun fell before forces of light who stood against her darkness.

The three men were easy enough: him, Henry Stewart, and Domin. That had been his original thought, at least. But he couldn't discount the lost Prince Edward as the potential Fisher King being one of the three. And what about Telesm or Lucien? Jairus believed that God lined things up just so, and the extra numbers bothered him. There were extra women, too. Cassandra, Amy, and Mary were all strong in their own ways, but none of them were fighters as such. He could imagine someone like the Morrigan fighting, but she might not even be on their side in this conflict. Which of the ladies would stand up to the might of the Carmun? And what might it cost them?

Chapter Twenty-One

Henry watched the English countryside slide by the train windows. In London, the only indication that anything was amiss was his nagging sense that the magic of the land was dulled and off balance—and the appearance of Faerie creatures, including Georgina Weaver's sighting of the white stag. But out near the Cotswolds, the Carmun's touch stained the land. Blight crept over fields of crops, with stalks of grain and even thick hedgerows browning and withering in an undulating pattern like the waves of the sea touching the shore.

"That's ugly," Jairus said, his hard expression making it clear he didn't just mean the brown spreading over the fields.

Henry nodded. This close, he could feel the land crying out for help, slowly smothering under the touch of the Carmun's poison. He had been uneasy about leaving Cassandra behind in London, but now he was grateful.

When they disembarked in Cirencester, the sensation of unease hit Henry with full force, tightening his stomach. The people in the town felt it, too. He could see it in their hunched shoulders and the wary, even hostile, looks they gave the outsiders. Fitzhugh had warned them the Carmun sowed hatred and despair along with plague and famine. Many of the houses were marked with signs of quarantine.

A young boy approached Henry, his eyes downcast. "Please, sir, can I shine your boots for a penny? My family has nothing to eat. Our crop's been ruined, and my pa is ill."

Henry felt as though he'd been punched in the gut. How many times had he ruined a family's crops on Titania's whim? How many children had he left hungry? He pulled all the coins from his pocket and offered them to the confused boy.

"For a debt I owe," Henry said.

The boy took the money, hesitating as though it were Fay currency that might turn to acorns. Then he mumbled a thanks and rushed toward the baker's.

"We need to move quickly," Domin said in a low voice. "The sooner we can reinforce the Fisher King, the sooner we can end this."

Henry hated to leave people in distress, but Domin was right. There was nothing he could do here.

Domin guided them out of the town on foot. Trees shaded their paths, the branches shuddering sometimes as if quaking in fear. Or begging for help.

As they walked, Henry heard the trickle of several springs. Even more, he felt them—the fresh, clean water bubbling up from the earth, anxious for its journey across England to the sea. Yet even the water spoke of darkness—not the natural darkness of rest and restoration, but something poisonous seeping deep into the land.

"There." Domin pointed to an ancient hawthorn tree standing guard above one of the springs, its branches bowed as if its delicate leaves were too heavy a burden.

"How do we open the way?" Jairus asked, frowning at the water bubbling up beneath the tree.

"Normally, only members of Thames's court would be able to," Domin said. "I tried calling him from here, and he did not respond."

"Sounds like he doesn't want to help," Jairus said.

Henry knelt and dipped his fingers in the icy water. A shiver raced to his heart. "I'm not certain. The water feels...wrong. I wonder if he is poisoned or under siege like Queen Mab."

"Can you open the way then?" Jairus asked.

"Maybe. My magic is Seelie like his, and I can speak to the water."

Henry trailed his fingers through the icy water that sprung up from somewhere deep beneath the earth. Shimmers of magic clung to it. Yes, the Lord of the Thames's kingdom was beyond this spring—through it—but Henry had to convince the magic that he was a friend.

If it were Faerie magic alone, he might have tried to force it to obey him as he had learned to do with Titania's magic. But the water's energy was almost alive, slippery and dangerous. He dared not push it.

Instead, he worked with it, letting his mind travel deep into the earth where it trickled through ancient stone that had never dreamed of sunlight. The water didn't love the darkness. It wanted freedom and light. And there was a poison in the dark now, something to flee from. But there were many paths the water could take to the surface. Magic called it to one in particular—one that led deep into the caverns of the earth—but Henry gave the water another nudge. After all, one path was as good as another. The water heeded his suggestion, bubbling down deeper into the mouth of the spring, and then rising from another opening nearby.

The empty mouth of the spring waited for them, and Henry could feel the press of Faerie magic. It was easy enough to push it aside like a curtain. The veil between worlds opened to admit them. Dark, water-stained stone steps led down into the cold depths of the earth.

"Careful," Henry said. "They'll be slippery."

Jairus raised his lantern, and it cast eerie patterns of light and shadow on the slick-looking steps. They picked their way down the black stairs into the cold embrace of Thames's realm.

At the bottom of the steps, the path broadened into a wide corridor. Faint, blue-green light reflected off the stone path. But there were no Fay about. No signs of life. The only sounds were the footsteps of Henry and his friends echoing off the high walls. An unpleasant scent laced the air, like stagnant water and rotting plants. A cold deeper than the chill of the damp cavern filled Henry. Were they too late for Thames? What would happen to England without the power of the mighty river he shepherded?

The corridor opened into a vast cavern. Ribs of stone extended upward, and in the spaces between, light filtered down, shimmering and rippling over the surfaces of the room.

"It's water!" Jairus breathed. "We're under the water."

He was right. Henry craned his neck to stare up at the dome overhead. The dancing light filtered through water held back by... What? Only magic, as far as Henry could tell. Hopefully, that meant that Thames was not defeated. If he was, the magic could give way at any moment and the river would crush them in an icy torrent. Henry might be able to divert it, but he had never tried to control that much water.

Only after Henry's eyes adjusted did he realize a throne stood at the far end of the room, one of stone with a rippling pattern as though centuries of lapping waves had carved its form. A young man sat on the throne, his fingers gripping its arms as he watched the strangers enter his realm. He had dark blond hair and a weak chin, but there was steel in his eyes and in his posture, even at that distance. Somehow, Henry had expected something different from the Lord of the Thames. The young man was regal but didn't carry the sense of age he expected from a Faerie Lord.

Domin and Jairus also noticed the throne and turned to it. Domin looked about to whisper something to them, but the young man interrupted him.

"What has brought you to the Court of Lord Thames?"

His voice, though not deep or commanding, filled the huge chamber.

Henry glanced at Domin, who stepped forward. He was more a diplomat than Henry could ever hope to be.

"We have come to address Lord Thames in the matter of the Fisher King."

Domin's words carried through the cavern and reverberated around them into a terrible stillness. Henry hoped they had not made a mistake.

"The Fisher King," the young man said thoughtfully. "The Fay speak often of him in secret counsels on the edge of twilight." He studied Domin and Jairus, but his attention fell on Henry. "Have you come on behalf of your Lady?"

Henry winced inwardly at the reminder that he was not free. "No, my lord. I come on my own behalf. On behalf of the peoples of Britain."

"And you have the right to do so?" the young lord asked, an edge of mockery in his voice.

"I am a royal changeling, Henry Stuart, and I am not a puppet of the Lords and Ladies."

Domin motioned Henry to stay quiet and turned back to the throne. "Where is the Lord of the Thames?"

The young man on the throne stiffened, and Henry looked at Domin in surprise. This was not Thames, then. So, who was he?

"You may address your questions to me," the young man said.

"No," Domin's voice echoed off the stone ribs of the chamber. "I will speak only to Lord Thames."

"My father is not accepting audiences," the young man said.

"Your father is dying," Domin replied, his tone gentle despite the blunt words. "We may be his last hope—and yours as well."

The young man on the throne went pale at Domin's words, and the waters overhead surged against the dome as if to wash the words away. But then the young man stood, and the waters calmed.

"What do you know of it?" he asked.

"I know that Lord Thames has fought a long and tiring battle against incursions and pollutions in his domain, and now, a more immediate danger threatens the last of his strength."

The young man stared at them for a long moment, his face hard.

Then something in his eyes flickered, and he gestured them forward. "You wish to see Lord Thames? Then you shall. Follow me."

Henry looked to Domin and Jairus and then followed with them where the young man led. He guided them into a room off of the main chamber that seemed to be molded from water. The river flowed around them, forming the walls, and a spring bubbled up from the floor to form a sort of cushion. On that cushion, a man rested—or rather, a Fay.

Henry paused at seeing him. The Faerie Lords he had known had all been as timeless as the Ladies. But Thames was old. Not as ancient as he might have looked if he had lived as long as the river flowed, but his beard and hair were long and white, and his pale skin bore wrinkles near his eyes and on his forehead. No smile lines marked his face. This was not a Faerie Lord who smiled often. Being linked to the mighty power of a river ought to make one strong, but the river had suffered much over the centuries, and Lord Thames had felt the struggle of the river against man and nature. His hands and wrists looked frail where they showed beneath his robes, and his emaciated body rested heavily against its cushion of water.

Thames opened his eyes and regarded his visitors with weary resignation.

"Why have you come?" he rasped. "Have the other Lords and Ladies sent you to gloat?"

"No, my lord," Henry said quickly. "No one sent us, and all the Fay are in danger. Queen Mab's realm is under siege by an enemy—the witch Carmun—and the other kingdoms will soon follow."

Thames grunted.

"We are seeking to restore the Fisher King, and we believe there may be changelings in your court who can aid us."

The ancient Faerie Lord fixed Henry with a dangerous look, one grounded deep in the fury of many mighty waters. "I have no wish to speak of such things."

"But we must speak of it," Henry said. "Lest the power of the land be overthrown and the Dark Lady take control of it."

"I agree," the young man said. "Father Thames, I believe it is time we discuss things that have long gone unsaid."

"Boy—" Thames warned.

The young man turned to Henry. "I am Edward of the

House of York, royal changeling in the household of the Lord of the Thames. And I wish to hear what you have to say."

Henry stared at Edward—the most senior of all the royal changelings, the one with the oldest claim to the throne, dating back four centuries. Yet he suddenly felt a twinge of regret at what he had to ask. It would be a heavy burden if Edward had to take the mantle of the Fisher King. Probably a lonely one as well. Yet Henry did not think it wise to take the role himself, not when Titania might still control him. Not when Cassandra also needed him. And the changelings.

"The Fisher King is weak, maybe dying," Henry said. "And a terrible blight is infecting the land. We hope to find the Fisher King and heal him. But if we cannot heal him, a royal changeling must take his place."

"You claimed to also be a royal changeling," Edward said, eyes narrow.

Henry sighed. "I am. But I am under the control of The Lady of the Woods. If I took the Fisher King's place, she would try to use me."

Thames grunted at that, a frown creasing his face.

"And you don't fear my father's influence on me?" Edward asked.

Henry glanced at the aging Faerie Lord, who had closed his eyes again. "I was led to understand that Lord Thames would be more sympathetic to our cause and less likely to turn it to his advantage."

He might not even have the strength. Lord Thames was a warning of what would come to all the Fay if magic eroded and their domains were desecrated.

"You are correct," Edward relented. "My father takes little interest in things beyond his domain. We have much to occupy our time in this realm, trying to keep the River Thames alive. As you can see, our efforts take a terrible toll. My father suffers greatly, and I would see his health restored. The renewed strength of the Fisher King would benefit us all."

Henry nodded, letting himself hope. Edward might be an ally after all.

Edward turned to Thames, studying him with a worried expression. "Father?"

"You know I will not stop you, my son. You may choose what you think is best."

Henry did his best not to gawk at this compassionate response. Thames had not kidnapped the Lost Princes to be his servants. He had truly taken them in as his children. Or Edward, at least. There was no sign of the younger brother.

Edward knelt beside Thames and clasped his hand, his face worried as he studied his Faerie father. Then he slowly shook his head.

"No," Edward said, "I cannot leave." He looked to Henry. "It is a constant battle to keep the river alive. It weakens my lord, and without my support, I fear what would happen, not just to him, but to his domains."

"The Fisher King could help strengthen Thames's domain," Henry said.

Edward looked with fondness on his Faerie father. "But what might happen in the interval between when I leave and when we find the Fisher King? What if we fail to restore or replace the Fisher King or the witch attacks this realm, and my father is left helpless? No, I cannot risk it, and England cannot afford for Thames to fall."

"What will happen, then, when the Carmun reaches London?" Henry asked. "When her blight infects your waters?"

He and Edward locked stares as if each daring the other to back down.

"I don't know," Edward finally said. "I only know that my duty is here. In the human world, do they still tell the story of the dog who held a bone in his mouth until he saw his reflection in the water?"

"He grabbed for the reflection of the bone," Domin said. "And in so doing, he dropped the bone he had and lost them both."

Henry frowned, but he couldn't argue. There was a chance that they could heal the Fisher King. But there was a chance they would fail. Thames's hold on his power was clearly weak, and Henry could not blame Edward for not wanting to see his realm fall.

"There were two princes in the tower, though," Domin said in the quiet.

Edward's gaze snapped to Domin, then he shook his head. "We cannot be of any help to you here. I think you had best continue on your quest. I wish you luck, however, in restoring the health of the Fisher King." His face softened again. "For all our sakes."

Chapter Twenty-Two

Henry trudged back into the human world, the lingering dampness of Thames's realm making him shiver despite the summer sun. Henry shielded his eyes against its unfiltered glare. Once his friends were out of the tunnel, the water rippled back up to hide the entrance.

"We'll just have to find a way to restore the Fisher King's health," Henry said.

"There's always the Grail," Jairus said.

But Domin only frowned, worry in his eyes and the set of his shoulders. Henry looked once more around at the trees. How long before blight touched this place? The sickness was close, creeping nearer with every breath. Titania would not have Henry hurt the trees or the land if he took the mantle of the Fisher King. But she had already forced him to hurt humans in the past. It would be that much worse if he had more power.

A crow's caw broke the quiet. The huge black bird watched them from a nearby branch, its sharp eye fixed on them. It cawed again and flapped off as if to tattle.

"Not her again," Jairus mumbled.

"It might be just a crow," Henry said.

But he knew it wasn't.

Domin scowled and led them forward. Around a bend in the path, the Morrigan stood waiting.

She wore a long black dress that trailed into the leaves. At least it wasn't her armor, and her sword was nowhere to be seen. The crow landed on her shoulder, and she scratched its head.

"Domin," she said with a smirk. "You're looking unwell."

Jairus drew his shotgun. "What do you want? We have things to be doing."

Her smirk widened into a grin. "Darling human. You never cease to amuse me. But I bring a message for Henry Stewart."

Henry braced himself. Was Titania summoning him to fight? He didn't know if he could resist her—or if he should, in the circumstances. They did have to stand against the Carmun, but he had hoped to do it his way. His friends would go on without him if needed, though.

"What is it then?" Henry asked.

The Morrigan tsked. "Not very polite, princeling. Don't you humans warn against slaying the messenger?"

"For whom do you act?" Domin asked.

Henry braced himself for the answer.

She tilted her head. "For the dead. Those who walk the Twilight Path are restless. They beg: Do not forget us."

Henry stared at her. "That's your message? But..." Titania summoning Henry to war would please the Morrigan. This, though? "Why do you choose to bring me their message?"

She studied him, stroking the crow on her shoulder. "Contrary to what many believe, I do have some feeling for those who die in battle. Especially those who die nobly. Their sacrifice is sweet to me."

"But not those who die of plagues or blights," Henry said.

One corner of her mouth curled up. "True. Such deaths bring nothing to me. It would be unfortunate to lose this entire island to an ancient enemy. I would much rather see an honest fight."

Henry considered her words. "Did you witness the Carmun's last appearance? You are a spirit. You have existed many centuries."

Her eyes grew distant. "True. So much blood has soaked into these islands, and I have witnessed all of it."

"How did they defeat her?" Jairus asked, grasping the direction of Henry's questions.

"You don't know?" she asked with a sly smile.

"A female Fay and three males to counter the witch and her three sons," Jairus said. "But what did they do?"

"They could not kill her sons, bound with deep magic as they were. One cannot destroy darkness or pain. But they banished the sickness from Ireland and imprisoned the witch."

Jairus shifted impatiently. "What weapon—"

"Words," the Morrigan said disdainfully. "Of all the beautiful weapons in the world, that is what they chose. They did not believe they could defeat the Carmun in battle, so they tricked her sons into a bargain: they would depart Ireland forever, and in exchange for their safe passage, they left their mother as a hostage. This the champions accomplished through the power of their individual strengths: Poetry, satiric speech, wisdom—and light."

"They used poetry?" Jairus asked, looking down at his shotgun in dismay.

"They weren't all Fay," Domin said, his eyes widening. "At least some of them were humans or were changelings. They must have been to master creative powers like poetry."

Or like satire, Henry realized. Cutting words. As Lucien had. But he dared not say it out loud. The Fay needed to forget that Lucien existed. If the Dark Lady realized that Lucien might help her against the Carmun—and perhaps help her to replace or control the Fisher King—or if the other Faerie Queens realized it, Lucien's freedom and perhaps his life would be over.

"I warn you," the Morrigan said, "this witch is formidable. She is not likely to allow herself to be defeated the same way again. War is coming." The Morrigan studied each of them as though taking their measure. "A great and terrible war. You will all have to make choices. Choices that will break your mortal hearts. And I would hate to see any of you choose poorly."

She fixed her gaze on Henry, and a chill ran through him. She reminded him of his promise to the dead—his promise to fight Titania. He could not allow Titania to use him, no matter what it cost him.

The Morrigan swept them a bow—a sincere gesture, Henry thought—and then she dissolved into crows and filled the sky above them with flashing black wings.

"What was that?" asked a small voice.

Henry gave a start and turned to see a boy standing behind them—a boy about twelve who looked a great deal like a younger version of Edward.

The boy, finding himself under scrutiny, straightened and wet his lips. "I am Richard of Shrewsbury, Duke of York, a royal changeling, and I will accompany you on your quest for the Fisher King."

Henry gave a start. The second Lost Prince.

"Does Lord Thames know of your decision?" Domin asked.

Richard looked guilty for a moment, but then he lifted his

chin. "He has said I may do as I wish, as long as I do not leave the Thames."

"But..." Henry looked around. They were at the headwater of the Thames, but they were unlikely to find the Fisher King along its shores.

"Oh, I know how Faerie promises work," Richard said. "So, I don't let the Thames leave me." He displayed the ends of his cloak, which dripped with river water.

Jairus laughed. "Ah, yes, Richard! I thought you were familiar! You're the soggy...uh, the lad who rescued the changeling."

"Yes. My father and brother have many troubles—so many that they don't notice much else." His lower lip jutted out defiantly. "But I notice. I have long been aware of the interest of the Lords and Ladies in royal changelings, and you have provided me answers. I am ready to act."

His words were mature—Henry had to remind himself that this "boy" was older than he was—but everything in his bearing was childish. His eyes, especially, looked frightened despite his brave posturing. Still, they needed all the allies they could muster.

Richard seemed to sense his hesitation. He stepped forward, head high. "I am a prince of Britain. I watched my mortal father fight to bring stability to our land, and I've watched my elder brother fight to keep the Thames flowing as the lifeblood of this country." He gestured, and the springs all around them shot a shower of water into the air, where it hovered like a rainstorm frozen in place. "I am the forgotten prince, but I have not forgotten where I came from. I ask for the chance to prove myself."

Henry exchanged a glance with Domin and Jairus, who expressed no objection. The Morrigan said they would all have to make choices, and that must include Richard. Henry only hoped this wouldn't be one of the heartbreaking ones. With a heavy feeling, he turned back to the boy.

"If your father will not stop you, then neither will we," Henry said. "Come, we have a long train ride back to London."

Richard scoffed and whipped at the water floating overhead, sending it spiraling to the ground. "I do not ride on trains. Find me a boat, and I will have us to London in a trice."

Chapter Twenty-Three

Domin had been skeptical of Richard's plan for floating to London, but after walking to Ashton Keynes and buying a row boat from a lad who seemed happy for the exchange, they whisked down the river at unnatural speed. Domin could not quite bring himself to enjoy being at the mercy of someone else's powers, but the river was more comfortable than a train with its iron bolts and rails. Only the locks controlling the flow of the river slowed them down, and Richard looked very dark about each of them.

"I could open them and force our way through," Richard grumbled.

Jairus chuckled. "Better not."

"It's more attention than we want," Henry said.

Richard folded his arms. "Someday, I would see the river run free again."

Domin caught Henry's uneasy look. In a way, that's what the Fay wanted as well—for the natural forces they ruled to throw off all human restraints.

Richard stared into the water sliding away beneath the boat. "I can feel the witch you fear. Her power is like the locks. It's slowing all the energy in the land."

"That's why we need the Fisher King." Henry had to raise his voice to be heard over the wind whipping past them.

"What will happen after we defeat this witch, then?" Richard asked. He looked at Henry. "Will you return to your Lady's court?"

"Not if I can help it," Henry said. "I wish to be free of her. Perhaps I will help other changelings. Perhaps I will simply retire to a few years of peace."

Richard looked perplexed by that, and he turned to Domin and Jairus. "Do you also wish to retire from the fight?"

"There will always be monsters to fight," Jairus said, and though he tried to appear cheerful, his voice was weary.

Domin didn't answer. He knew that Henry's chances of breaking from Titania were small, but restoring the Fisher King would shift many things. What if Titania did ignore Henry, let him have his freedom, even for a time? Domin would still be bound to Henry, but he wouldn't be needed. He might even be in the way of whatever domestic bliss Henry dreamed of. And if Henry did manage to break free and become a solitary Fay protecting the changelings, Domin's role would become auxiliary. He would always be Henry's friend, but he might not truly have a place anymore. Like most daemons, he would fade into the background.

And that was assuming he didn't need someone to rip the magical blade out of his chest to defeat the Carmun.

He rubbed the spot just above his heart where the sliver of iron rested, a constant presence like a ringing in his ears or cold fingers that never warmed. Perhaps it was his time to fade. He had lived centuries. Much more time than most people had—even many Fay.

And yet... And yet he was not finished living. It had been easy to put off thinking of the future when he thought he had practically forever, but when the days dimmed, he wanted to make the most of the light. He sometimes had to refrain from demanding that Henry try to remove the splinter of iron. Better to take the chance for renewed life than to die slowly. He told himself he didn't care about losing his Faerie half, but how could he not mourn something that had been a part of him? Not a part he had always been proud of, but one he had used to good effect. How he missed being able to run with the feet of a wolf or leap with a panther's strength. He had even tried flying once as a giant eagle, long ago. It had been glorious, and he had assumed he would be able to do it again.

He had breathed magic, let it run through his blood, and it was hard to think of becoming...nothing. A ghost in the wind. He had enjoyed good years, many of them, though often lonely. He had done much he could be proud of. Known many sorrows and triumphs and friends. He did not fear death—he had seen that it was only another step on a path whose end he didn't know. But he did fear the nothingness of fading away. Of becoming some insubstantial spirit only watching from a distance.

Dusk fell, cloaking the countryside in a darkness that seemed to hold many shadows and many eyes. Richard guided them around occasional islands rising from the waters like the backs of primeval monsters. The glow of London rose in the distance, a false dawn. Lights from barges and buildings on the outskirts of the city glittered over the water like a thousand will o' the wisps.

Jairus stirred and squinted at the shore, his hand drifting toward his pistol. "I don't like the feeling I get here. Something's wrong."

Richard's eyes narrowed. "You're correct. I sense the touch of an Unseelie Fay on these waters."

"This close to London?" Henry asked. "The church bells ought to keep them away."

Domin scanned the shore, reaching deep, trying to summon powers he'd used for so long he felt like he'd lost a hand without them. He could sense his vanishing abilities still trying to work, but the weight of the iron pressed too heavily on him.

"A very powerful Unseelie creature could venture this close to London," Domin said. "If it was trying to escape the Carmun—trading one danger for another. But the iron and bells will make it almost mad."

"Sounds like our evening is just beginning." Jairus readied his shotgun.

Richard steered them to a dock in the East End, and they hurried ashore, abandoning the boat for some lucky lad to discover.

"It won't be near St. Paul's," Domin said. "Or any of the large, ancient churches."

"We're in the right part of town, then," Jairus said.

The East End was not home to such notable churches—or their bells. The residents in the poorest areas of the city were always the most vulnerable.

"How do we track something if we don't even know what it is?" Henry asked.

He glanced at Domin, the unspoken question in his eyes: Can you still sense anything?

But Domin couldn't. Other than a vague sense of unease, he could not tell if any Fay were near or what court they belonged to. Everything was fading.

Jairus whistled and pointed to the ground. "Well, that's not normal."

Huge, wet pawprints marked the street, larger than a man's hands—as large as a dinner plate.

"That's one big...whatever it is," Jairus said. He grinned and hefted his shotgun. "This way!"

Domin paused a moment to study the pawprints, too large even for a hell hound. And it was Unseelie?

A howl reverberated off the crowded buildings of the East End—a deep, mournful sound that went on and on.

All four of them froze, shaken by the sound. Richard swallowed several times and stared longingly back at the river.

Domin knew the visceral fear beneath the monster's howl.

"It's a Cu Sith," Domin said. He caught Jairus's curious look and added, "A wolf-like beast that feeds on terror. It normally dwells far from cities—in the mountains."

"It's hurt by iron?" Jairus asked.

"It's Fay."

Jairus raised his shotgun. "Then let's find it before it feasts."

Jairus led them as they tracked the beast through the narrow alleys. He paused to free a tuft of fur from a crooked fence, holding it up to show the greenish sheen in the glow of the gaslamps.

"I thought you said it was a big wolf." Jairus waved the green fur.

Domin sighed. "A giant, dark green wolf. Yes."

Jairus stared at the tuft of fur, then shook his hand clean and wiped it on his shirt. "Well, it's sure to stand out, at least."

In the quiet following its howl, the Cu Sith moved silently

—as silent as an unexpected death—but its paw prints were those of an animal moving slowly, almost drunkenly. Probably disoriented by the iron and church bells of London. Only great danger to its own life would have driven such a wild Unseelie creature from the highland mountains to a city far from its home.

The men rounded a corner, and the Cu Sith stood in the street before them, as large as a bull, covered in thick, dark fur that shone with a green luster in the city lights. Its attention was focused on one of the many pubs in the East End.

Jairus fired. The shot echoed off the tall buildings. The iron shot hit the Cu Sith, and the animal snarled and whipped around to face them. It shook itself and bared its teeth, their long points yellow in the dim light.

"The fur," Henry said. "It's protecting it."

"It's like fighting a bear!" Jairus grinned. "Only bigger."

Henry summoned a storm heralded by a blast of wind that stunk of the Thames, and he drew his rowan stake, coating its pointed tip with a blade of ice.

Richard stood frozen at the sight of the giant beast.

The Cu Sith turned its head toward the young prince, drawn to his fear. It huffed, and the stink of rotten flesh rode on its breath.

Jairus fired his second barrel, then Henry charged.

The Cu Sith swatted Henry aside, and he reeled against the stone wall of the pub and to the ground. Domin felt the flash of pain but likewise knew that Henry had no serious injuries. Jairus swung at the creature with his gun, but it sent him sprawling as well. The American slammed into the pub window, and the glass shattered, showering the street with glittering shards.

The people in the pub called out in surprise and annoyance.

And Richard stood there, his gaze fixed on the Cu Sith.

The Cu Sith took another step toward the prince.

Domin dodged in and grabbed Henry's fallen stake. The ice had shattered, but the rowan would still hurt an Unseelie creature. He smashed the stick into the Cu Sith's nose.

Its huge, golden eyes fixed on Domin. He had his own fears, and they would taste just as meaty to the Cu Sith as Richard's.

It howled again. The sound shivered through Domin, and the men and women in the pub threw themselves to the ground and went silent in terror.

Domin jabbed the Cu Sith in the throat. He dodged a swipe of its paw, rolling out of the way. Then he ran.

The Cu Sith gave chase. Its paws were silent on the street, but its warm, stinking breath followed Domin as he dodged through dark alleys and streets shrouded in fog. A sense of danger—of terror—radiated from the beast's presence. Some deep, animal part of Domin quavered at that sense of Unseelie power, but he welcomed it. It meant the Cu Sith pursued him and not his friends.

He raced farther from the populated areas of the city into a warren of warehouses locked up for the night. Fog swirled around him, blinded him. He cursed his senses for failing him, the splinter of iron for sucking away his strength.

In the darkness, the Cu Sith hunted. Its Unseelie bloodlust, fed by the suffering of London, gave it the strength of a desperate animal.

Domin slowed, his chest tight. It was not a sensation he was used to, and he had to catch his breath. The pain near his heart spiked, and he wondered if the iron would pierce his heart and kill him before the Cu Sith could.

The fog swirled unnaturally. Domin bent low and snuck

forward. A glimpse of green fur bristled through the curtains of fog.

The Cu Sith howled again, a terrible wail, a cry of being forgotten and dying unmourned. The howl went on and on, its echo seeming to answer itself on every side. It reverberated in Domin's ears, and he froze in place. To hear the Cu Sith's howl three times meant certain death. As strong as Domin once was, the Cu Sith was stronger—a manifestation of the most primal fears in every living creature's heart. The daemon part of Domin was grateful Henry was safe, and Jairus and Richard, too.

But the Fay part of him bristled at the indignity. He was Domin, son of an ancient Faerie Lady—one whose mighty realm far to the east pierced the sky with sharp, unforgiving mountains. The Cu Sith ought to have backed away in respect if not bowed before him. Domin wasn't proud of everything he had done with his strength, but he *was* strong. A touch of Telesm's arrogance ran through Domin as well. He usually tried to silence it, but now he wondered if he had been too quick to allow the Fay to forget who he was. If *he* had been too quick to forget.

The Cu Sith appeared from the mists. Its green coat shone strangely in London's dirty light, its huge form blocking any possible escape. Domin sometimes had taken the form of a wolf because it had come naturally to him—a fierce predator of his adopted home, as the panther reminded him of his native lands. But this creature was both more than a wolf and less than one. So much larger and more dangerous, and yet without any of the admirable pack instincts that made wolves a part of the natural world. The Cu Sith only wanted to feed on fear and death, and London was fertile ground for its hunting. Domin could not let it get any farther.

He braced himself, awaiting the attack.

The Cu Sith leapt, its movement so silent it almost might have been a dream.

Domin could no longer take a wolf's form, but he could still move with speed. He darted from the huge claws of the Cu Sith and whipped the sharpened end of the rowan stake around, slicing the creature's leg.

It danced back, unused to quarry that returned blows. The Cu Sith shook its wounded leg, then snarled and lunged for Domin.

He jabbed the stake into the Cu Sith's jaw.

The creature tried to wail again, but Domin held the stake in place, pinning its mouth shut. The Cu Sith's blood trickled down his hand, sticky and warm.

The Cu Sith jerked free, mouth dripping blood, and Domin held up the stake again.

"You do not belong here, Unseelie creature. The church bells and the iron will torment you."

The Cu Sith swiped at its bleeding mouth and growled. Almost a whine.

Domin twirled the stake. Where to send this creature? He had no ability to banish it from the human world, and it would not return to anywhere the Carmun's power had touched. The distant stink of the Thames gave him an idea.

"There are islands in the river," Domin said. "Bide your time on one of those until the blight has passed, and I will not harm you further."

The Cu Sith bared its teeth.

Domin brandished the stake. "I protect the people of this place, Cu Sith. You will not hunt here."

The Cu Sith huffed. It lowered its head and bounded away for the Thames.

Domin let out a slow breath and wiped his hands clean. He was smiling. Almost as manic as Jairus Hale. But he felt more real, standing up to the Cu Sith, knowing he could still protect his friends. He had not faded away yet, and he would fight for a little more time to live.

Chapter Twenty-Four

Night had settled over the city when Amy finally heard the front door. She had not been able to settle herself enough to dress for bed, so she hurried down the stairs in time to see Henry and Domin guide a wary boy into the house with them. Jairus followed behind, shotgun in hand.

Her attention fixed on the boy. He was not what she imagined of Prince Edward. Was this the younger brother? He only looked a few years older than the nine he'd been when he vanished from the tower. She was too young to have known the Plantagenets, but he reminded her of the pictures of the family —rather weak in appearance. Their weak features were misleading, given how ferociously they had fought over Britain's soil.

The boy carried himself like a prince, an image of pride. But beneath it, Amy saw his uncertainty and fear. Even shame. The haughtiness was nothing more than a poorly fitted mask.

He had no trouble stepping across the threshold. Might not have even been aware of the wards. So, he meant no harm to any of them. It was the Carmun and the Unseelie court that would fear him, she hoped.

Domin stepped up beside Amy and gave her a warm look. Amy resisted the urge to reach out to grab his hand or touch his arm. Both because it would not look seemly, especially in front of a stranger, and also because she might feel things he did not intend for her to know. He had respected her privacy when he might have breached it, and now she would do the same.

Domin turned to the boy. "Amy, may I introduce Richard of Shrewsbury, Duke of York. Richard, this is our host, Amy, Lady St. Clair."

Richard gave her a nod, not at all struck by her appearance. Used to the Fay, then, and not impressed by them. That was good.

"Is this where I'll be staying?" He surveyed the neat house with a look of mild disdain.

Amy bristled a little, then soothed herself. If he had been living with a Fay lord, he would be used to the kind of splendor that Amy could not—dared not—replicate within her walls.

"This place is protected," Henry said.

"I thought we were going to fight," Richard said. "I know I did not comport myself well against that wolf creature—"

Amy raised her eyebrows at Domin and the other men, realizing they did look like they'd experienced a mishap or two that day.

"—but I will prove myself. On the field of battle, if need be."

Domin sighed silently—a movement Amy felt but did not hear. "If we must fight, we want to do so from a position of strength. Something we don't yet have. We will have to deal with the Faerie courts and the Carmun, and both are formidable. We need the Fisher King."

Richard nodded. "And if we cannot heal him, then I will take his place, and the Fay will have to obey me."

"I'm not sure it's quite that simple," Henry said.

Domin shifted. "We don't yet understand all that the Fisher King can do. Stop the Carmun, we hope. But he must keep a balance with the Fay. Even the Unseelie ones."

Richard's eyes flashed at that. Amy understood. She hated the Unseelie Fay, too. Maybe it would be good to see them defeated once and for all.

"If you will show me to my chambers, I will rest and contemplate the future," Richard said.

"About the chambers..." Amy put on her best conciliatory expression. "We don't have an empty room, but there are several places you can choose to sleep. Well, only one in a chamber as such."

Richard looked alarmed. He glanced at Henry. "Perhaps I can share with the other royal changeling? That would be acceptable."

Amy tried not to laugh at the look of alarm on Henry's face. They couldn't tell Richard why he would not be sharing space with Henry, not unless they trusted him with Cassandra's secrets as well.

"Nope, you'll be bunking with me," Jairus said from behind them.

Now, it was Richard's turn to look alarmed. "With the...the..."

"American. Yup. Oh, though I guess America wasn't a thing when you were last among us mortals."

"I was going to say commoner," Richard said.

"As common as they come," Jairus said, rocking on his heels. "But you'd probably prefer me over Telesm 'My-father-was-a-Persian-prince.' He doesn't keep his room neat with all his magical bric-a-brac. I wonder how Domin endures it. And Lucien agreed to sleep in the nursery with the young changeling he rescued. The child has nightmares and, uh, things get uncomfortably warm when he's upset. Lucien's good at finding the words to calm him, but I doubt you want to sleep there."

Richard looked completely bemused. "This is the strangest house I've ever set foot in."

"Probably," Jairus said.

Richard eyed him. "You are human, at least. And my mother was not royalty."

"Well then." Jairus repressed a chuckle. "Come along. I'll show you to our 'chambers.'"

Henry hurried away as well, no doubt anxious to check on Cassandra.

Amy turned to Domin. "Richard, not Edward?"

"Edward is shouldering many of the duties of the Lord of the Thames. He did not dare leave Thames's court. Richard left, I believe, against the will of his elder brother."

"Is he going to be of any use as an ally?"

"We cannot discount the importance of any help we find, and he is a royal changeling." Domin sighed and ran his fingers through his hair. "He is young, sheltered." He gave Amy a rueful smile. "I had forgotten what it was like at the courts."

She laughed. "Yes, thank goodness we are away from them."

"You never let yourself become like the courtly Fay, though," Domin said. "Never cruel. Even when it would have benefitted you. I always admired that about you. When I was with the Fay, I was not so strong-minded."

Amy flushed. "I made my share of mistakes, as you well know. And I never felt welcome in the courts. That made it easier to turn my back on them, though it still wasn't simple." She smiled a little. "You were spoiled, I imagine."

"Yes, I suppose I was. A favorite of my mother, as long as I served her court. Now...I am glad that I cannot return there. But it helps me understand Richard. It is difficult when one has been catered to—doted on—and then has to learn to serve others in turn."

"But that shows there's hope for Richard," Amy said. "To be less of a prig."

Domin chuckled. "Hope for all of us to be wiser and braver, I suppose. He is frightened, but I believe he will find his way. Though none of us did it alone, did we?"

He looked off into the distance, and Amy imagined that he was thinking of the woman he had once loved. She stepped back, but he caught her hand. It surprised her, and by his expression, it surprised him, too.

"What's wrong?" he asked.

"I don't want to think about...about the past," Amy said.

"You're right. The present is what matters. And the future."

Amy relaxed. Domin did not drop her hand, and she didn't want him to.

"It's hard to imagine the future," Amy said. "Everything is changing, isn't it?"

"Yes, I suspect our world is a collapsing house of cards, and when the cards finish falling, the pattern they make will be much different." He rubbed at his chest with his free hand, just above his heart.

Amy tightened her grip on his hand. "Have you considered that the Fisher King—the Grail—might be able to heal you?"

"I have wondered, but I suspect it is not so straightforward. The Fay can heal—they even have stories of objects that grant extended life—but there is always a cost. And I don't think the Grail is an object to trifle with for personal desires."

"What do you desire, then?" Amy asked.

Domin looked surprised by the question. "I hope to see Henry safe, of course. And his goal to help the changelings is an admirable one. I'm not sure if he has the strength to defy Titania, but I hope he does."

"As do I," Amy said. "But I meant what you want for yourself."

Domin went very still, then he furrowed his brow. "It has been so long since I've considered such things."

"Yet if Henry succeeds in becoming a Faerie Lord, your protection will become redundant, won't it?"

"It will."

"Then what do you wish for?"

He stared at her for a long moment—long enough to make her cheeks redden. She was trying not to sense his emotions, but they rushed over her: curiosity, longing, hope awakening like the buds on a tree after a long winter.

His voice was low when he spoke. "I suppose I will help protect...someone else. As my Faerie magic fades, my desire to protect—to fight for things I care about—becomes stronger. Though, if the blade begins to devour my daemon magic as well—"

"No!" Amy tightened her grip on his hand. "We will not let that happen. We will find a way to remove the shard. You'll be around for centuries more to protect the changelings or...or... just to be here. To be you. That's all I would ask of you."

"Really?" Domin asked. He pulled her closer, ever so slightly. "I suppose that's all you've ever asked...even when..." He hesitated, and Amy guessed he was thinking of the time she had tricked him and betrayed his trust. "Well, you never did ask anything of me."

"I've never wanted anything of you except just...you. As you are."

"I am not what I was."

"Yes, you are! Regardless of your magic, you're still yourself. You are strong and wise, and I don't want to think of this world without you in it."

Amy had stepped closer as she spoke, and now she rested her hand on his cheek, staring into his bright green eyes. His pupils dilated until Amy could see her reflection in them.

Domin raised his hand slowly and traced his finger down Amy's cheek. "Your optimism never fails to amaze me."

"Oh," Amy whispered, not able to take a deep enough breath to say anything more.

She trailed her fingers down Domin's throat, coming to rest on his fast-beating pulse. Then she continued the path over his chest to his biceps, the muscles firm through his shirtsleeves. Good heavens, he was strong. She let her gaze drop from his eyes to rest on his lips.

Domin brushed his finger down her face and ran his thumb over her lower lip. She sighed and closed her eyes, wanting nothing but to feel his touch. To savor it.

"Amy," Domin whispered, his breath on her cheek.

"Mmm," she responded, leaning into him.

He sighed and pulled Amy against his chest, her head resting under his chin.

"Amy," he said again, low, quiet, but an undercurrent of anguish in his voice. "I don't know if I can offer you anything. Not anything that you deserve."

Amy chuckled ruefully, listening to the fast pounding of Domin's heart. "I don't know if I want what I *deserve*. But I do know I want you to be a part of whatever comes next for me."

Domin sighed, the sound rumbling in her ears. "I...I can only promise to try."

"Then that's all I need."

He caressed her chin, tilting her head up. Their gazes met again, Domin's questioning. Amy stood on her tiptoes and closed her eyes. Domin's lips found hers, a gentle brush at first. He pulled her closer and kissed her again, softly. She returned the slow kisses, swept up in the heady rush of kissing Domin. She pulled him closer, tightening her grip on his arm. He wrapped his other arm around her waist and held her against him, and she lost herself completely in his embrace and his kisses. Nothing in the future could be bleak as long as she was in Domin's arms.

Chapter Twenty-Five

Amy stood with her friends around a table in the dining room looking at a map of England. They'd marked the places they knew the Carmun had struck, dark blotches on the cream-colored paper. Jairus was explaining where he'd encountered Fay trying to enter London, with Lucien adding his observations, but Amy kept glancing at Domin, thinking about that kiss. Was he thinking of it, too? Did he want to kiss her again? His gaze slid to her from time to time, and a faint smile played on his lips.

Telesm slammed his hand on the table.

Amy jumped, flushing with a sudden guilty fear that Telesm knew what she was thinking. But one look at his face erased any thoughts of herself or Domin. Telesm had gone ghastly pale, the scar on his face bright red against the pallor of his skin. Jairus fumbled for his pistol.

"Telesm?" Domin asked.

"Someone is attacking my refuge," Telesm said, his voice strained.

"Surely they can't get past those lions," Cassandra said.

"They…" Telesm winced as though he had been struck. "They already have. How…"

His eyes rolled back, and he sank to the floor.

"Telesm!" Domin shook him gently, trying to rouse his half-brother.

Henry knelt beside Telesm, checking his pulse and examining his eyes, which jerked side to side, unseeing.

"It must be something magical," Henry said. "I don't know how to treat it."

"He tied so much of his will—himself—up in those protections," Domin said.

Jairus gripped his pistol. "All those magical weapons stored there…"

"But no Fay has ever been strong enough to breach his defenses," Amy said.

The Fay had tried. They coveted the strange and dangerous powers of the objects Telesm protected.

"Not the Fay, then." Domin stood, hefting Telesm up to rest in a chair. "We have to see what's happened there. Amy, will you open the gateway to Telesm's clearing?"

Amy was afraid to—afraid to know what power might have been enough to challenge Telesm's—but she trusted Domin, so she nodded and hurried out to her garden. The others followed close behind. She stood before her hawthorn tree and concentrated on Telesm's clearing, pushing magic into the memory to make it real. The gateway opened beneath the spreading branches of the tree.

Henry looked to Cassandra. "Stay here with Mary and Lucien and watch over Telesm."

Cassandra's eyes flashed with worry, but she nodded her agreement.

Henry, Jairus, and Domin hurried through the gateway. Amy hesitated a moment and then followed. They might need her to open the gateway again if it closed, and she had to know who had broken through Telesm's careful defenses—defenses that were the basis for her own.

And she wanted to be there for Domin if the situation was dire.

She stepped through the portal and feared for a moment that she had opened the wrong gateway. This was not the beautiful clearing with its roses and cottage. It was an ashy wasteland like something from the Unseelie Kingdom. No, it wasn't ash. It was more like decay—like everything had aged and rotted to ruins and dust. A musty scent filled the air. Only the remnants of the pedestals where the lions had once stood and the crumbled foundations of the cottage convinced her that this was Telesm's small domain.

"What happened here?" Jairus said. "I've seen battlefield destruction, but this—"

"It's magical destruction. Much worse than what humans have dreamed up," Domin said, his voice tight.

He walked carefully across the blackened ground. Piles of debris marked where the cottage had once guarded magical treasures.

Amy hesitated to follow, fearing the lions, but then she realized with a lurch that they were no more. Fire didn't burn forever, earth crumbled, even water dried up. The magic was gone.

"The blight," Henry whispered. "This is the work of the Carmun."

"She really can destroy the Fay, then," Amy whispered. "She can destroy both our worlds."

"But why start here?" Jairus asked. "I don't think she even knew about Telesm."

Domin muttered something that very well could have been swearing in a long-dead language. "But the Grigori must have heard something about it. The weapons Telesm had stored here..." He dug through the debris, trying to sift it, though it flowed through his fingers like black sand. "It could have been only a threat—a show of power—or a guarantee that we couldn't use those weapons against her. There's no way to know if they destroyed it all or if they took something."

The others followed after him, looking through the rubble for any clue about what the Carmun had done. The place was dead. Utterly dead. Except...

Amy shifted a rotten timber that crumbled under her touch, and a stone face stared back at her from the ground. She gasped and drew back.

Domin came to her side. "Oh, no. Ankhira." He knelt beside the ruined statue. "Telesm had always hoped to find a cure for the basilisk's curse."

"She's gone now," Amy said, her voice catching in her throat—both at Domin's pain and at thinking of the poor girl whose spirit she had sensed trapped beneath the stone.

Domin looked at her, his face etched with grief. "You're certain? Better for her to rest than to be still trapped and broken into pieces."

Amy shuddered at the thought. She knelt beside Domin and placed her fingers gently on the girl's stone face.

She had forgotten that some traces of the person's feelings upon death remained when they were gone. The girl had not forgotten it, though. She had roused from her centuries-long sleep enough to watch what had happened, recording it like a scribe making note of her doom. Amy tried to read the emotions the girl had left for her to find. Anger at the violation of her peace and of Telesm's home. Horror at the realization that she was helpless. Hope that someone would know what had happened here. Peace and acceptance of her rest finally come. Sorrow that she would not see Telesm again.

Not the end. Find me. Fight.

Amy gasped and pulled away.

Domin caught her shoulder, pulled her into an embrace. "You didn't have to do that. Was her end terrible?"

Amy let out a slow breath, aware that Henry and Jairus were watching. "No. There was no pain, at least. Only a sense of helplessness and frustration. I think she expected someone Fay to find her, though. She wanted me to know."

Amy quickly recounted what she had felt and heard.

"Find her? Are we supposed to go to the Twilight Path again?" Jairus asked warily.

"I don't know," Amy said. "I don't think so. It felt more like she was trying to hold on. To linger."

Jairus looked around the clearing. "Well, her ghost isn't here or I would see her. Sense her, at least."

"What does all of this mean?" Henry asked. "For us? For Telesm?"

Domin's shoulders sagged. "This attack was a serious blow to my brother. His will was tied to the magic of this place, and it's gone now. Physically, he will recover eventually since he survived the initial attack, but losing Ankhira will be another, deeper wound."

"And the Carmun may have any number of terrible weapons," Amy said quietly.

Weapons so awful that Telesm had locked them away from the world. That he had only considered letting Domin and the others use because of the danger the Carmun posed. Now, the

Carmun and her twisted Grigori "sons" might have that power added to their own.

And if Telesm's sanctuary could fall, so could any place in Elfland or Britain. The safety of Amy's house was only an illusion before the might of the Carmun. Even without Ankhira's urging, Amy knew they would have to fight. And what chance did they have against the Carmun?

Chapter Twenty-Six

Cassandra huddled by the light in the sitting room, surrounded by books that referenced the Fisher King or the Holy Grail. The stillness in Amy's house was broken only by the ticking of the clock whose spell protected them.

For the moment.

Telesm faded in and out of consciousness upstairs in his room. Amy tended to him, while Mary, looking paler than usual, ran whatever errands Amy required. Domin, Jairus, and Henry had gone looking for Spring-heeled Jack and any stray Faerie creatures who found their way to London.

Since the attack on Telesm's sanctuary, Cassandra wanted nothing more than to keep all of her friends together and safe. And she fretted about her sisters. Henry had brought rain to London to encourage people to stay inside, but her sisters were stubborn when it came to Society life. Georgina still refused to speak to Cassandra, so all Cassandra could do was try to find an end to the threat. She wanted to be by Henry's side, but she would be a distraction. Yet it frightened her—the thought that he was already a little farther from her, and their enemies so terribly strong.

Cassandra focused on the books, willing them to tell her something about healing the Fisher King. Most of the stories were about King Arthur and his knights, with much obsession over worthiness. Cassandra couldn't do much with that. They had to help the Fisher King. None of them were perfect Galahads, and it had always been her understanding from sermons that no human could be. They would just have to be good enough.

A pounding on the door made her start. She looked around, but unless Lucien had returned from whatever mysterious errands kept him occupied, she was the only one available. The wards should protect her from anyone who meant her harm, but she wasn't keen on opening the door to a stranger.

The pounding came again.

"Cassandra!" a female voice called.

She limped quickly to the front door and pulled it open. Georgie stood there in her evening dress, a broken umbrella in hand, and she clutched Sophie, whose blonde curls sagged and dripped in the rain.

"Cassie!" Sophie gulped. "It...it had these teeth. A monster!"

Georgina steadied their older sister and met Cassandra's eyes, her chin raised defiantly. "I think it was a spriggan."

Cassandra stared in surprise for a moment, then pulled her sisters into the house.

"Did you say a spriggan?" Amy asked from the stairs. She hurried closer and repeated herself to Georgina.

Georgina nodded, her eyes still glinting with defiance. "And

Robert Ashby is out there trying to fend it off. We ran this way for help."

"Oh, dear!" Amy said. She looked to Cassandra. "Spriggan are Seelie, but very troublesome. And, they grow larger the angrier they get."

Sophie gulped rapidly and looked as though she might faint at Amy's words, but Georgina gave Cassandra a challenging glare.

"What do we do against it?" Cassandra asked.

Amy frowned, then pulled off the necklace she wore. "Try to bribe it." She looked back to Georgina. "Where—"

A gunshot echoed across the square.

Amy ran outside, and Cassandra limped behind her. An almost skeletal figure, pulled tall and thin like stretched taffy, lurched across the damp square. Its head was too large for its body, and it did indeed have sharp teeth when it hissed at them.

Robert stood guard in front of the house, holding a pistol. When had he started carrying a gun? He shot at the creature again.

In the doorway, Sophie screamed and covered her ears.

The creature shrieked and stretched even taller. With one hand, it grasped one of the young trees growing along the square and uprooted it.

Robert raised the gun again.

"It's not going to work," Cassandra called to Robert over the ringing in her ears. "It needs to be silver and iron."

"I gathered as much from your American friend," Robert said. "But I haven't figured out the trick of that yet. Still, the bullets slow it down."

"And make it angrier!" Amy motioned for Robert to be still and hurried past him.

She strode up to the enraged spriggan, holding out her

offering of a necklace. The spriggan raised the tree like a club, but Amy didn't flinch from it. Cassandra couldn't hear Amy's words, but the elf remained calm—if perhaps a bit exasperated —shaking the necklace at the spriggan and apparently scolding it like a naughty child.

The spriggan slowly shrank, looking less stretched out and more like a very wrinkled old man. Finally, when it was smaller than Amy, she held out the necklace. The spriggan grabbed the necklace, clutching it to its chest, and scurried off into the rain.

A tingle of magic washed over Cassandra. Robert blinked and lowered his gun. "Oh, it was just the storm."

Cassandra wanted to roll her eyes at him, but she knew she was fortunate not to be so affected by Amy's Faerie magic.

"Just the storm," Sophie repeated, serenity settling over her features.

"No!" Georgina said too loudly. "What are you saying? That was not just the storm."

Sophie smiled. "Everything is fine, Georgie. We can forget it."

Georgina looked to Cassandra. "I will not forget it. Amy is a Fay, isn't she? That was Faerie magic!"

"Your imagination is running away with you," Sophie scolded.

"No, it's not," Georgina said, and she glared at Cassandra.

Cassandra pressed her lips together and looked to the hole in the ground where the spriggan had uprooted the tree.

Amy guided Robert and the others back into the house and blotted her face with a handkerchief.

"I'm sorry," she whispered to Cassandra. "I had to make the neighbors forget so they didn't panic. Your sisters..."

Cassandra knew. It was her choice.

She limped back up to Sophie and Georgina. "Georgie's right, Sophie. That was not just the storm."

"But..." Sophie cast Robert a perplexed look.

Robert's eyes had a bit of a glazed look, but Amy gave his arm a push. "Wake up. You know what you saw. I shouldn't be able to convince you otherwise."

He flinched and blinked hard. Then he looked chagrinned. "Unless I wanted to forget."

"What are you all talking about?" Sophie demanded, her voice reaching a desperate pitch.

Cassandra sighed and whispered to Robert. "You think we can just keep this from Sophie forever?" After all, that was what she had been trying to do.

Robert lowered his eyes. "Maybe not. But...I love your sister. I want to cherish and protect her."

Cassandra frowned, some of her dislike of Robert evaporating under his admission of love for Sophie. "Do you respect her?"

He straightened like a soldier coming to attention. "Of course!"

"Then I think you have to show your love by trusting her."

"I want to keep her safe."

"That's good, but she has a right to know what you're keeping her safe from. Tell her about the monsters, and then do your best to protect her from them."

"What are you talking about so quietly?" Sophie asked, her eyes narrow.

Cassandra gave Robert a meaningful look.

Robert sighed. "That thing back there was exactly what it looked like: a monster."

"That's not funny!" Sophie said. "I don't like to be laughed at."

She glared at Cassandra, but there was fear behind her accusatory look. Was she more afraid that Robert was lying, or that he was telling the truth?

It didn't matter. Sophie and Georgina deserved to know. Cassandra took Sophie's arm and guided her to the sitting room. Georgina followed closely, trying to catch what she could of the conversation. Robert trailed behind like a bedraggled dog, and Amy stationed herself in the doorway.

"He's not laughing at you," Cassandra said, showing Sophie to a chair. "None of us are. You remember Mr. Rushford?"

Sophie's lip curled back in disdain, and she lifted her nose. "Of course I do." She shuddered. "He was a dreadful man."

Georgina flipped through the books on the table and gave Cassandra a sharp look.

"Well, as part of his science, Rushford wanted to study magic," Robert said softly. "He was a friend of my father's, remember? I saw it myself."

"What does that mean, to study magic?" Sophie asked.

"Magic is a real force in this world. Hidden, but powerful," Robert said. "He thought by studying it, he could also control it."

Sophie still looked more angry than frightened. She didn't believe them.

Cassandra hurried on. "He tried to summon an ancient spirit. One that he thought would make him powerful."

Sophie's brows drew together. This was closer to the world she understood. "Do you mean like witchcraft? Summoning a ghost or a...a demon."

"Very much like that," Cassandra said.

"Last year," Sophie said slowly, "you said there were ghosts in London. I still half thought it had to be some kind of prank or...or nightmare."

"It was very real, I'm afraid," Cassandra said. "And so is this."

"But guns can't stop ghosts!" Sophie said, gesturing to Robert's pistol.

He sighed and looked down at the useless firearm. "No, not really. It might give them pause, but that creature is still out there."

Disbelief and fear warred on Sophie's features. Finally, her gaze hardened. "Then how do we protect ourselves?"

Robert smiled a little. "I knew you were brave! But we're not the best people to fight these creatures. Some of your sister's friends are better suited to it than I, I'm afraid."

Sophie looked to Cassandra. "Some of your friends. Like... like Lady St. Claire?"

She glanced at Amy, who nodded. Sophie looked aghast.

Cassandra faced both her sisters. "And Henry Stewart. Even Jairus Hale. Yes. They know how to fight the monsters."

"And you?" Sophie asked Cassandra.

Cassandra sighed. "I know a little: how to keep myself safe. And that's what you must learn as well. Use iron and silver against the monsters. Stay indoors where you can, and do not invite any strangers in."

Sophie huddled close to Robert. "For how long?"

Robert, Cassandra, and Amy exchanged worried looks.

"I hope not much longer," Cassandra said. "Those who are better equipped to manage these things are dealing with it."

Sophie smiled weakly. "Good, because I would rather go home and forget about all of this."

Robert nodded. "I will protect you from it."

Cassandra sighed. Sophie knew enough to make her choice, and she couldn't blame her for wanting to ignore it all. But

Cassandra couldn't ignore it. She had to face it to keep people like her sister safe.

Georgina stood, one of Cassandra's books in hand. "I am tired of trying to forget it. I am tired of the nightmares. You—" She glared and Cassandra and drew a deep breath. "You are always trying to cut me out of everything. Well, I can help, too. I'm not going to be left behind anymore."

"Georgie," Cassandra said, a tortured whisper. Then she raised her voice so Georgina might hear the words as well as read them from her lips. "I'm not trying to leave you behind."

"Whether you're trying or not," Georgina said, "that's what you're doing. You're leaving me. Well, I won't have it."

"It's dangerous," Cassandra said. "So dangerous."

"Then you need more help. I can read books, too. That's what I've been doing, ever since I started to suspect. I recognized the spriggan, and I knew to bring Sir Robert and Sophie here."

"You did well," Amy said.

She had, Cassandra knew. And she also knew she couldn't always protect her sisters by hiding things from them. Especially now, with so much danger creeping its way into London.

"You're right," Cassandra said. "You can help, and if you wish to—knowing it's dangerous—then I welcome it."

Georgina grinned and hugged the book, but Cassandra's stomach felt made of lead. No matter how she tried to protect her sisters, the danger was everywhere, too much for her to keep them safe. Robert would keep Sophie far from trouble, but Georgina was stepping into the thick of it.

Chapter Twenty-Seven

Henry had never been so glad for London's church bells. It meant that the Fay they had encountered in London were Seelie, more likely to cause mischief than any real harm. They had come across some pixies tying the bootlaces of men drinking in the tavern, and an offended brownie tangling the manes of a set of horses outside a club on St. James Street. Now, as the sun set and mist rolled off the river, will o' the wisps flashed from the fog, threatening to lead people into the water. Henry had eased the rain to a sprinkle to make their search less soggy, but he wondered if he ought to bring it back in full force to keep people inside.

And for all their searching, they found no sign of Spring-heeled Jack. Henry wondered if he might have left London, but since it was one of the safer places from the Carmun thus far, he couldn't imagine where else Jack would go. And they needed that magical knife now more than ever if the Carmun had magical weapons of her own. Henry guessed what Domin was planning, and he would not allow Domin to sacrifice himself to provide them with the splinter of enchanted iron next to his heart.

Henry's feet ached from patrolling the uneven streets all day, but as he trotted wearily down the street with Jairus, Domin, and Richard, something prickled at the back of his mind, bringing his senses to full alert. The sensation wove through the fog to give it a clammy, grasping feel. The air stank more than London's usual odor of river rot and coal smoke.

Henry stopped. "Wait!"

Jairus immediately paused and rested his hand on his gun, and Domin scanned the shadows.

Richard scoffed. "Don't tell me you need to catch your breath. I'm the elder royal changeling, and I could run all night."

Henry huffed. "There's something else here. Can't you feel it? Or smell it?"

"Yes," Domin said.

"Me, too," Jairus said. "The dead are stirring. Something is upsetting them."

Richard looked skeptical, but he turned back.

"The Wild Hunt again?" Jairus asked Henry.

"I don't—"

A chill rushed up Henry's spine, and he whipped around, blasting the fog away with a ferocious wind. A dark figure moved up the street toward them. It did not pause at the blast of wind, nor appear to care about the four people standing in its path. It continued forward, its passage silent except for the clanking of the sheathed cutlass against its side. It was dressed like a British sailor, but nothing about the way it moved was natural.

"Stewart?" Jairus asked.

Henry shook his head. He didn't know what this was, but

with each step it took, cold dread coiled through his arms and legs. This thing was...sickness, wrongness.

"It's not Fay," Richard said, his voice low.

The figure turned its head toward them at the sound. As it did, Henry caught sight of the blood. The front of the figure's shirt was black with it, and its throat had been sliced open.

"Revenant!" Domin hissed.

"One of the Morrigan's?" Jairus asked, pulling his shotgun.

"Maybe." Henry remembered the giant boar the Morrigan had reanimated. But the Morrigan had inhabited that body. Henry saw no sign of crows.

"This is not her usual style," Domin said.

Henry pulled all the cold through him and shot icy shards at the dead sailor, but the revenant didn't slow.

Jairus fired his gun, blasting the creature with iron shot.

It continued walking.

Richard's eyes were wide, and he looked at Henry as if seeking direction.

"Not the Morrigan," Henry said. "But I'd wager it can burn."

Henry summoned the fire from the gaslamp, causing it to flare.

Domin caught Henry's arm. "Do you want to set London ablaze?"

Henry grimaced. Right, if the fire didn't stop the thing, it would shamble through the city like a walking torch.

Jairus charged the revenant and slammed it in the face with the butt of his gun, making the thing's head snap to the side. He grabbed the revenant's sword from its sheath and danced out of the creature's reach.

"What are you doing?" Henry called.

"Very few things survive having their head removed," Jairus informed him cheerily.

He raced forward and sliced down with the sword before the revenant could react, finishing the cut that had killed the man. The head rolled away from the body.

But the body remained standing, staggering onward.

Richard looked like he might be ill. Henry was very glad he hadn't set the corpse on fire.

"That's a problem," Jairus said.

"It reminds me of the Carmun," Henry said. "The way it feels. Don't let it touch you."

Jairus nodded and took a swing at the thing's arm, but it jerked away from him and flung its other arm out to grasp for Jairus. He skittered back.

"We need more than one sword," Jairus suggested.

Henry readied his ice dirk.

"And an idea of what to do with the body once we've...dealt with it?" Henry asked. "If it's infected by the Carmun in some way, we can't just leave it here."

"Not to mention it's not a pretty sight," Jairus said, managing a shallow wound on the thing's leg.

"Once it's stopped moving, *then* you can burn it," Domin said with a smirk.

Before Henry could think of a sarcastic reply, the sound of hoofbeats distracted him. Was some hapless rider going to stumble across this fiasco?

But the horse that cantered toward them was black, and the musty scent of fall rode with her.

"Pooka!" Henry called, not entirely certain if he was hailing her or warning the others.

She reared and brought her hooves down on the revenant's back. The body collapsed to the street, and the pooka stretched out her neck and breathed on the revenant. Its movements stopped, and it dissolved into dust.

"You made that look easy," Jairus said.

The pooka reared and transformed into the shape of a woman, her long black hair curtaining her face. "It was simple for me. My power is to bring an end to things whose times have come, and that thing's time was well past."

"Did you return to help us?" Henry asked.

"No. I returned once again to warn you. The Lady of the Woods is on the move. She is setting forth to summon you to the most terrible battle of our age."

Henry stepped back, going cold. "You are not part of her court."

"Which is why I can warn you. My Lady does not wish to see her Unseelie sister queen triumph and take the Fisher King's throne, but she would prefer Titania did not gain such power either. Your fate depends on what you choose to do with this knowledge."

Henry bowed his head in acknowledgment of her warning, but he felt as though he were baring his neck for the executioner. Despite what the pooka said, he was running out of choices and out of time.

Chapter Twenty-Eight

Henry could find nothing to say on the walk home. They saw no other revenants, but that first was a herald of things to come. And Henry felt his friends watching him, their worry not lightening his own. He sensed Richard, in particular, studying him fearfully. What could any of them do? War was at hand. Titania would come to claim him. He could try to break from her hold. If he failed, she would either kill him or force him to fight for the Fisher King's throne.

And he did not think he would succeed in breaking free from her. He dared not even prod at her magic now, in case it brought her attention to him. The dead walked. The Carmun spread her sickness across the land. Too much was at stake to bicker with Titania. Henry might only have a few more hours to pretend he was free—perhaps even to live.

They climbed the front stairs of Amy's house, the lights inside beckoning, promising a few more moments of joy. Cassandra waited for him inside. Cassandra and their unborn child—the light of a future he might never see. But he would see Cassandra safe, no matter what it cost him. And he would savor whatever time he had left with her.

Amy met them at the door, and worry washed over her expression. "What happened out there?"

"New monsters," Jairus said. "Bad ones."

Cassandra hurried into the entryway behind Amy, and Henry's throat tightened. How was he going to tell Cassandra? What could he do to protect her once he was gone?

Georgina was there, too. Standing just behind Cassandra. Henry tensed. Jairus had mentioned monsters in front of her.

Cassandra glanced at her sister and back at the men, her eyes full of worry. "She knows."

Amy nodded. "We had an eventful time here while you were gone."

Jairus laughed ruefully. "It could have been worse for all of us, I suppose."

Henry managed a small smile, but then he turned serious again. "The Carmun has devised a new threat. It's..." His gaze darted around the others gathered there, but he knew they couldn't hold back information. "She managed to raise the dead. Created a revenant. Probably more than one."

"Long dead, or recently killed?" Telesm's voice came from the sitting room, weak but clear.

Henry recoiled from the question, but Jairus was quick to answer. "Recently killed. His clothes were modern, and his injuries were...not far gone."

No need to be gruesome in front of the ladies.

They all pressed into the sitting room where Telesm sat in a chair with a cup of tea, looking uncharacteristically domestic in a dressing gown.

Telesm frowned at his tea then took another sip. "Any signs of vampirism?"

"His throat was cut, but his blood was...there," Henry said.

"Are vampires real?" Cassandra asked.

Telesm looked up at the question. "After a manner. It's possible for a spirit to inhabit a body—"

"Yeah, like the Morrigan's trick," Jairus said, waving a dismissive hand. "And some need blood to maintain the illusion of life. But I've seen vampires, and this was different."

"This wasn't the Morrigan, either." Henry sat heavily and took Cassandra's hand. "The body didn't stop moving, even when we destroyed it."

"I think I know what the Carmun might have done," Telesm said, his expression grim now. "It's not good news."

"Of course it's not," Jairus said.

Telesm nodded. "One of the...one of the items I was protecting was an ancient staff called Lorg Mor imbued with powers from the Underworld. One end could kill enemies, and the other could return them to life, though as mindless warriors in thrall to the bearer of the staff."

Jairus sat heavily, too. "A deathless army. Good heavens. How do we defeat that?"

"Our only hope is to find the Fisher King," Henry said. He met Cassandra's eyes. "And there's more bad news."

"Oh?" Cassandra asked quietly.

"The pooka saved us from the revenant. She warned me that T— the Lady of the Woods is coming to claim me."

"I won't let her in!" Amy said.

Telesm nodded. "The wards are strong. I think they would hold against her. For now." Gloom sank over his features again.

Henry's heart warmed to think of his friends' willingness to stand by him, but then he shook his head. "We would all be trapped in here. Under siege while Jane sets off to defeat the Fisher King and take his place." He glanced at Richard. "If the

Lady of the Woods forces me to fight, I will swear only to stop Jane. I will not fight you."

Richard nodded, looking pale, as though the weight of what he proposed to do was beginning to press on his shoulders.

"We should run," Cassandra said. "Find the Fisher King as quickly as possible. We can strengthen him or help Richard replace him before *she* even comes this way."

Henry took her hands. "That's our best hope. But how do we find the white stag?"

"The white stag?" Georgina cut in, obviously struggling to follow the conversation. "Is that what you said? I saw it. Did Mr. Hale tell you?"

She looked to Jairus, who nodded.

"The Fisher King is seeking help." Domin rubbed just above his heart.

"We shouldn't delay," Henry said. "The longer we wait, the more dangerous it will be out there."

And the more chance that Titania would find him.

"We need to go looking for it tonight," Henry said.

"After what we just saw?" Jairus asked. "And you said I was crazy."

Henry smirked at him. "You are. But the stag is the only way to find the Fisher King. If the Carmun is raising the dead, we're out of time. We have to find him."

"I'm ready," Richard said, his voice cracking a little.

"I can help," Cassandra said quietly. "It has often appeared to me."

Henry wanted to object—wanted to keep her safe—but Domin said, "That's true. The stag has an interest in you."

"Very well," Henry said.

Cassandra took her cane. She looked to Mary and Amy.

"Some of us need to stay to protect the changelings," Amy said quietly.

"I'm not staying behind again!" Georgina protested.

"Georgie—" Cassandra reached for her sister.

"No!" Georgie pulled her arm away. "You keep leaving me, and I'm tired of it. You get married without telling me. You have all these secrets. We did everything together. And now, you're abandoning me again."

"I'm sorry," Cassandra whispered to her sister. "You're right. I have not been fair to you. I wanted to protect you, but leaving you alone is no protection. I won't stop you from coming if the men don't object. But I want you to fully understand. We're facing a...a witch. She's not human, and her power is terrible. She is spreading plague and blight, and she will kill us if she can. The things we are facing are worse than any of your nightmares. And I don't want to lose you."

Georgina threw herself into Cassandra's arms. "I don't want to lose you, either. I have seen those nightmares. I have painted them. How will I ever get them out of my mind if I don't face them?"

Cassandra nodded, but Henry, with his hand on her back, felt a shiver race through her.

"You'll all need weapons," Telesm said. "We lost my most powerful items, but I did bring some here with me before..." He sighed deeply, pain lining his face. "One moment."

He made his way slowly up the stairs, Domin hurrying to assist him. The rest stood uneasily, shifting in impatience as fog swirled outside the window, until Telesm and Domin returned, their arms laden with an assortment of weapons and other items. Telesm carried the shield that Cassandra had used against the hell hounds, and Domin had Jairus's blade.

"These weapons you know," Telesm said. "I wish I had

something that would counter the Carmun's staff, but you will have to find that answer yourself. There are other weapons in this world more powerful than any I could forge or steal away." He hesitated, then motioned for Domin to hand a sheathed blade to Henry. "This sword can burn as you wield it. The more terrible the foe, the brighter the flame. I think you'll be able to put it to good effect."

Henry nodded and took the sword carefully. He felt the fire within it—a spark from the forge always burning at its core. It sang to him a song of courage, and of noble deaths against dreadful enemies.

Telesm turned to Domin and unfolded a leather breastplate to reveal a short lance with a spade-shaped point.

Domin took a step back. "Are those—"

"Ankhira's dragon scale breastplate and Bradamante's lance. Yes. I didn't tell you I had them... Well, I don't regret it, either. But you can use them now. Few things can pierce this armor, and the lance will always hit its mark."

Domin eyed the items with something between sorrow and wariness, then he sighed. "Very well. But Richard wears the breastplate."

"I don't care about protecting Richard," Telesm said. "I care about protecting you."

"I appreciate that, but Richard has to survive if any of us will."

Richard looked chagrined by this talk, but he accepted the breastplate when Domin held it out to him. It was too large for the young man, but he strapped it on.

"And for the young human lady, a ring," Telesm said, holding a silver ring bearing a small pearl in the center to Georgina. "Another relic of older days, but it will make you difficult for the Fay to notice and give you extra protections against their enchantments. It only works for humans, more's the pity."

Georgina looked uncertain if she had heard correctly, but she slipped the ring on her finger.

Amy gasped. "It works! I don't see her. Well, if I concentrate very hard..."

Georgina still appeared baffled, and she looked no different to Henry, but he was glad Cassandra's sister had some protection against the Fay.

Something like an electric shock blasted over Henry's skin, and Amy gasped and took an unsteady step.

"What's wrong?" Mary asked.

Amy grasped her forehead. "I'm not sure. I—"

A ferocious bark rose from the back door.

"We're under attack," Telesm said, clutching the other items in his arms.

Henry grasped Cassandra's hand. Their time was over.

Chapter Twenty-Nine

Henry's hand tightened on Cassandra's, then it slipped away from her grasp, leaving her fingers cold. He marched to the back door where the commotion was. Cassandra reached after him, wanting to beg him to stay by her side. But he was hurrying away, and with her limp, she could not keep up as he stepped into the threshold of the back door and paused there to unsheathe his sword.

Cassandra reached the door behind Amy, Henry, and Telesm, with Domin and Jairus just behind her. Mary and Lucien hung back.

A growl from outside rumbled through the glass in the windows and trembled its way up Cassandra's legs.

"What is that monster?" Cassandra asked.

Amy's eyes were huge, and she turned to look at Telesm. "I think...I think it's our guardian."

"See, it works perfectly," Telesm said.

Cassandra peered out to see the enormous slate-gray dog standing before the back door and growling.

"It grows in proportion to the threat," Telesm said.

"Then what's out there?" Mary breathed.

"Amy!" called Titania's voice. "What is the meaning of this?"

Amy gasped and looked at the others. "My mother!"

"She means you harm," Telesm warned.

"So I gathered," she said drily. She raised her voice and called. "Just a precaution, Mother. Give me a moment."

"I will not stand for this insolent delay," Titania responded. "I am here to collect Henry Stewart."

Cassandra felt like she had been punched, and she watched Henry's shoulders tighten. He glanced at her quickly, his eyes full of too much to be spoken, and he gestured for her to stay back.

Amy walked outside and put a hand on the dog's giant flank. It sat, and Cassandra could see Titania now, standing in the garden and looking as sharp and cold as bare branches against a winter sky. The rain had stopped, but the night sky was heavy with clouds.

Henry squared his shoulders and walked down the stairs to the garden. Domin slipped past the rest of them to stand beside him.

"I am here," Henry said. "You have come about Jane and the Fisher King? I am willing to discuss the situation."

"I am not here to discuss anything with you. I will command, and you will obey."

"I have gained some measure of my own power. I am not a tool to be wielded at your will."

Titania gestured, and Henry grunted in pain. "You belong to me, Henry Stewart. I should not have let you forget it."

Henry staggered at whatever force Titania exerted over him,

though he managed to stay standing, apparently with great effort. Cassandra balled her hands into fists.

Domin took a step forward, but Titania gestured for him to halt. "I have not forgotten your threats, outcast, but I also know that your power is fading." She held up her arm, displaying her pale blue tattoo. "Even you cannot forever prevent me from claiming what is mine."

Domin moved toward Titania, but she made another gesture at Henry, and he screamed and dropped Telesm's sword. Domin paused, clearly uncertain of his ability to protect Henry against whatever Titania was doing to him.

Slowly, painfully, Henry moved closer to the Lady of the Woods, drawn by an invisible tether he fought with every step. The Seelie Queen's mouth curled in a horrible grin. Overhead, clouds churned ominously. Was Henry going to battle her? Cassandra wanted to believe he was strong enough to overcome the Faerie Queen, but he was already losing.

Vines shot from the ground and wrapped around Henry's wrists. They pulled down, though he fought them, and the ground shook, either with his fury or Titania's. Lightning flashed, and the clouds overhead whirled into a funnel, lashing the garden with a roaring wind. Still, the vines dragged him down, forcing him to his knees.

"Now you will remember who owns you," Titania called. "You belong to me."

The words jolted Cassandra, made her lift Telesm's shield and take a step forward involuntarily.

Henry jerked at the vines, trying to break free. Another bolt of lightning shot from the sky. Titania swept it aside, and it hit the hawthorn tree, exploding through it and catching it on fire.

"Stop!" Amy screamed.

Jairus raised his shotgun.

Domin charged Titania, but she slammed him in the chest, sending him gasping back.

"No!" Amy rushed to Domin's side.

Cassandra pushed her way past Telesm, struggling to keep the shield level, and came to a stop next to Henry.

"Henry doesn't belong to you," Cassandra said over the rushing of the wind and the crackling of the hawthorn tree.

Titania laughed. "Your infatuation gives you no claim on him."

Cassandra smiled back, remembering the story of Tam Lin. Of how the changeling's human lover saved him by refusing to release him. She loosened her grip on the shield with her good hand and grabbed Henry's shoulder.

"I'm not *infatuated* with him," Cassandra said. "I am married to him. The Fay respect human law, do they not? And acting according to human law, he gave himself to me."

Titania's expression of glee froze. Henry looked up at Cassandra, eyes wide.

Cassandra grasped his shoulder tighter. "I have a claim on him, too. My husband according to the laws of Scotland."

"You!" Titania breathed, and Cassandra wasn't sure if her wrath was directed at Henry or Cassandra—or both. "How dare you!"

Henry smiled weakly, his lips pale. "She's right. You'll never be able to bring me completely under your control. You own a part of my allegiance, but not the better part of it."

He ripped his hands free of the vines and struggled to his feet to grasp Cassandra's hand. She squeezed, determined not to let go no matter what Titania threw at them. When their fingers laced together, a blue band encircled her third finger like a tattoo of a ring—her oath with Henry. The same mark appeared on his finger.

Titania lashed out, and vines sprang from the ground, but Henry froze them, withering them in place. Then he gestured again, and the fire engulfing the hawthorn tree died down to embers. She glared at him.

He grinned at Titania. "I've realized something that's been bothering me since I met the Ghillie Dubh. His magic is not strong, but he's a solitary Fay—strong enough to stay free from the courts. And I wondered how he managed it. But now, I think I know. The answer is love. Caring enough about something outside of yourself that you can cling to it and never fall into the clutches of the courts. That's the secret to strength."

"I will show you strength!" Titania said, her face red with fury.

Henry lurched as Titania tugged at his magic. Cassandra felt it—felt the searing pain as the magic tore through Henry. But she also felt the pull reach her and slow. The pain eased. She was anchoring Henry, counterbalancing Titania's hold on him.

Titania snarled and stepped forward.

"Run!" Henry called, grabbing his fallen sword.

He half-dragged Cassandra back into the house, and once they were all inside, Amy slammed the door and bolted it.

The stone dog leapt back into action, snarling and rending at something large and green that rose from the garden.

"Oh, dear," Amy said. "Now she's very angry."

"We need to go. Now!" Henry said. "We have to find the Fisher King."

"She will follow us," Amy said. "She will not let this go."

"Then we will have to move very quickly," Henry snapped.

"Actually..." Amy stilled and tilted her head. "I may have an idea. Something that will at least slow her while the rest of you escape."

Domin looked at Amy. "I'm not sure you should stand against her."

"I'm not going to challenge her directly. But I think the wards here can entangle her for a time. Especially if Mary, Lucien, and Telesm help me. That will let the rest of you reach the Fisher King." Amy glanced at Richard, who looked small in his oversized breastplate.

Domin looked torn, but he squeezed Amy's hands and met her gaze. "Catch up with us as quickly as you can escape her. Telesm can help you track us."

"I will see you again," Amy said, though it sounded more like a question than a statement.

"We just need the white stag," Jairus said.

"We have to hope it's looking for us as desperately as we're looking for it," Henry said.

And with that, they hefted their weapons and hurried out the front door, leaving Amy to deal with the Lady of the Woods.

Chapter Thirty

Jairus hated it, breaking up their group. As he hurried into the night, he dared one look back at the lights of Amy's house, silently wishing Amy luck in whatever scheme she enacted. Something whispered he would never again return to those warm lights blazing against the darkness. He swallowed against the cold lump in his chest. He could not let sadness or fear stand in the way of their mission. That had been an advantage of hunting alone—fewer distractions.

His gaze drifted to Georgina Weaver, whose face was set in determination, but he forced himself to stay focused. This was not a time for distractions. He wondered if there was ever a time for the sorts of distractions that made his chest feel warm and light. Of course, Cassandra had just saved Henry—saved all of them—from Titania through love. So maybe, it wasn't as much a distraction as he had always thought.

Jairus hefted his sword, keeping it ready in one hand with his shotgun in the other. Henry clung to his sword, and Domin wielded a lance as tall as he was. They would have looked preposterous, but there was no one on the streets to judge them. London seemed to sense that a new threat walked the night. Even without Henry's rain storm, the city was unnaturally quiet.

Georgina hung close to Jairus. He didn't think she knew that Domin wasn't human, but she might have sensed it given her Sabbath-born abilities. It had taken Jairus a while to become comfortable with that fact, and Georgina was bearing up well under the new world she was just discovering.

"This way," Georgina said, her voice a little too loud in the darkness of the London streets. "If we're going where I saw the stag last time."

With no better ideas, they followed her lead. Only the occasional gaslamp pierced the fog that drifted over London, creating odd, eerie halos that did nothing to dispel the darkness.

Georgina brought them to the square where she had seen the stag. "I saw it right over there. It was gone when Mr. Hale brought me back, but maybe it comes this way often."

"Let's listen," Domin suggested.

Georgina scowled at that, but the rest of them stood very still.

"I hear hoofbeats," Domin said. "That way!"

They hurried after the ghostly sound, and Jairus hoped they were chasing the stag and not some phantom. Yet the sound was uneven—the steps of a wounded animal. The sounds led them to another square with dark and shuttered houses. No sign of the stag.

A whooshing sound drew Jairus's attention up in time to see something move on the rooftop above them. He raised his gun, and the others looked as well.

Spring-heeled Jack poked his head over the edge of the roof.

"Oy there, mate. No need to point a gun at ol' Jack. It won't do much against me anyhow."

"This one will," Jairus said. "It's full of iron shot."

Jack grinned down at them. "You lot are full of tricks. I bet you have some tricks against the monsters walking the streets now, too."

Domin gave Jack a speculative look. "Is that why you're hiding on the roof?"

"I'm no fool. Those things will kill me, and so will you! I know you've been 'unting for me."

"I'm not looking for revenge," Domin said. "I wasn't out to hurt you, but you'll have no such assurance from the monsters coming here. Even hiding on the roof won't save you if we don't stop the witch that summoned the blight."

"And what do you want from me, then?"

"The rest of the knife, Jack. Give me the rest of the knife that destroys magic."

"So you can use it on me?"

"No, so we can use it on the witch," Domin called up.

"Why should I 'elp you? I might 'ave more uses for such a powerful weapon."

"Because it will also help you. Unless you plan to help us against the witch?"

Jairus sincerely hoped not.

Jack was silent for a long moment. Domin stood very still—his worry only evident in the stiffness of his shoulders. If Jack wouldn't give them the knife, the only piece left of it was next to Domin's heart.

"You have to swear to me you won't harm me, nor none of your friends, neither," Jack said.

"I swear I will not seek revenge on you, nor allow my friends to do so," Domin said. "I promise not to harm you unless you threaten me or someone I care for."

Another long silence.

"Send one of the ladies over. I'll give it to them."

"You can hand it to me," Jairus called.

"But I don't want to steal a kiss from you," Jack said with a chuckle.

"No, you'd better not!" Jairus said.

"Jack!" Domin said. "Time is of the essence."

"Alright, I'll tell you the truth. I don't 'ave it anymore."

Domin hissed quietly. "What did you do with it?"

"I melted it down to nothing. I'd 'ad my fun with it, and I didn't want to risk it 'urting me again."

Domin sagged, and his skin went gray in the dim light.

"You still promised not to 'urt me, don't forget," Jack called.

"It doesn't matter," Domin said dully. "The real threat is out there, and we have one less way to fight it."

"Only one less," Henry said firmly. "We haven't lost yet. Come, Jack! Make yourself useful. We're looking for the white stag. Can you see it from up there?"

"In this fog? Ha! But I see it from time to time by that park over yonder."

"Come!" Henry called the others.

Georgina, who looked baffled, followed the others obediently, scanning the fog.

"There!" she said, pointing to a flash of white.

They ran into the thick darkness, but Jairus slowed, sensing something amiss.

"Wait!" Jairus called. "We're running blind."

A wind whipped past them, clearing the fog enough to show them the street ahead.

Three hellhounds waited for them. Behind the beasts, cornered, stood the white stag, the blood forever oozing down its leg. Jairus lifted his gun, training the barrel on the closest dog. The swish of a blade nearby reminded him that Henry and Domin only had edged weapons. Domin wouldn't be changing shape to charge into battle against the hellhounds. Henry's sword blazed to life, bright yellow flame licking up the metal and illuminating the hell hounds.

Jairus aimed his gun, careful to avoid the stag, and fired.

The rear hellhound whimpered and collapsed. It did not yet turn to dust, so it might not be dead.

Henry and Domin rushed past Jairus, sword and lance swinging. Richard moved to help, but Jairus put out a hand to stop the boy.

"Can't have you injured," Jairus said. And the boy *would* be injured fighting hellhounds.

Richard frowned and glanced at Cassandra and Georgina on either side of him. Cassandra had her shield raised, protecting the boy prince. Richard might not like it, but he had a different role.

Jairus locked gazes with the white stag—its eyes more intelligent than any beast.

Angel.

The word floated through his thoughts, and even as it did, he knew it wasn't quite correct. It was only his mind trying to make sense of the message. The stag wasn't an angel in the normal sense of the word, but it was a messenger, and they needed to hear its message.

He glanced over his shoulder to where Cassandra ushered her sister behind her.

"Guide the stag free!" Jairus called.

Then he jumped into the fight to clear the way. The first

hellhound he had shot twitched and started to rise, but he slammed it with the iron-cased butt of his rifle and then fired into the other hound that turned on him. It crumpled. Out of iron shot, he stepped forward, prepared to use his gun like a club. Henry's burning sword blistered the hound nearest him.

Jairus glanced back to be sure the ladies were safe. Georgina looked a little pale, but she carefully avoided watching the carnage of the fight. Instead, she kept her eyes fixed on Cassandra, who bowed and then reached out a hand for the stag.

The stag shied, and Jairus feared for a moment that it would bolt. Another hellhound commanded his attention, and he turned back to pound it with the butt of his rifle until Domin leapt in and sliced its head from its body. It crumpled to dust.

Movement caught the corner of Jairus's eye. The white stag limped after Cassandra and Georgina. Georgina had a hand resting on the stag's neck, and Cassandra gently beckoned it forward. Richard watched with wide eyes. Jairus let out a sigh of relief.

Domin sliced down the last of the hellhounds, and the men turned to follow them.

The stag led them back toward the park, breaking free from Cassandra and Georgina to bound ahead. They followed as well as they could, their boots rustling over the grass. Dark trees and shrubbery lurked on the edges of the light from Henry's sword.

A blur of white caught Jairus's eye. "There!"

The stag stood at the edge of the water. Light shimmered off the unquiet surface. The stag stepped into the lake. Its hooves created ripples that reflected a different landscape—one with the ruins of a great castle. It stopped to stare at them, as though waiting to guide them forward.

Henry bowed, and the others followed his example.

"Take us to the king," Henry said, his voice questioning, not commanding.

The stag returned his bow, dipping its great horned head, then limped ahead, the blood still oozing down its leg. Rushford had wounded it, and it had never healed, maybe because it was weakening, as the Fisher King was.

The stag walked deeper into the water, then it vanished.

"Oh!" Georgina said. "Where did it go?"

"There must be a gateway here," Henry said. "We have to follow."

"Where are we going, then?" Jairus asked.

"I have no idea, but we must follow the stag."

Henry and Cassandra led the way, Domin close behind. Richard squared his shoulders and followed. Jairus paused to reload his shotgun.

Georgina hesitated at the edge of the lake. She watched the strange, rippling castle reflected unclearly in the water, then looked to Jairus.

"What will it be like?" she asked.

"Dangerous," he said without hesitation. She deserved the truth. "Perhaps also beautiful, or at least awe-inspiring. We can't know until we step through."

She swallowed. "I'm not a coward."

"Definitely not!"

"I don't know..." She shifted her feet out of reach of the lapping waves of the lake. "I just don't want to be left behind."

There was no turning back for her now—not that night, at least—but Jairus didn't need to rub that salt in. He holstered his shotgun and offered his arm.

"How about we go together?"

A blush pinked her cheeks in the dim light, and she nodded. "Thank you. I'd like that."

She took his arm, her touch shy but warm through Jairus's sleeve.

He glanced back once at the hazy outline of London in the distance. Then he gripped his sword with his free hand and stepped into the water, as prepared as he could be for whatever they might face.

Chapter Thirty-One

Henry followed the white stag into the water, expecting to see a hawthorn tree somewhere nearby. But this was not a Faerie portal. His stomach lurched, and he had a sense he'd fallen some great distance, though he was still walking through dark, calf-deep water, surrounded by fog so thick he tasted it with each breath. It reminded Henry of the Twilight Path. He grabbed Cassandra's hand, and she gripped back hard. No indication that she was going to vanish like everyone had in the Twilight Vale. They walked together through a strange fog, the only sound the quiet splash of their feet through the water, and Henry felt almost as though he were floating, like he moved in some kind of dream. Only Cassandra's warm hand in his convinced him anything in that world was real.

And then the mist cleared. It was not night there, but an indeterminate gray dusk. Stone walls rose before them, the ruins of some ancient fortress slowly decaying back into the earth. Moss clambered over the crumbling stones, and the air was still but cool. The light, Henry realized, came from the stones themselves, a beacon against the night. The sound of lapping waters broke the quiet. They were on an island, though Henry could not guess where. Beyond the island, all grew dark again. He sensed his connection to the land's energies, so they were still in the human world, yet this felt like a place set apart.

Domin, Richard, Jairus, and Georgina fanned out around Henry and Cassandra, all wrapped in a hallowed quiet.

An old man sat on one of the stones by the broken entry arch, his shaggy hair white and his beard neatly combed. He wore only a long robe without ornament, but he bore a look of both power and fatigue. A dried trail of blood marked his leg, matching the wound of the white stag.

"You are the Fisher King," Henry said. It wasn't a question. He sensed it like he felt the hum of his pulse or the power of the magic in that place singing through his blood.

"I am," the old man replied. "I am Owain Glyndŵr, once a king of the Britons, and now a guardian of the land's magic."

"Owain Glyndŵr." Henry frowned. "But..."

The medieval Welsh prince had vanished over four hundred years earlier, but he was still young compared to the first stories of the Fisher King.

"Yes, I am not the first Fisher King, nor will I be the last. I took this role when I found Arthur's cave, and the ancient warrior himself ready to rest at last. He, I believe, took the role from the ancient king Bran, who once healed the land from the Carmun's depredations."

"That must be a heavy burden," Henry said slowly. "You are wounded and alone."

Owain's eyes flashed. "I am wounded *because* I am alone. Once, I had grail knights and ladies around me, and together we protected the land and bore the pains and joys of guardianship. But even the magic of the Fisher King does not grant immortality, and I have said goodbye to each of them. So few believe in magic anymore that none have come to join me or take my place. I sent my stag to the children and grandchildren of England's queen, but they do not heed it."

"You are not alone anymore," Henry said. "My friends and I have come to aid you. The Fay wish to replace you with one of their own."

"I know. I feel them drawing near. They would commit a grave mistake. The Fay have the power allotted to them and should have no more."

"I agree," Henry said. "That is why my friends and I will protect you. Some of us have Faerie magic, but we will not yield to the Lords and Ladies."

The Fisher King sighed, and the air around them stirred. In the distance, a crow cawed. "It would be better if none of you had ties to them, but the world changes, and so does the Fisher King and his court."

"Certainly, we can restore you to health," Cassandra said.

The Fisher King chuckled drily. "Were you my age, you might not wish to be restored. I will not live forever, young lady. Britain's magic needs a new shepherd."

Henry nodded and glanced to Richard. It was good they had him, though the young prince looked like he might be ill.

"Are you the one who seeks to take my place?" the Fisher King asked Henry. "I sense the ancient British blood in your veins, and your ties to the power of the land."

"There is someone with an older claim than mine: Richard of the House of York."

The Fisher King grunted and wrinkled his face, suddenly looking like nothing more than an irritable old man. "A Plantagenet! It had to be a Norman, I suppose."

"I beg your pardon!" Richard sputtered.

"I was still young in my role as Fisher King when your War of the Roses spilled blood on my fields and rivers."

Richard folded his arms. "That was none of my doing."

The Fisher King nodded. "You don't crave bloodshed, but you're willing to fight. That is good."

"He was raised by the Lord of the Thames," Henry said. "He cares about this land, and he will fight for it."

The Fisher King met his eyes. "There is more to this role than fighting. There are elements of love and sacrifice involved in being a ruler of any kind, and especially when the life and well-being of the land are involved. For instance, I would be willing to relinquish my role to a Norman when the time comes."

Henry smiled. "I'm sure he will make a good Fisher King."

He had to. Though Henry felt a little guilty at his relief that Richard could take the role, his belief in Richard was sincere. The prince acted arrogant, but his heart was good.

"I will do my best, sir," Richard said, his shoulders straight but his voice trembling slightly.

"No need to frighten the child," said a cold female voice behind them. "I will save you the trouble and become the Fisher Queen."

Henry turned, drawing his sword. Domin already had his lance raised, and Jairus lifted his shotgun.

Jane rode toward them on her black stag. Her armor glinted in the pale light. Behind her, a bridge of solid black ice joined the Fisher King's island to the land beyond.

Jairus fired at Jane. Her stag reared, intercepting the shot, and dapples of red appeared across its chest.

Domin and Henry charged. Henry raised the sword, willing it to burn. Blue flames shot up the metal. Henry swung and connected with the stag, the blue and red colliding in a blast of color and heat.

Jane screamed and tried to steer her mount away from Domin's magic lance, but it struck her chest and sent her sprawling sideways off the stag.

She vanished along with her mount.

Henry brandished the sword like a torch, expecting her to reappear behind him.

"She cannot dismount in the mortal realm," Domin said, "and the Fisher King's realm is part of the mortal world. But she will return."

Henry looked at the bridge Jane had constructed and moved to destroy it.

"Wait!" Jairus called. "Listen!"

The distant ring of voices and swords reached them despite the darkness beyond the island.

"Yes," Owain said. "The Fay—Seelie and Unseelie—have brought their battle to the threshold of my realm."

"Henry," Richard hissed.

Henry paused, and he knew exactly what Richard would say. He felt it himself. The sickness growing close. Heavier. While the Fay fought each other, the Carmun approached.

Henry turned to the Fisher King, but the old man simply watched him sadly, not speaking. This was their chance, but what was he supposed to do with it?

"The Grail," Cassandra prompted.

"Where is the Grail?" Henry asked the Fisher King. "Can't we use it to save you?"

Henry felt a jolt deep in his gut, and his vision went dark. When his sight cleared again, they stood on the outskirts of the Faerie battle, the water separating them from the Fisher King's island.

"What..." Henry looked at his friends in confusion.

"You asked the wrong question," Cassandra said. "In the stories, there's always a certain question that heals the Fisher King or reveals the Grail. But it's different depending on the story."

"Of course." Henry had known that. But it was one thing to read about a legend in a book and another to be in the midst of one and have to remember each detail.

"How do we get back?" Jairus asked.

"We have to fight our way back," Domin said. "And we have to hope we reach him before Jane or any of the Fay."

Chapter Thirty-Two

Amy's ears ached from the dinging of the clock and the pressure brought by the warding spells holding Titania back. Her mother's magic thrummed against the house. A row of yew trees sprouted outside the window and cracked the glass, and the stone dog snarled and tore at vines attempting to hold it in place.

"You said you had a plan?" Telesm asked. "As soon as she realizes the others have fled, she'll leave her vines to crush the house and go after them."

Amy released a slow breath. Her plans usually did not go as she wished them to. But all she had to do was buy Domin and the others some time. "She's not going anywhere. We will trap her."

"Trap a Faerie queen?" Telesm asked. He didn't sound skeptical, only curious. And amused.

"Yes." Amy looked around the house. As much as she had disliked the legacy of her late human husband, she had grown to care for this house and all the memories it held. Domin had kissed her right in that corridor.

Another window shattered as a strangling vine sought a way past the wards.

"How?" Mary asked, her voice small but certain.

Amy faced Telesm, watching his reaction to see if her idea was feasible. "We lower the wards on the house. Let her step inside—and then put the wards back up."

Telesm's eyes sparkled. "You are a good student after all. That's a clever idea—the spell will hold her fast if you and your changeling companions have the will to oppose her."

He glanced at Mary and Lucien, and both nodded.

Amy thought of Domin and her other friends. "We'll hold her, and then we can negotiate her freedom." Amy's chest trembled at the thought of trapping her mother—Titania's fury would be terrible. But this was her chance to forge her own path and to help her friends be free as well. "Yes, we will do it. You will help us?"

"Your will must be strong—at least as strong as Domin believed it to be."

Amy nodded. Never had she wanted anything more.

Telesm went on. "Someone—I think Mary would be best—must stop the hands of the clock. Hold them in place. You, Amy, must hold the magic inside you until she has walked so far into the house that she cannot walk out. And Titania must enter uninvited or the wards will be nullified."

"I have invited her in before."

"Not since you placed the wards. The previous invitation may allow her entry to the building, but not past the wards. You have to provoke her to enter without repeating your invitation, though."

Amy drew a shaky breath. "Very well. Lucien, go and fetch

young Will. Keep him close. And order my cook and my maid to flee. I'm not sure what will happen here, but I don't want anyone hurt."

Lucien raced to the stairs.

Telesm nodded to Mary, and she darted down the sitting room where the clock ticked its protective spell. After a moment, the ticking stopped. The quiet pounded against Amy's mind, and a surge of panic welled up inside of her. Titania might kill them all.

Telesm nodded to her. "Start with the dog. Command it to return to stone."

Amy concentrated on the dog. She could feel its protectiveness—an extension of her own. She spoke patience to it. Its barking stopped, but it still loomed behind the house. She couldn't stop thinking about her friends still in this house. About what Titania would do to them. What she had done to Henry and even Amy.

Wait. Patience. Have faith.

The dog slowly grew smaller, finally returning to its stone form by the back door.

Telesm nodded his approval.

Titania walked to the back door and threw it open, but she stayed beyond the threshold. She looked disdainfully at the dog. "Telesm is cowering here after his sanctuary was destroyed, I see."

Amy avoided looking at Telesm, but she sensed that Titania's barb had hit its mark. "Telesm is helping us to fight the Carmun. Her invasion of his sanctuary should warn you that we cannot afford to fight each other."

"I don't need your pathetic advice. I have come for Henry." Titania held up her arm, showing the faded tattoo on her wrist. "Domin's end approaches, and Henry will serve me."

Amy couldn't lie and say that Henry was there. She had to dodge the truth. "No, you are weakening. Your grip on your power and on Henry are loosening. Look at how his mortal bride defied you."

"Silence, brat! Henry will kneel before me again. He may dislike it, but the Dark Lady marches on the Fisher King's throne, and I'm certain he would rather my court control the Fisher King than hers. I may even keep his human plaything alive as a reward for his obedience. She will provide a useful pawn."

"You're welcome to try to force Henry," Lucien said, stepping forward with Will. "But he is ready to break from you and become the Lord of the Changelings. We are here, an army of us, and we will not let you take him."

Oh, yes. Lucien could lie, and he had been taught to use words as weapons.

Titania looked for a moment as though one of the chairs in the room had spoken to her. But then a wicked smile spread over her face. "You are an Unseelie changeling, not one of mine. But I can still make you suffer. Do you honestly think you— even all of you—can stand against me?"

Lucien folded his arms. "Yes."

Her mouth curled into a snarl. "Henry may try hiding behind changeling children as he hid behind Domin, but he will have to face me."

Titania stepped into the back corridor. A zap of energy raced through Amy, the magic surging to escape and drive Titania away. Amy trembled, uncertain if her magic was strong enough against her mother. But it wasn't only her magic. Mary and Lucien had helped. Telesm had strengthened it. And she had done it for her friends. Her love for them was stronger than her fear of her mother.

Amy backed away, pulling Lucien and Will with her. Titania followed them, her face terrible and inhuman in her fury, like the reaching shadows of a darkening wood, the fangs of predators who stalked the forest paths.

Amy put Lucien and Will behind her and walked her mother back toward the dusty ballroom. Mirrors along the walls echoed back images of grasping tree branches and predatory eyes. The greenery outside stirred at Titania's fury.

Titania stepped into the center of the ballroom.

"Now!" Telesm shouted.

Amy released her hold on the wards. She gasped as the power surged through her, and Lucien, joined to her through the spell, jolted as though shocked. The images in the mirrors changed, swirling and erasing the images of distant Faerie woods. Instead, they reflected Titania's many cruelties. Her torture of changelings, her betrayals of fellow Fay to solidify her power, her vengeance against innocent humans who had unknowingly offended her.

Titania froze, bound by the spell, her expression a terrible mask of rage. Lines creased her face, her illusion of eternal youth fading, her hair shooting through with white like the snows of the Winter Kingdom blowing over the forests.

"What have you done?" Titania gasped through clenched jaws.

"She has trapped you," Telesm said. "Or rather, you have trapped yourself. You violated the peace of this sanctuary."

"Set me free!"

"No," Amy said quietly.

"You think your magic is stronger than mine?" Titania snarled.

"No," Amy said, trying to ignore the terrible images swirling in the mirrors. "I'm certain it's not. But my heart is stronger than yours, despite all the times you tried to break it. To break me."

"If I broke you, it means you were weak." Vines climbed from the mirrors. Began snaking their way around the room. Poisonous spines emerged from their tendrils, gripping the walls, tearing the paper away.

Amy was weak. She always had been. Her mother was right. The vines thickened, tangled across the walls. Amy was trapped with her mother. She wished Domin were there. Even with his injury, he was strong. Yet his strength came not through being cruel and powerful, but through being caring and wise.

Amy met her mother's eyes. "You're wrong. Strong things often break. Great oaks lose branches and even heartwood. Walls that stopped armies crumble. The iron of humans rusts away. The strong think their strength can save them from the inevitable and trust in it alone, and they become brittle. Fragile. But weak things *bend*. They move with the elements and learn to survive. It allows them to keep growing and later become strong themselves—strong and also wise."

"You and your emotions!" Titania sneered.

But her vines had stopped. Their tendrils found cracks in the walls and clung on, but they were no longer expanding.

"The emotions you sneer at are what have you trapped. It was love that made the protections that bind you here. Love and hope and determination. I am not stronger than you, but those things are."

"You think you can claim my kingdom? You cannot even protect your own little dominion here."

Titania was correct, Amy knew. Even if her mother withdrew all the vines, the walls were cracked and the floor was broken. This house would crumble, and the protections they had put on it would no longer matter. Amy's heart twisted at the thought of losing everything. So much work to rebuild her life, all crumbling away before her eyes.

But she wasn't losing everything. She was saving her friends. And wasn't that what the house had always been about?

"I don't care about your kingdom," Amy said. "Someone will take your place if you don't return. You can be replaced just as the Fisher King can be. But you will never control the Fisher King. We found another to take his throne."

"I will kill Henry."

"No, you will set him free."

A nasty grin split Titania's face. "I will take my power back and he will die."

"Only if you wish to die as well," Amy said. "No, you will let go of the threads of Henry's power. You will release your hold on all of your changelings."

Titania's face went white with rage. "What right have you to demand such a thing of me?"

"You never had the right to hold them. You stole every one of them from their lives and their families, and now you will release them without taking back the magic that keeps them alive."

"That magic is a gift!"

"And they have paid for it with their servitude to you. So, you will let them choose what to do with it from here. And you will swear never to seek vengeance on them or on me or anyone who has dwelt in this house. Them or those they love. Those are the conditions of your freedom."

Lucien stepped forward with Will at his side and Mary peeking out from behind him.

"You have come to gloat, I suppose," Titania snapped at them.

"Only to see justice done," Lucien said. "Would you like to

discuss gifts? The Dark Lady made my words a weapon, but now I choose how I use them. My gift helped trap you. And Will here was cast off by some Faerie Queen. Perhaps you? He has magic he doesn't know how to control. He burns things. Would it serve justice if he burned you? Would that be right, for a Faerie Queen to be destroyed by the pain she caused?"

Titania wrestled against her invisible bonds, her eyes flashing with fear. "You would not be so foolish. With the Carmun attacking, it would throw the magical world into disarray."

Lucien laughed. "I would not ask Will to hurt you or anyone, but not because of the Faerie world. It is because he should not carry the burden of such a brutal act at such a young age. That is something you might not be capable of understanding, but I think you can understand this: the world is shifting. The Fay will never be as strong as they once were, and if they do not learn how to bend, they will break. They may even be broken by the changelings they value so little."

Titania was silent for a long moment, no doubt trying to wriggle her way free from the spell. Finally, she bowed her head. "Very well. I swear as my daughter bids me. I release my hold on the changelings in my care, and I swear not to seek vengeance on them or on the current or former occupants of this house or their loved ones."

Amy nodded and pulled the magic back, holding its force in her chest. The cracked mirrors returned to reflecting the room, casting back hundreds of images of withering vines and the defeated Faerie Queen.

Titania said nothing, only turned her back on Amy and strode through one of the broken windows to the garden. With the hawthorn tree destroyed, she would have to find another way back to the Faerie realms, but that was not Amy's concern.

The house trembled as the vines and trees withdrew from its walls.

"Oh, you forgot something," Telesm said.

"What?" Amy asked, her heart pounding.

"You didn't protect the house itself. We need to move outside."

They hurried for the front door, avoiding whatever Titania might be doing in the garden.

"We will have to follow the Lady of the Woods," Mary said.

"Why?" Amy asked.

"She won't tell the changelings that they're free."

"And the Dark Lady is marching after the Fisher King," Lucien added. "We have to warn Henry and the others, too."

"How will we find them?" Amy asked.

"We don't have to," Telesm said. "The Dark Lady's forces will lead us to them."

"We will go to the changelings, then," Lucien said. "Mary and I. You two go and tell Henry what has happened."

They reached the square and turned to look back at the house. Something cracked with a blistering pop, and the roof sagged. Amy felt her spell dissolving as the house and its clock splintered and fell. Her chest lurched, and she turned away, unable to watch her home crumble. She instead faced the foggy night and turned her thoughts to the rest of her friends out there somewhere, fighting against the darkness.

Chapter Thirty-Three

Henry did not ignite his sword as they fought their way through the Fay. Great bonfires illuminated the battlefield, along with flashes of magic. Henry, Domin, and Jairus led the way, weapons drawn, while Cassandra used her shield to protect Richard and Georgina. Around them, trolls, goblins, red caps, and all manner of other Faerie creatures shrieked and roared and tried to tear each other to pieces. Henry thought their best hope was to slip through without drawing too much attention. They had to return to the Fisher King before Jane returned or one of the Fay took him captive.

"Maybe we can convince them to stop," Richard said, flinching away from the din of the fighting. "They know about the Carmun. They can't be so stubborn and foolish that they would let her win instead of working together against her."

Henry grimaced at Richard's naivety about the Fay. The prince had grown up in a sheltered court—proof that not all the Fay were terrible. But many of the ones with power held that position through cruelty. How was Richard supposed to deal with them as Fisher King when he was so innocent?

"This is brutal even for the Fay," Domin said. "I think it's the Carmun's influence, hatred and desperation making the fighting more savage."

Henry spotted Fitzhugh in the midst of the fighting ahead of them and turned quickly away. If he saw them... Then what? Fitzhugh wasn't Henry's friend; Henry knew that well enough. But he was a little more clear-sighted than most of the Fay. Maybe it was his human blood, or simply his understanding of the human world. And maybe Richard wasn't entirely wrong. Maybe they could convince some of the Fay to stand with them against the Carmun.

"Jairus, Cassandra, Miss Georgina, watch over Richard," Henry called. "Get him to the Fisher King. Domin, let's catch Fitzhugh!"

Domin nodded and shoved back a hobgoblin who came too close. Richard looked confused, but Jairus dragged him back and lifted his sword, ready to protect the prince.

Domin and Henry cut their way through the melee, chasing Fitzhugh as he cut a path toward the bridge connecting the field to the Fisher King's island.

"There!" Domin pointed to where Fitzhugh wielded a longsword against a being that seemed to be made of ice.

Henry froze the ice creature into place. Fitzhugh brought his blade around to smash the creature, but Domin stepped in to block the fatal blow with his lance.

Fitzhugh snarled and drew his sword back. "I should have known you weren't trying to help. What are you doing?"

"We are trying to warn you," Henry said. "The Carmun is coming in this direction."

Fitzhugh's expression fell, and he looked to the south. "Yes, I sense it."

"Can we turn the Fay to fight against the Carmun?"

Fitzhugh scowled. "They think the solution is to claim the Fisher King's power against her. Bloodlust has overtaken them, and they'll be happy to see their opponents fall to the blight."

"We're all going to fall to the blight," Henry said.

"I hate to agree with you..." Fitzhugh glanced once again to the south. "But we probably are. The Fay are not as strong as we once were. I don't know if any of us can imprison the witch again. That's why they're so desperate for the Fisher King's power."

"But it wasn't just the Fay who stopped her in the past," Henry said. "It was changelings, too."

Fitzhugh parried a blow from a troll and slashed its leg, sending it reeling back.

"Changelings, you say?" he asked.

"The Morrigan gave us that hint," Henry said.

A sluagh reeled in their direction. Henry turned to face the host of damned souls. He scrambled to pull energy in so he could wield it against them.

The energy came easily—too easily. He pulled at the sluagh, too, dragging them off course. Closer to him. They hissed and shrieked, mad with the fury of battle. Henry sucked in a sharp breath and whipped the energy out, sending them whirling away.

He stared at his hands. Something was different. He took stock of the energy around him—

And he felt no trace of Titania.

The only magic flowing through him was his own—the magic that came from his connection to the land.

He was free. He didn't understand how, but Titania no longer held a chain around him.

Fitzhugh looked at him, eyes wide. "How did you do that?"

"I don't know," Henry said, turning his hands back and forth in wonder.

"Well, you'd best take advantage of it while you can," Fitzhugh said. "You could take charge of the changelings. Lead them to freedom, or against the Carmun if you think that's the solution."

With a lurch, all the possibilities flowed through Henry's mind. He *could* lead the changelings, try to protect them from the Lords and Ladies. He could live a normal life with Cassandra.

But he couldn't do any of those things while the Carmun threatened them. And he did not want to lead innocent children against a witch. No, he should spare them from such a fate if he could.

He glanced back at Richard and Cassandra with her shield up protecting the young prince. He should spare all of them. But there was only one way to do that. Something snagged and tore in his chest, a blossoming hope ripped from him. That sense of freedom, so glorious for the few moments it had lasted. But what good was his freedom if it meant watching many others still in chains? It was the one thing that was truly his own, and he knew what he had to do with it.

He looked at Domin, who watched him with a deep sorrow. Henry cast a quick glance at the bridge of ice, and Domin returned a curt nod. This was what Henry had to do, and Domin—true friend that he was—understood and would help him.

"I'm going to the Fisher King," Henry said. He looked over

his shoulder at the fighting between him and the bridge. "But now, every Fay is my enemy."

Fitzhugh looked...disappointed was the only way Henry could make sense of it. But only for a moment, and then he laughed. "We always were, as you well know."

"You're not trying to stop me."

"But don't expect me to help you either."

Henry nodded and turned with Domin to fight his way through to the Fisher King.

They sliced and dodged their way through the clash of Faerie creatures. Some knew Domin and avoided him out of old habit. None seemed very interested in them. Henry felt a surge of hope as they neared the bridge.

But a troop of dark elves stood guard before the bridge, ancient Unseelie creatures, every shadow and sinew of their bodies full of suffering.

Domin charged the dark elves with his lance. Henry ignited his sword and followed.

The first creature tried to deflect Domin's lance with a sword made of magic and shadow, but Domin's lance neatly wove under the sword and struck home.

The dark elves focused their attention on Domin. Domin motioned for Henry to run for the bridge.

Henry hesitated at leaving his friend, and in that moment of indecision, one of the dark elves charged him. Henry struck back with his flaming sword, and the clash of the two weapons sent a shower of sparks into the air.

The dark elf's blows came fast, each strike hammering against Henry's blocks, making his arms ache with the effort of parrying. He managed to step back, catch his breath, and draw on the chill in the air. He sent a blast of ice shards into the dark elf's face and raised his sword to strike.

And another dark elf caught him with a blow, slicing into his side. Henry gasped at the deathly cold of the cut from the shadow blade.

Henry stumbled away from his new opponent, trying to watch both of their blades.

Domin's lance burst through the second dark elf's chest.

The creature shrieked and clutched the lance, trying to tear itself free, and its companion spun to face Domin.

Henry pressed his injury, warm blood oozing over his fingers.

"Go!" Domin called.

Henry gritted his teeth, holding his bleeding side. Domin could still fight, even if he didn't have the power he once did. And they would all die if Henry didn't get to the Fisher King and stop the Carmun.

He managed only a few steps before a different wave of power washed over the field. He clutched his sword and looked up to where a dark, whirling portal opened in front of him. Unseelie magic poured from it, a direct connection to the Unseelie realm opened in this place of suffering. Was Jane returning? Henry stumbled for the bridge. He had to reach it before Jane or any of the Unseelie Fay.

Chapter Thirty-Four

Mary trembled as she followed Amy through the gateway to Elfland. It was an unfamiliar gateway on the edge of London, but Amy said she was *fairly* certain it could take them to the Lady of the Woods' kingdom.

Prepared for whatever horrors they might face, Mary straightened her back. They could do this. Lucien took her hand, and she gripped it tightly, not pulling away. It felt right, not just because a Faerie changeling and a human one were facing the Fay together, but because it was Lucien, who seemed to understand her better than anyone else. They had reason to fear—Titania had promised not to hurt them, but there were many other Fay in the Otherworld—yet they would not shrink from their task.

Mary paused for a moment when she stepped through the gateway, stunned. She had feared the woods near Drixton, even when flowers bloomed a tapestry of colors across its floor. But the beauty of the Kingdom of the Woods stole her breath. Birds and butterflies filled the air, and the trees and ground bloomed, mingling into a wild mixture of color like someone had tossed buckets of flowers over everything.

But then, she noticed the shadows. Deep, creeping shadows with sharp angles cut through the understory of the trees, as though the beauty was only a trap to lure in unsuspecting prey.

Mary shivered.

Once they all stood among the ever-flowering trees of the Forest Kingdom, Amy turned to face them. Telesm had come as well, his expression more serious than Mary had ever seen it, guiding little Will.

"I will tell my mother's changelings that they are free and lead them from her kingdom if they wish it," Amy said.

"And where will you take them?" Telesm asked. "Most are too old to return to the human world."

"What about your clearing?" Amy asked. "Just for the moment."

Telesm grimaced. "There's nothing left there. No cottage. No protective spells. They won't be safe there. Or comfortable."

"They'll be safer and more comfortable than they were as thralls to the Fay," Lucien said. "They can help you build your sanctuary again. Or, if you don't want to rebuild, you can teach them how to do it."

Telesm was silent for a long moment, studying Lucien. Finally, he turned to Amy. "Very well. Take them to my clearing. We will...see what comes of it."

Amy smiled brightly at him, then she looked to Lucien and Mary. "Are you certain you want to go to the Unseelie Kingdom?"

"Yes," Lucien said. "I believe many of the changelings there will be willing to fight—to take any chance to survive and be free—and the Dark Lady will have left few to watch them."

Amy looked worried, but she nodded. "You can open the way?"

Lucien raised his chin. "Of course. I have grown quite good at opening the gates."

"I will hope to see you again soon, then," Amy whispered to both of them.

Lucien turned back to the hawthorn marking the gateway and placed a hand on it.

"There is suffering enough here," he said.

Amy nodded, her eyes tight with pain.

Lucien touched the ground, and it yawned open, a dark descent into the Unseelie kingdom. He looked back to Mary and held out his hand once again.

She took it, and they stepped into the blackness.

It was a thick, pressing kind of dark, cloying and humid, like a giant tongue slurping over her. And then they stepped through into the cold of the Unseelie Kingdom, surrounded by the black trees with their lifeless gold leaves and the ground mulched with bones. Mary shivered and wiped her free hand on her dress. Silence greeted them.

Lucien tightened his grip. "The whole Unseelie Kingdom seems to have marched away."

"Let's find the changelings!"

They hurried past the gothic eating hall and back to the outdoor kitchens. There were fewer changelings there this time.

Lucien frowned. "She must have taken some to serve her army along the way.

"We'll do what we can," Mary said, trying to mask her disappointment.

The changelings mostly ignored them until Lucien stepped close enough to be recognized. Then some of them stopped their work to watch him.

"Did she catch you again?" one young man whispered.

Lucien smiled grimly. "I'll never let her catch me again. I'm still free. And I've learned how to move between worlds. I learned it from the Lady of the Wood's royal changeling, Henry Stuart."

They all looked at him now, various levels of skepticism and wistfulness on their faces.

Mary stepped forward. "We have forced the Lady of the Woods to release all of her changelings."

Several of the changelings gasped. Some shook their heads in disbelief.

"It's true," Lucien said. "And if you want to be free, this is your opportunity. We're going to help Henry Stuart save the Fisher King. And then, maybe he can protect us from The Dark Lady."

"No one can protect us from her," one female changeling said, keeping her eyes down.

"I'm willing to try," said the young man. "If others have done it, I'm willing to fight for my chance."

Lucien smiled. "Any who wish for their opportunity, follow us."

One by one, each of the changelings put down their spoons and rags and came to stand around Lucien. A few wielded kitchen knives and brooms as weapons. Lucien nodded at them, and they turned to leave, creeping away from the Unseelie hall with its many spires and toward the woods and the hope of freedom.

A figure moved through the gloom. A Fay. There was no mistaking her ethereal grace.

"One of the Unseelie," Lucien whispered. "Be ready to fight."

"Wait!" Something about the Fay was familiar to Mary. "I

think that's...that's my Faerie mother."

"She's holding a child," Lucien muttered.

"She'll force us back to work," another changeling groaned.

"Quiet!" Lucien said.

They went silent and watched.

The Weeping Woman paused, sensing if not seeing the group gathered there.

"I will go speak to her," Mary said, emotions warring in her chest.

Her Faerie mother was in thrall to the Unseelie Queen and might be planning some trap for Mary and her friends. But maybe her mother would help her again, as she had once before. She wanted her mother to be...to be *good*. To be heroic in some way. As if it could make Mary more heroic as well. She knew she had to be her own person regardless of what either of her parents chose. Still, she would like to see her mother free. It hurt her to think of some part of her—some person whom she believed had good in her—in the grasp of the Unseelie Queen.

The Weeping Woman stepped gingerly forward like a doe uncertain of her steps. She held an infant in her arms.

Mary stepped forward, tearing her gaze from the little child to the Weeping Woman.

"You look well," the Weeping Woman said.

"Thank you. I am."

"The human world can be cruel to Fay."

Mary nodded. "Sometimes, but it can also be beautiful. And it's possible to avoid the worst of the iron and other things that harm Fay."

"But the magic is...wrong. Weakening. The Lords and Ladies are dwindling. They will not allow that to stand."

The Weeping Woman lowered her head, pain creasing her features. Mary realized she was under a geas not to reveal certain things. Just as Fitzhugh was. That tickled her memory of when Fitzhugh had spoken to her. Told her the name Maude.

Finally, the Weeping Woman spoke. "My Lady has long anticipated this danger—the failing of Faerie magic as human influence grows. She has a plan to retain her strength—she always does—but it will not be pleasant for the human world."

Mary shivered and looked at the infant her mother cradled. "We know about the Fisher King. But why the other changelings?"

The Weeping Woman's face contorted, and her mouth moved as she sought words against the geas that bound her. Mary's heart ached, but she did not know how to help. Her mother had to win this fight alone.

"Court. Knights. Powers." The Weeping Woman gasped, and fresh tears coursed down her cheeks. "Stop. Jane."

Mary rushed forward and seized her arm. "Thank you. I can see those words cost you."

The Weeping Woman looked down at where Mary clutched her arm, her expression confused. How rarely must she experience a touch in kindness? "I only wish that you will not have to suffer as I have." She blinked as though coming back to herself and looked down at the infant in her arms. "You are trying to free the changelings. I will have to try to stop you. She ordered me to guard them. But I don't wish to succeed. And I did not want you to miss this one. Jane took it on St. John's Eve. It could still go back to its parents. I cannot give it to you. You will have to take it from me."

Mary did so, afraid her mother would fight her in some way, but the Weeping Woman stood very still, almost trembling with the effort not to struggle.

Mary cradled the child against her chest.

"This was kind of you," Mary said. "We will do all we can to help this child find his human family again. You have done a good turn."

"Have I?" The Weeping Woman looked pleased.

"Yes. I don't think you are as lost as you believe. And I have something that might help you."

"You do?" The Weeping Woman looked down at Mary's hand as though expecting to see a dagger or a talisman.

"It's your name. Maude."

The Weeping Woman stared at her, confused. Mary's heart sank. That had not been Fitzhugh's meaning after all.

Then, the Weeping Woman's eyes filled with tears, and she gasped. "Maude! Yes, yes, I do remember. That was what they once called me. But the Dark Lady stole it. How did you get it back from her?"

Mary wasn't entirely certain if the stealing of a name was real or symbolic, but either way, she would not betray Fitzhugh's act, self-interested as it might have been. She shook her head.

"I cannot say. Just take your name, Maude, and find yourself again."

"Maude, Maude, Maude," she repeated the name as though making certain she would not forget it.

"Can your queen steal it from you again?" Mary asked, suddenly afraid. Certainly, the Unseelie Queen would not respond with mercy if she knew Maude had her name back.

Maude smiled. "Only if she knows, and I'll be sure that she doesn't. Thank you for giving me back a part of myself. I will make good use of it. I will start by closing my eyes and saying it to myself many, many times."

With that, she curtseyed low—which made Mary very uncomfortable—and turned her back on Mary, shutting her eyes as she promised.

Mary stood there awkwardly for a moment, then she realized.

She motioned for Lucien and the others to hurry. Maude was still under orders to stop them, but the anchor of her name gave her the power to fight—to delay a little.

They rushed past her for the woods. Lucien guided them to a place where he could open a gateway.

"To Telesm's domain?" Mary asked.

"I don't know how to get there," Lucien said. "But I could find the place where the Fay are fighting. There will be suffering. We could join them there and find our friends."

Mary looked back at the others, then down at the child snuggled in her arms. "Not everyone may want to fight."

"But most of us do!" called a girl from the back. "Those that don't can make their own way, but if this is our chance to be free, I want to take it."

The other changelings cheered.

Lucien and Mary looked at each other.

"Open the gate," Mary said.

Lucien nodded, and Mary passed the infant off to an older boy who looked frightened.

"Your job is to keep this little one safe," she whispered. "Can you do that?"

The boy looked at the child, then he straightened and nodded firmly.

"Ready?" Lucien called.

Mary wasn't, but she stepped up next to Lucien and took his hand as he opened the gateway to the battlefield.

Chapter Thirty-Five

Henry raised his sword, his arm aching, ready to face whatever issued from the Unseelie portal. A wave of dizziness rolled over him. Blood seeped down his side from his injury. He was in no condition to fight, and these fresh Unseelie forces would overwhelm him. Overwhelm his friends. He had to clear the way. Jairus, Cassandra, and Georgina were far back with Richard. If Henry died, at least Richard could still take the Fisher King's place. Maybe that was Henry's role: to open the way for Richard. He steeled himself, ready to rush forward.

The first figures he saw were familiar. Lucien and Mary raced through the portal. Were they fleeing from some Unseelie foe?

But they didn't look frightened. They looked determined.

Behind them flowed a stream of...children. Children of all ages dressed in rags but holding kitchen knives and staffs of black wood from the Unseelie forest.

Another gateway opened, this one behind Henry. He whirled and saw Amy charge through on her Faerie pony, a group of older children—changelings—in tow. Telesm brought up the rear.

What on earth had happened?

"Amy!" Henry called.

Amy turned in his direction, grinning broadly. "You're free, aren't you? All of my mother's changelings are free!"

"How—" Henry began, but they didn't have time. Not then.

Titania's changelings flowed past, holding various implements taken from her kingdom: sharpened poles, knives, even pruning hooks. They joined up with those who followed Lucien and Mary. But most were so young. They divided themselves, the older forming a loose phalanx with their makeshift weapons, the younger huddling together for protection.

"They're not trained to fight," Henry said.

Amy glanced back at the changelings. "Let them decide what they're willing to risk."

Henry grimaced as the changelings turned to face the Faerie forces. Amy moved her pony in front of them, ready to lead the way if they charged.

Henry turned for the bridge, but a cold wave slammed into his back, sending shivers over his skin.

The Fay nearby had taken little notice of the children, but a stir moved through the fight. The Dark Lady marched toward the changelings, wielding a barbed spear made of bone and stained with the blood of many foes. She drove back both her own people and her enemies to reach the changelings. Fay fell back before her, and the fighting slowed as attention turned to her.

The dark elves, those still on their feet, tried to retreat to the bridge, but Domin held them off, forcing them to engage with his lance.

Henry looked between the bridge and the Dark Lady. How could he leave the changelings to face the most terrible of Faerie Queens?

The Dark Lady looked past Amy. Her gaze fell on Lucien, and her eyes narrowed. "I know you. You should have been grateful I allowed you a place in my court and a piece of my magic. Now, you will have nothing!"

She gestured, and Lucien doubled over in agony.

Henry gathered energy to throw at the Dark Lady, but it felt slippery in his grasp. His injured side throbbed, and his head grew light.

Fitzhugh stepped forward and yanked at the Dark Lady's spear, knocking her off balance.

"No," Fitzhugh said. "You cannot have him. He should have been Nannette's. He should have been mine."

"I don't belong to anyone!" Lucien yelled.

The Dark Lady raised her free hand, tugging at her spear. "You both belong to me!"

"Never again," Fitzhugh said. And he wrested the spear free.

She shrieked and lunged for the spear with both hands. He made a slicing motion with his hand, and Henry felt the wave of Unseelie magic roll away from him. The Fay behind the Dark Lady screamed at its touch and fell writhing to the ground.

The Dark Lady gasped at the touch of pure suffering. Her pale face went blotchy with rage.

Fitzhugh grinned. "You have lost your hold on me. And I will not let you hurt my son, either."

He spun the spear toward her, but she struck out with her own wave of Unseelie magic. Fitzhugh stumbled and dropped the spear. Henry felt the echoes of the magic, a pain so sharp his eyes watered.

Fitzhugh and the Dark Lady lunged for the spear, tugging it between them and hurling pain at one another. The Dark Lady grimaced in rage, her face almost skeletal. Fury and suffering radiated from her, driving back the watching Fay of every court. But Fitzhugh had learned to endure suffering over the centuries, and he possessed a defiance and human stubbornness that the Dark Lady could not match.

She struck out at Lucien, and Fitzhugh screamed in fury and jerked the bone spear from her grasp, then shoved it into her side.

Henry forced himself to look away. Fitzhugh's rage let him break free from his Lady for the moment, but it might not let him defeat her. Even if it did, it would leave Fitzhugh as a Dark Lord, a terrible prospect.

Henry caught sight of another figure watching from across the field.

Jane on her stag.

She had made her way back, and he had to stop her. Had to reach the Fisher King first.

Henry turned his back on the fight. Turned his back on the changelings and on Cassandra and Domin and everyone he cared about. He had to, to save them. He wanted to say goodbye. He wanted to scream for everything he would lose, for all the days and all the dreams that would never be his.

But his throat was dry, his skin clammy and cold. All he could do was stumble forward, ignoring the pain of his injury, grateful to be forgotten for a few moments.

He reached the bridge. The ice was slick—but sticky where he tried to grasp the rail with his bloody hand. He fell to his knees and crawled across to the Fisher King's island.

Everything was going cold and distant. Dark. But Cassandra was out there in the midst of the fight, as were his friends. And all the changelings. Even Fitzhugh had sacrificed to get Henry this far. Jane would be there soon. He thought he heard the hooves of her stag. Or was that Annwn and his hounds come for Henry? He couldn't stop now.

He pulled himself to his feet. His limbs felt heavy. So heavy. How much blood had he lost? Too much.

"No!" Jane screamed. "It's mine."

Henry clutched his sword, ready to protect the Fisher King. Jane's stag kicked him, knocking him to the ground. Black spots swam over his vision. He could just see Jane charging the Fisher King.

"Don't!" Henry called. Or slurred. He was so dizzy. So cold.

She turned her sword on the Fisher King. "Yield to me."

The Fisher King smiled sadly and shook his head. "That is not the way of the Fisher King."

Jane snarled, and the sky rumbled overhead. "Then you will die. But first, you will tell me, how do I become the Fisher Queen?"

She straightened with a gasp, and then she and her stag vanished.

Henry blinked, wondering if all of this was a strange dream.

"She asked the wrong question," the Fisher King said. "Her thought was only for herself. But she may be more clever next time."

Henry grunted. He pulled himself up and stumbled to where the Fisher King lay. They stared at each other for a long moment, two dying men.

"I know what I must do," Henry said.

The Fisher King nodded.

"I must ask a question, and I must mean it whole-heartedly.

And yet the answer will draw me away from my mortal life—from the people I care about."

"Yes," the Fisher King said.

Henry closed his eyes and took a deep breath. He had longed to reclaim the human part of himself, and now it bled away. He pictured Cassandra. He pictured his friends. This would separate him from them, but it would also let him protect them. And he pictured all the people he had hurt when he served Titania. All the wrongs that he wished he could make right. He couldn't change anything about the past, but he could make certain that nothing like that happened again. And the changelings... He didn't owe the same kind of debt to them, but he wanted to help them as well. This was the path—the only path still open to him. He had been on it all along, all the branches and courses it might have taken streamed together into this moment.

He looked up into the old man's eyes. "How may I serve Britain?"

The old king smiled. "Accept the mantle of the Fisher King and drink from the cup."

"The..." Henry's gaze fell on a well behind the Fisher King, and beside it, a simple chalice. His eyes widened. "The Holy Grail?"

The Fisher King choked out a dry laugh. "Don't let the legends around it frighten you. They say both too much and too little."

Henry pushed himself up, caught himself on the broken wall of the castle, leaving a trail of blood in his wake. He groped his way forward to the cup and took it in his hand. It felt so ordinary. Just smooth metal, polished over many decades. Centuries. And yet, it was warm, and perhaps a little heavier than it had any right to be.

"It will not make you immortal," the old king said behind him. "But it will heal your deadly wounds and extend your life. Change your nature, though not your essence. And it will bind you to the task the Grail sets for you—in your case, to become the Fisher King."

Henry nodded and dipped the cup into the dark, cold waters of the well. In the cup, the water was pure and clear. Henry closed his eyes and drank.

The water was cold flowing down his throat. So cold it burned. He gasped at the sensation and opened his eyes, but everything was black.

No.

He could see. He could see everything—all the magic flowing through the land, the energy, each life in the land a spot of light, large or small. It was so much, he could not make sense of it. He squeezed his eyes shut, willing it all to go away.

And it settled. Settled deep inside him. Somehow, something in him shifted and opened up to make room for it all. Some place in his mind and heart he hadn't known existed. The strangest thing was, he was still himself. He had thought becoming the Fisher King would make him someone different. He was still him, he just saw and felt more than he used to.

When he dared look up again, he could see normally, but everything felt different. Brighter and bigger, filled with flecks of life, each one precious. While most of those spots of life knew and cared nothing about him, some shone more vibrantly than the others, as if they reached toward him. Some deep thread that tied them all together. He knew each one of them. Cassandra. Domin. Amy. Jairus. Even Mary, Lucien, and Telesm.

He looked at the Fisher King.

"You will have to find your court," the Fisher King said.

"Choose carefully. I am only weak because I am alone. Together, with the right companions, you will heal the blight and heal the land."

The Fisher King needed a court. People to help serve the land and its magic. No wonder the Fay had wanted more human changelings—the Fay would wish for the magic to be strong without being bound to service themselves.

"I...I don't know what I'm to do," Henry said. "You will teach me, won't you?"

"No. My fight is done. It was a noble one, and I have earned my rest. That is the way of this world. The land cannot begin to heal until the old king passes and the new takes his place."

The Fisher King stood and groped his way forward to a fissure in the stones. A breeze wafted from it that smelled of the Twilight Path.

"Wait!" Henry called.

"I have waited too long. Trust yourself and the land's magic."

And with that, Owain Glyndŵr stepped out of the human world.

Henry gritted his teeth, then turned back to look over the island fortress. *His* island fortress. The scent of the bonfires on the battlefield wafted over him, and beyond, a foul wind warned him of the Carmun's approach. He forced himself to take a slow breath. He had to trust himself.

Chapter Thirty-Six

Amy had to look away from the fight between Fitzhugh and the Dark Lady. The destruction they wrought had brought the fighting between the Fay to a halt.

She had thought for a terrible moment that Fitzhugh would win. He seemed to be winning. But then, it was as though his will faltered. And now, equally terrible, Amy was certain the Dark Lady would destroy him. Perhaps torture him first, but definitely kill him when she was done. And Jane had vanished, riding toward the Fisher King's island. It looked as though the Dark Lady would win the day. It would be her who faced the Carmun. Amy wondered if their battle would leave anything left of Britain to save.

Quiet fell over the field as the Dark Lady pummeled Fitzhugh with wave after wave of torturous magic. But a crisp sound like a trumpet's call echoed over them. No, more like the clear ringing of a metal cup when struck. The Fay didn't seem to hear. But Cassandra turned to the noise, as did Jairus and Richard, and even Georgina Weaver with her deafness. Telesm had slipped off somewhere, either with the changelings or with Domin.

"We need to go," Cassandra said. "I think the Fisher King is summoning us."

"Yes," Amy agreed. She looked to her pony Isabel. "I can carry one. Prince Richard?"

Richard shook his head and gestured to Cassandra. "No, you'll be faster on horseback. The American, your sister, and I can go quickly on foot."

Amy nodded and helped Cassandra onto Isabel. She cast one last look at Fitzhugh, sunk on the ground at the Dark Lady's feet, and she would have sworn that he was smiling. The best she could do for him now was to help Henry and the Fisher King stop the Dark Lady and the Carmun.

She spurred Isabel into action, with Cassandra clinging to her back. They cantered past the Fay to the bridge. It had been made of ice before, but now it was solid stone. That seemed a promising sign. They crossed it and found Henry standing alone in front of the Fisher King's castle.

Cassandra slid from Isabel's back, and Henry hurried forward to help steady her when she reached the ground.

"Henry?" Cassandra asked. "What of the Fisher King?"

"He is gone," Henry said, his voice tight. "And I...I drank from the Grail. I have taken his place. I am free from Titania, but I have pledged my life to this new course."

Cassandra went pale, and she clutched Henry's arm. "But... Then you're the Fisher King?"

"I don't know yet what it means for us." Henry's voice was full of anguish.

Amy's heart twisted for them.

"We heard your call," Amy said softly. "The horn."

"I did not blow a horn," Henry said. He looked back at the

metal cup sitting on the stone behind him. "But the Fisher King —the previous Fisher King—said I would not be alone." He tilted his head. "I keep thinking...I need a Grail Maiden?"

Cassandra looked at him hopefully, but he shook his head slightly, sorrow in his eyes.

"Mary, perhaps?" Amy asked.

Mary was the only maiden of her acquaintance. Or Georgina Weaver, but that would be unimaginably cruel to Cassandra if her sister could join Henry and she could not.

"No, that doesn't feel right." He looked at Amy. "I think the Grail wants you."

Amy shifted and looked down. "I am no maiden. I am a widow, as you well know."

Henry shook his head. "Maiden is not the proper term, but there are words in my head I don't quite know how to express, and they're coming out in heroic nonsense. I need someone who can see into the hearts of others. Someone who will know who should drink from the Grail."

"Domin is the one who sees into hearts," Amy said quietly.

"Not anymore. He... His future is murky." Henry's voice caught. "But you see into hearts not through magic, but because you have learned from your own heart to fairly judge the hearts of others. And you triumphed over your mother. You're brave enough to help protect the Grail. Not just the Grail—this land and everyone in it."

Goose flesh prickled over Amy's skin. Was that really her? But when she looked to the Grail, she would swear it was singing. Calling her.

Henry stepped aside to let Amy pass. She hesitated, glancing uncertainly at Cassandra. Cassandra's eyes brimmed with tears, but she managed a smile for Amy.

Amy nodded and took the Grail. The water in it was clear,

yet the light flashed off it strangely, as though something lay hidden within. She lifted the cool metal to her lips and sipped.

She gasped and nearly dropped the Grail. The water was cold and pure, and it coursed through her. As it did, it uncovered and then washed away pain and weariness she did not even know she carried.

And she saw everything a little more clearly because of it— the struggles and weaknesses of her friends, but also their goodness and courage. Amy had always been able to see more in the world than humans—she imagined because of her combined sensitivity to magic and emotions—but now, it was like she had been walking with her head down and only this moment lifted her eyes to look. Lights danced through everyone, some brighter than others, and it spoke to her. She wondered if this was how it was for Domin. How it had been. How painful, to have such sight stolen from him. It was beautiful and heartbreaking.

"Is this how everything looks to you?" Amy asked Henry. "So bright?"

"Only for a moment at the beginning. Then it settled into more of a feeling, for me at least."

Amy turned, and a billowing wave of darkness on the horizon made her stop cold. "Something is wrong."

"The Carmun approaches," Henry said. "I need to face her."

"Not alone," Amy said. "It's like in the old stories. A woman and three men to face the witch and her three sons."

Henry glanced at Cassandra, who looked perplexed, then back at Amy. "You're going to stand with me against her, then?"

Amy laughed. "Not me." She searched, trying to find the right people—the ones who could fight the darkness approaching on the horizon. And then she looked back into the water in the Grail, and images danced over the water like scattered reflections. "You need Grail Knights."

"People with magic," Henry said. "The Morrigan mentioned poetry, wisdom, and, uh satire. They battled her with words, I think. Maybe Lucien?"

Amy shook her head. "The world was different then, and so was the threat. Words helped them fight darkness in those times, and they were of the Faerie world, used to making bargains. Now, we need something different. After all, the Carmun has a physical weapon this time, and a terrible one. We need..." She looked at the Grail's faint images. "Faith to counter despair. Loyalty and love to counter hatred. Healing and hope to counter destruction."

Jairus and Richard hurried over the bridge with Georgina Weaver, and the light from them made Amy blink and then smile.

"There is one of your knights, if he will accept the task." Amy strode forward holding the Grail.

She reached Jairus. Blood spattered his face and shirt, but none of it seemed to be his. His eyes fell on the Grail, and he froze, his entire attention fixed on it. It knew him. Amy could feel it. And the light in him burned. She'd had no doubt he would be worthy of it. He was practically a Grail Knight already. But now she could see it, the glow around him like armor.

"Is that what I think it is?" Jairus asked.

"It is. Drink from the Grail and become one of its knights. You will step away from this world to fight for it. The battle is a noble one, but sometimes lonely."

Amy held the grail out in both hands, and it showed images of immense joy and exquisite sorrow. And she waited. Because she understood that the next step had to be his.

He hesitated. She felt it. He glanced back to where Georgina stood, her expression confused. His eyes turned wistful for a moment, but then he sighed and turned back to Amy, his jaw set in determination.

"I accept the call."

"Your faith will help counter the despair brought by the Carmun. Drink, and become a Knight of the Grail."

Jairus nodded and took the Grail from Amy's hands. He tilted his head and drank deeply. He drew a sharp breath as the water coursed through him.

Then he smiled. "Amazing!" His smile faded. "The Carmun is almost here. I can see the darkness now."

But they needed two more knights. The images in the Grail's water swirled and rippled. The Grail was searching for someone—searching for its next knight, a person who could stand against the Carmun.

Amy knew what she wished, but she also knew she could not force the Grail to do as she wanted. She had chosen to serve it, and she had to obey.

There. She smiled, almost laughed in relief. A knight to stand for love and loyalty. Across the bridge, Domin had dispatched all the dark elves and now fought a half-circle of goblins trying to make their way to the Fisher King's island. He held them off with Telesm by his side, though blood dripped from his many wounds. With another sweep of his lance, he killed two of the goblins. Telesm injured another, and the rest fled.

He wiped his forehead with his sleeve and turned. When he saw Amy, he took a step forward, stumbling a little. Telesm caught him and helped him across the bridge.

Domin limped up to them, leaning heavily on Telesm, his

face pale with loss of blood and magic. He straightened and studied the Grail in Amy's hands, then locked eyes with Henry.

"It will heal you," Henry said, coming up beside Amy. "At least of your current wounds. And it will commit you to always serve Britain. You will be bound by a different oath, and I don't think it will restore your Faerie magic. You will age slowly, and eventually die."

Domin hesitated. Amy bit her lip, trying to keep her desires to herself. This was a choice Domin had to make.

"If...if it makes a difference, I will not be offended if you do not wish to accept," Henry said. "You have served my bloodline and kept your previous oath nobly. I know that oath is important to you, and this one would supersede it. You will continue to be my friend no matter what you choose."

Domin took a deep breath. "I am daemon. It is my nature to protect. Britain is not my homeland, but I am fond of it. Sometimes, our course may change from the one we set out on. Yes, I can see a new future in protecting this land."

He met Amy's eyes as he said this, and his words, *a new future* soared through her. A future they would face together.

"Then drink!" Amy prompted. "Your loyalty and love will serve against the hatred sown by the Carmun."

Domin smiled a little and took a sip from the cup. He closed his eyes for a moment, and a new flush of health warmed his skin. He opened his eyes and blinked in wonder.

Then he hissed, pain lancing over his features.

"The knife shard?" Telesm asked.

"Take it out," Domin said to Henry.

"Are you—"

"Yes. The Grail's magic is trying to remove it. Take it out."

Henry pulled out his knife. With one last concerned look at

his friend, he cut into his back. Domin grunted at the pain, and Amy grasped his hand with her free one.

"There!" Henry gingerly held up the sliver of knife blade that could eat through magic, then placed it in his pocket.

Domin sighed deeply, then worry creased his brow. "Most of my Fay magic is gone. Perhaps all of it."

"And we don't have much time to discover what that leaves you with," Telesm said.

"But we need one more knight." Amy scanned all of their faces.

"Don't even think of asking," Telesm said, folding his arms.

Amy laughed. "I didn't plan to."

Richard watched with wide eyes, then he looked at the Grail. "Is it time for me to serve the Fisher King?"

Amy smiled at him. "No. At least not as one of his knights."

Richard looked at the cup and then at Amy and Jairus. "Is it wrong that I'm relieved? I wanted to prove myself, but I'm not certain I'm ready yet for this."

"That's wise," Amy said, "to know when the time isn't right for you."

"And that's only for this moment," Henry said. "Those of us who accept the call of the Fisher King will live longer, but someday we will wish to walk the Twilight Path, and on that day, perhaps you will be ready to return here and take my place."

Richard nodded.

Amy looked into the Grail water, trying to decipher the rippled images. When the image cleared, she was confused for a moment, then the warmth of rightness flowed over her. "Oh, of course! We need someone who can bring life and hope to bear against the grimness of the blight. That's you, Cassandra."

Chapter Thirty-Seven

Cassandra stared at Amy, not comprehending. She had watched with a mix of joy and anguish as the Grail selected its champions. Henry was free now. He would watch over all of them. But he would be cut off from her.

Unless she fought beside him.

Henry took Cassandra's hand, jolting her out of her stunned state. "You want Cassandra to fight?"

"A true mother, filled with life, against a false mother filled with death. Yes. She is meant to drink from the Grail and stand beside you against the Carmun."

Henry looked to Cassandra, his eyes full of longing and fear. "I want you by my side, but you'll be leaving behind your human life. I never wanted you to be trapped by magic. I wanted both of us to be free."

Cassandra smiled. "I never want to be separated from you. Besides, it's not a trap if I have a choice."

"You're leaving me again!" Georgina said, her eyes wide with anguish.

Cassandra's chest tightened. "Oh, Georgie. I will always be your sister. I will always love you. But we must choose the paths our lives will follow. And they will not always be the same."

She wrapped her sister in a fierce embrace.

Georgina squeezed her hard, then pulled back to look at her. "It frightens me."

"I know," Cassandra said. "It frightens me, too, but we can't let fear rule our lives."

Georgina took a deep breath, then nodded. "Perhaps you are right. I will try to be brave, too."

Cassandra squeezed her sister's hands, then looked back to Amy and Henry. "But what of our child?"

"Your drinking of the waters won't hurt him," Amy said. "Because it has to be a choice. It might give him some extra wisdom, but he will make his own decisions someday."

Cassandra nodded. "Then give me the cup." She met Henry's eyes. "I choose this."

And she drank. The water was cold, refreshing. It did not erase her limp or her weaknesses—those injuries were old and had become a part of her—but she could feel its magic filling the gaps, as if light and hope poured through her and strengthened her. She squeezed her eyes shut and opened them to find the world...brighter. She didn't have another word for it. It was the same world, but the loveliest parts of it drew her gaze.

"Beautiful," she whispered.

"We have our knights," Jairus said, "but we also need a sorceress, and those seem to be in short supply."

Amy looked into the Grail and laughed. "We have our 'sorceress.' It's Henry."

Jairus stared and then guffawed.

"Me?" Henry asked.

"Yes, the Fisher King. A weather mage and guardian of the land to counter the magic that disrupts and devours Britain."

Henry looked uncertain, but Cassandra took his arm and gave him a confident nod. His magic was strong enough. She knew it.

"That's it," Amy said. "You have your four to stand against the Carmun's four."

Henry nodded. "And she approaches."

He took Cassandra's hand, and they all walked across the bridge, Amy carrying the Grail, and Telesm, Richard, and Georgina trailing them.

The dusky light of the Fisher King's island faded into the harsh nighttime battlefield lit by fires. The ground was scattered with the bodies of fallen Fay. So much life lost, so pointlessly. Cassandra's eyes burned for them, but she didn't slow.

Henry still didn't know how to defeat the Carmun, but he had a shard of magic-eating knife in his pocket and Cassandra and his friends by his side. He had hope.

The Dark Lady waited for them, Jane on her stag by the Unseelie Queen's side.

"Titania may think she has won," the Dark Lady called, "but we only have to kill you, and Jane may claim the Fisher King's throne."

Henry stepped forward. "Titania no longer controls me, and Jane will never be the Fisher Queen."

Jane spurred her stag forward, but Henry had only to think it, and the ground softened, sucking the creature's legs in.

Jane screamed in fury, and the clouds overhead rumbled with thunder. The hair on Henry's arms prickled to attention, and the air crackled with energy. Everything moved slowly, forks of lightning piercing the sky. But lightning was not Henry's enemy. He merely pushed the energy aside, and it exploded in front of Jane. Her stag bellowed.

A sharp, cold wind blew at Henry's back, and he smiled.

"Jane Tudor, you have stolen from the land of Annwn. It is time for you to return to the Wild Hunt and learn a new purpose."

Jane's eyes went wide, and she looked about as if considering jumping from her trapped stag.

But she was too late. Annwn's hounds, always seeking lost souls, bayed over the sounds of the storm. The clouds roiled, and the sky filled with the call of the horn.

Jane froze, terror in her eyes. Then the clouds descended around her, and when they lifted, she was gone, along with her stag.

The Dark Lady snarled and advanced on Henry, the air around her charged with suffering.

Henry saw deeper, though. Suffering was a part of life, but only a part. By embracing Unseelie magic, the Dark Lady had cut herself off from so much more. He reached beyond air and water and fire and found the pure energies flowing through the land—forces of life and healing and growth. And he wrapped them around the Unseelie Queen, cutting her off from the suffering she sought.

Her eyes widened, and she shook herself, trying to find her way back to the suffering that gave her power. But Henry would not give it to her. He surrounded her with threads of beauty and peace, silken cords she could not break. She screamed.

"Release me, Henry Stewart!"

"There has been enough misery here today," Henry told

her. "Return to your realm, and leave your changelings alive, unharmed, and forever free."

She struggled, trying to throw off his hold. But Henry held her fast. She howled in rage and stumbled to her knees.

"Very well. I will go," she breathed. "And leave the brats for you to manage."

Henry let out a slow breath and released her.

She roared up, her eyes glittering with hatred. Henry braced himself, wondering if she would try to break her vow. But then she vanished in a whirl of dark energy.

Henry rolled his shoulders, trying to shake out the tension.

"That seemed too easy," Jairus said.

Henry ran his fingers through his hair. "It lies in the Fisher King's duties to keep the Fay in check. I understand the rules of her world. The Carmun will be different."

Out of the corner of his eye, he noticed the changelings standing together, Mary and Lucien in front as if guarding the children. There were so many of them, free now but lost in this world.

Cassandra beckoned to her sister and pointed at the changelings. "Stay with them. Help them," she mouthed.

Georgina looked like she might argue, but then she nodded grudgingly and hurried over to join Mary and Lucien. The Fay wouldn't notice Georgina with her enchanted ring, but that would do little to keep the changelings safe if Henry failed to stop the Carmun. Even when Telesm and Richard hung back by the children, Henry didn't feel they were protected enough.

"Wait!" Henry called to Amy. "Where's Fitzhugh?"

Amy frowned but pointed down the battlefield. "He lost his battle with the Dark Lady. Even if he still lives, the Grail does not want him as a knight."

"He does live," Henry said. "I can feel it. And I'm not

leaving him behind. The land has another use for him if he accepts it." Sensing Amy's skepticism, he gently reminded her, "Willingness can matter as much as worthiness."

They traversed the eerie fields of death to where Fitzhugh rested against a splintered tree. The side of his face was cut and swollen, bruises forming under his eyes. His clothes were stained and stiff with blood, whether his own or others', Henry did not know.

"So, you are the Fisher King," Fitzhugh rasped.

"I am."

"Don't expect me to bow. I haven't the energy."

"I would not wish it even if you were at your best."

"Have you come to gloat then?" Fitzhugh's eyes were feverishly bright, and he scanned the field. "But I succeeded. The Dark Lady forgot her changelings completely."

"You should know I would not gloat, but you're correct that I am not finished with you. Drink from the Grail."

Fitzhugh's eyes narrowed. "Surely, that cup is not for me. I am Unseelie. And I don't have the stomach to be one of your courtiers."

"You were Unseelie for a time. You were Seelie once, too. What do you want to be now? I know you are not ready to die. I don't want you as part of my court, but the land aches for the children who are lost. The changelings. Those now free and those who will come later. I will not be able to take all of them into my care, though some might find their way to me. They need a guide. A figure who knows the darkness and can carry a light through it."

Fitzhugh frowned. "A guide for the lost. A solitary Fay? It would be a relief to have no queen to answer to."

"And in service to the land, the Lords and Ladies could have no power over you. To remain apart from the Fay, you have to care enough about something to stay free, and I think you do care about justice for the oppressed—and about your son and your lost love—enough to do that."

Fitzhugh grunted, then slowly held out his blood-stained hand. He paused. "But where am I to lead these lost children?"

"I am hopeful that Telesm may rebuild his sanctuary quickly once the Carmun is defeated."

Fitzhugh managed a raspy laugh. "You're dragging Telesm into this? That is worth staying on to see."

"There are also some human workhouses that need a good shaking up from time to time," Henry said.

Fitzhugh grinned wickedly at that. He wiped his hand clean and reached out for the cup. He took a careful sip, and a look of peace brought color back to his face as his wounds closed themselves.

"Guide the changelings to safety," Henry said.

"I'm still not bowing to you." Fitzhugh rose slowly to his feet.

Henry smirked. "I know. But I also know you will see that justice is done."

Fitzhugh nodded. "That I will. But you have a bigger problem."

Henry looked back over the field. Darkness spread over the edges of the horizon, snuffing out the fires of the battlefield. And where the Carmun's magic touched, the dead stirred, rising to fight again.

Cassandra took Henry's hand, and he squeezed tightly. Their time together might be short after all.

Chapter Thirty-Eight

Domin still felt the course of the Grail's water where it had rolled down his throat. Though the water had been cool, it hadn't chilled him. He had always been cold with the dagger's sliver eating away at his magic. He'd grown used to it and only feared the time when he felt nothing at all. But the water had poured warmth back into him. It was still spreading, strengthening and healing him.

But everything had shifted. Most of his Faerie magic was gone. And as much as he had despised it, he found he missed it. Missed the insights it gave him. When he looked at Amy, he could read the concern on her face, but he couldn't feel it. He couldn't feel the magic in the world around him as he once had.

At least he felt more solid and real than he had since the injury. Perhaps even before that. And he could see clearly again —see into the hearts of those around him. That had been a daemon ability, not a Fay one. He saw the courage radiating from Henry, Cassandra, and Jairus—even from where Fitzhugh helped Lucien, Mary, and the others round up the changelings and shepherd them away from the Carmun's path. And Amy's heart shone brighter than ever.

Amy took his hand as they strode across the battlefield toward the darkness that was deeper than night. He almost pulled away from her touch, afraid that his lingering pain would spill over into her, but that ability—that part of him—was gone forever now. Instead, comfort flowed from Amy into him, her emotions projecting out, and him too defenseless to stop them. He didn't want to. He longed for the comfort of her touch, the reassurance in her steady affection. He laced his fingers with hers.

"Thank you," Domin whispered.

"Are you well enough to fight?"

"I have to be, don't I?" He lifted their clasped hands so he could kiss her knuckles. "Have faith. The Carmun has been defeated in the past, and we have a Fisher King in full strength."

He glanced at his wrist. The binding mark of his oath with Titania had vanished. Henry didn't need it anymore. And Domin was no longer bound to Henry as a guardian. He was bound to him as a friend.

Henry and Cassandra, also hand in hand, walked forward, and Jairus strode beside them, shotgun in one hand and sword in the other.

Domin released Amy's hand. She was not meant for this fight. He jogged unsteadily toward the darkness on the horizon. It would be faster if he could change form. Wolf. Panther. Both were swift. But he couldn't find them within him. Being part daemon allowed him to change shape, but he had lost more than just his Faerie magic. Lost some part of who he was. Without it, he didn't know what he could do besides wield a sword and stand firm against the darkness. And that he would do.

He caught up with Jairus and Henry, who had both slowed their steps to match Cassandra's. Domin worried for her, but she held her head high and marched forward by Henry's side. She had always been brave, and now she felt it in herself. Jairus, too, had little fear.

But, Domin admitted to himself, he was afraid.

Henry met Domin's eyes and nodded once. He was confident now, the mantle of the Fisher King too large for him still, but he was quickly growing into it.

Domin walked with them, his steps unfaltering but not as sure.

"How do we stop them?" Jairus asked. "I feel...stronger, but not any smarter, more's the pity. I don't know how to fight darkness and blight."

Henry frowned. "I'm not entirely certain either. I can feel strength in the land. It wants to fight back. It's waiting for us to call it forward. I just don't know how to do it."

"So, we're playing it by ear?" Jairus asked, a grin creeping over his face. "Perfect. I knew I wasn't the only crazy one."

Henry laughed.

"She's almost here," Cassandra whispered, putting a hand on her belly.

All three men stepped closer to her, but she put up her hand. "Wait. It can't appear that I'm afraid. I can't be afraid. That's what she wants—fear, anger, hatred. I think it feeds her."

Henry nodded. "Like the Unseelie. The Carmun creates chaos and feasts on it."

"Evil always does." Jairus shrugged. "So, we fight it by..."

"Standing strong," Henry said. "We have to trust in our own abilities and in each other. The Grail hasn't made us different, but it has made us stronger. More of what we always were. Reach deep and find it—light against her darkness."

They all looked up. The Carmun and her so-called sons had almost reached them, darkness spreading around them in waves of blight, like the path of a fire. And with them marched an army of the undead.

Henry turned and faced the Carmun, his face like stone. The Carmun's army slowed. Henry stepped forward, made a sweeping gesture, and the ground jutted up before them.

"Your course of destruction ends here, sorceress," Henry said.

She smiled and called out, "The Fay who once cast me off and then imprisoned me were much older and more powerful than you. They are dead now, and I am still here."

"They are dead," Henry said, "And we are here in their place. You will learn to fear Man as you once feared Fay."

The Carmun straightened. "I do not fear anyone!"

"You lie," Jairus said with a smile. "Your power comes from your anger, and your anger comes from fear. When we show you your true face, you will wither and your own blight will consume you."

The Carmun's eyes widened. "No, it will consume you, consume this entire land and bring a reign of darkness and destruction to your world, and I will be its queen. The sun will never rise on Britain again."

The undead strode forward, struggling over the low wall Henry had created, or veering to find a way around it.

Henry summoned his ice dirk. He embedded the sliver of magic-eating metal in the tip of his weapon. He lifted his sword with his other hand, and white flame radiated from it. Cassandra raised her shield, and Jairus his sword.

Domin froze, reaching out around him, sensing. In the past, he would have taken a more suitable form for fighting, but none came to him now. Everything had changed. He had to pause. He had to listen and remember who he was at his core.

Britain was foreign to him, this chilly island far from his homeland in ancient Persia, the empire ruled by the Sassanid and lost long ago. Yet this was his home now, and he had come to care about it, though he resisted becoming attached because pain always came from loving and losing. But if he didn't care, then he also wasn't really living.

He did care. He cared about Henry, Cassandra, and Jairus. He cared about Amy until it formed an ache deep inside of him. He cared about Britain or he wouldn't have pledged himself to protect it. His daemon father had been the guardian of a bloodline, as Domin had chosen to be. But daemons could also protect a place. He could protect Britain, but he had to understand it to do so.

He knew Henry felt a connection to the energies of the land, and many Fay did as well, but Domin never had. Now, as he searched for it, he found it. The land had its own energy, its own heartbeat, almost like a living thing. And it was a living thing in pain.

He let himself feel the pain of the land, the wounds where the blight cut and sickened it. And he also felt its energy, its history, its countless joys and sorrows. Britain had been waiting for its champions. For its Grail Knights or anyone else who would fight for it. The Fay might have done it. They had their moment when they could have once again been strong. But they had been too busy with petty infighting and their own concerns to listen to the energies that fed them. They had only taken and not stopped to offer anything back. Now, the responsibility and the power belonged to Henry, to Cassandra, to Jairus, and to Domin.

He let it roll through him, and a new form came to him as

naturally as rivers rolled toward the sea. He smiled, a grin filled with sharp teeth, and his arms and legs stretched and grew talons. He had never been able to change into something much bigger than his natural form because he had been relying on his strength alone. But now, he was borrowing the strength of the island, and he grew larger and larger, unfurling enormous wings that bore him into the air.

Jairus whooped at the sight of the dragon rising into the sky. He had always hoped to see one, coming to Britain, though he hadn't expected it to be someone he knew. He would take what he could get.

After all, how did one fight darkness, disease, and blight? Telesm's sword was a good weapon, but neither blades nor guns could stop those foes.

Domin, in dragon form, swept over the decayed, lurching figures and breathed fire. The force and heat of it blasted over Jairus, and he turned his face from the furnace-like wave of hot air that rippled over the field. The fire crumbled some of the dead who were farther along in their decay, but many kept moving forward, dragging flame with them.

Henry gestured, and the flames sputtered out. The dead continued their path. And with them strode the Carmun and her three children, blighting everything they touched. Jairus tried charging against the Carmun, but the undead blocked his path. He couldn't defeat foes that he couldn't even reach. Domin passed over the field again, burning a path of destruction through the undead, but the Carmun touched the freshly fallen Fay with her staff, and they rose to join her army.

Movement at the edge of Jairus's vision distracted him for a moment. Ghosts. The dead were here, too, watching. The spirits he'd seen before didn't seem to pay much attention to the actions of the living, but these ghosts watched with interest. He knew they were the dead because he could see through them: some in recent clothing, others wearing armor in various stages of historical provenance, from redcoats to plated knights on horseback to Roman soldiers in leather armor.

And they all watched as he cut and thrust against the undead hordes. He could hack these enemies apart, but they kept coming for him.

On the edge of the field, he caught sight of black feathers. The Morrigan watched with a smirk, fully armored against the fight. Jairus growled with frustration. Of course, she would be enjoying this. Whether or not the Carmun's sons were truly apocalyptic horsemen, and whether or not she was, they were bringing battle. Yet even she had not been entirely heartless. She had appeared in the land of the dead and tried to help those who were trapped.

A prickling raced over Jairus's skin, and he glanced again at the dead all around him. Why were they here? Why were they so attentive? He looked again to the Morrigan. She met his eyes and gave a single nod.

Could the dead aid him? They were closer in nature to the undead and belonged to the same world.

He fended off a blow from a terrible undead Fay creature all tendons and claws. How did he call to the dead? He didn't have Annwn's horn. And he didn't dare stop fighting. Trying to summon the dead to his aid was a risk—a gamble. And he had given up gambling.

But that little voice in the back of his mind gave him a nudge. Maybe he had given up cards and betting, but life did require the occasional gamble after all.

Jairus thrust against his opponent, sending the creature crashing back into those behind him, and then he retreated a few steps to face the dead. A lad holding a tattered banner met his eyes, a bright glimmer in his gaze. And a figure in ancient armor stepped closer as if encouraging him to speak.

"What brings you here?" Jairus called, his voice carrying over the din of battle.

The dead fixed their attention on him, and an eerie wave swept over him, almost a sickness. It was not healthy for the living to have so much attention from the dead. Unless, maybe, one was a Knight of the Grail, and the dead only wanted a little direction.

"Perhaps you believe it's not your business to worry about the living," Jairus called. "The living don't give much heed to the dead anymore, after all."

The ghosts shifted, moved closer. Jairus resisted the urge to flinch from them. The figure in the ancient armor nodded. Jairus cleared his throat.

"But this isn't just about the living or the dead. This is about all of Britain. That witch would ensnare all, living and dead."

The spirits shifted uneasily, a cold breeze wafting around them.

"I don't know why you're still lingering here. I don't know how to set you free. But maybe, some of you still had work to do in this life, and it binds you to this place. Maybe this is your opportunity to fulfill debts to those long passed, to prove your honor to yourself or your kin, to leave this world with a deed that will let you hold your head high in the world to come."

The lad with the banner raised it aloft, and it snapped in a wind that Jairus could not feel.

The figure in ancient armor came forward. A female figure,

Jairus realized. She removed her leather helm, revealing a young face framed by short brown hair.

"I know you," he said. "But I don't know why."

"You saw me only in my stone sleep. I am Ankhira who fought beside Telesm and Domin long ago—another time when magic threatened the human world."

"The Carmun killed you," Jairus said.

"The Carmun destroyed my prison of stone, and I followed her here." She turned to the assembled spirits. "I followed her because I knew I could not rest until I had finished my fight. I have waited a thousand years to have a voice again—to be able to act again. I am no longer a prisoner of the past. Now, I choose to claim my future. Will you?"

The other spirits stirred, lifting spears, swords, and axes.

"It is time to earn your peace and your place in the next world!" Ankhira unsheathed a ghostly sword swirling with otherworldly mist.

"Save Britain," Jairus shouted to the spirits. "And save yourselves!"

He gestured with his sword, and the ghosts charged. They passed him like a cold wave, raising goosebumps on his skin. He could not hear the clash, but he felt the impact of it as the dead collided with the undead.

And the undead fell back before the weapons of the dead. Domin swept overhead, his massive wings lashing the field with a windstorm as he breathed fire into their ranks and the ghosts brought the undead to the ground. And as he watched, some of the ghosts vanished. Jairus was happy if they had found rest, but he hoped they didn't all vanish too quickly, not while the Carmun was still on the field.

∼

Cassandra stayed firmly behind her shield, not understanding what was happening around her. Domin had changed into...a dragon? She didn't know that was possible, but now he lanced the field with fire. Henry fought his way toward the Carmun with a whirl of wind, ice, and fire, and then Jairus started shouting and the deathless fell back before a force Cassandra could not see.

They might actually have a chance against the Carmun's undead forces, but the Carmun and her ghastly sons were not deterred. They marched on, surrounded by their undead thralls, and Henry showed signs of flagging. Even the Fisher King was not immortal or immune from fatigue.

And what of the Fisher King's consort? Cassandra didn't know what she was supposed to do. She protected Henry with the shield from any who tried to approach, but was that the extent of her abilities? Domin, Jairus, and Henry all seemed to have gained new powers as Fisher King and Grail Knights, but Cassandra felt no different. She still limped along, struggling to hold up the shield as her good arm grew tired.

Domin, in dragon form, landed beside them, swiping aside a path of undead with a taloned hand. The path to the Carmun and her three sons was clear.

Domin launched into the air to breathe fire over the Carmun, but she and her sons walked through the flames unscathed. The four figures seemed more shadow than substance. Cassandra could not guess which had once been Rushford. The Carmun's magic had consumed everything that had once been human of him and the other two Grigori.

Jairus jogged up to Henry, and together they charged the Carmun's sons.

Henry slashed the first one with the ice dirk holding the magic-eating knife. The shadow son screamed, and a glimpse of something human showed through the gash in the darkness encircling the figure. Henry shoved the flaming sword into the opening, and the light flashed, blasting away the creature and its darkness like an explosion of gunpowder.

"That's more like it!" Jairus yelled. "Hand me that dirk."

Henry passed it to Jairus, who charged against the second of the sons. The creature sent a whirlwind of shadow against Jairus. Cassandra flinched from the cold of it, the sense of despair emanating from the darkness. Jairus froze for a moment, then slashed into the swirling shadows. He shouted and lunged forward. The creature howled as the dirk struck home.

Henry followed through with a slash of his sword, and another of the creatures dissolved.

"No!" The Carmun's voice echoed over the field, chilling Cassandra.

A wave of darkness rolled over them. The third creature swiped at Jairus, knocking the ice dirk with its enchanted tip from his hand. He scrambled after it.

Domin swooped overhead, slashing at the Carmun with his talons. She lashed out, and threads of darkness wrapped his wings, sending him crashing into the remnants of the undead.

A tendril of darkness curled around Henry's foot and yanked him down, slamming his head against the ground. Cassandra gasped and rushed forward. The tendrils slithered up to Henry's throat, choking him. She tried to pull Henry free, but his skin was icy cold. She sliced at the darkness with the edge of the shield. The tendril fell back, curling warily like a snake poised to strike.

Blood seeped from the side of Henry's head, and deep blue-black injuries marked his skin where the darkness had touched him. He groaned, but his eyes stayed closed.

The sword lay by his hand, but it would do Cassandra no good—she didn't have the magic to ignite it.

"Wake up!" Cassandra hissed, rubbing his arms to warm him. "You have to wake up!"

"You're too late," the Carmun said.

Cassandra turned, holding up the shield.

The sorceress laughed. "Oh, that little trick might work against lesser creatures, but I'm not impressed by your bravery. In fact, I can see that you're terrified of me."

"Of course I'm frightened," Cassandra said, grateful that her voice didn't break. "But that doesn't mean I'm not brave."

She wasn't afraid of dying, not after walking in the Twilight Path or seeing the figure of death in the Winter Kingdom. But she was afraid of leaving Henry and her family defenseless. Of losing her child before he was even born. Her fears weren't for herself, but for those she loved. And that made her strong despite her weaknesses.

She stood straighter, holding the shield so it covered herself and Henry.

The Carmun raised her magical staff of twisted oak wood— the one that would kill them and then raise them again as mindless thralls. She brought it down with a sickening clank on the shield.

Light flashed, a blinding blast like a bolt of lightning. The shock reverberated through Cassandra's bones. She collapsed, blinded, struggling to lift the shield against the Carmun's next stroke.

But the shield was gone. Only the straps remained on her arm. She fumbled around, blinking hard to clear her eyes, and found a broken piece of it, the edge sharp where the shield had split into pieces.

~

The blast of magic shook Henry to his senses. He gasped and sat up, rubbing his aching throat. The cold of the Carmun's magic lingered, slowing his limbs and his mind. Cassandra lay nearby, her weak arm raised defensively as she patted blindly with her good hand for a weapon.

And the Carmun sprawled on the ground in front of them. Splinters of wood littered the space between them. The Carmun's staff, shattered by the impact with Cassandra's shield.

Henry's ears buzzed from the explosion, but beyond the ringing, he heard the Carmun's howl of agony and rage.

The Carmun rose unsteadily, and Henry pushed himself to his feet to match her.

"Henry!" Cassandra called, rubbing her eyes.

"I'm here!" Henry's voice came out raspy, not as strong as he hoped, but he stepped between the Carmun and his wife.

Wisps of darkness trailed from the Carmun, and she glared down at Henry, her eyes hollow pits in the strange angles of her face. The darkness pulled at him, threatening to suck him in and devour the last of his strength.

The grotesque form of her final son lumbered toward them with a halting gait, blocking them from where Jairus still scrambled after the lost fragment of magic-eating blade.

The earth around the Carmun and her son withered, the tiny lives of plants and insects smothered by her unnatural magic that sought only darkness and death. Henry felt the sting of each small light she extinguished.

The Carmun turned her gaze on Cassandra.

Something sharp and hot burned through Henry. No. The Carmun would not have any more lives. She would not have Cassandra.

Henry glanced at his sword, just out of reach. The Carmun noticed, and her lips twisted in a parody of a smile. Her son lurched toward the sword and sent curls of darkness to encircle the magic blade, pitting it with rust.

Henry swayed on his feet. What did he have left to throw at the Carmun? To heal the land? His hands were empty, his strength small compared to the vastness of her destruction. Death and blight and hopelessness lay all around him.

Shadows crawled toward Henry. Toward Cassandra. They veered around a piece of the broken shield as long as Henry's arm. It reflected the light of a nearby bonfire. A faint glimmer clung to its edge like a memory of magic.

Henry dove for the fragment of the shield, a long, slender piece of enchanted metal. The edge drew blood from his finger, so sharp he hardly felt the cut. He tore a silk handkerchief from his pocket and used it to grip the makeshift weapon. The shreds of its magic hummed through Henry, awakened and woven with Cassandra's bravery and love.

He was not alone. The world still held some light.

Henry lunged forward and shoved the piece of shield into the Carmun's gut. She shrieked and doubled over, light reflected from the shield burning through her. Henry yanked the broken shield free and brought it down on the Carmun's neck, severing her head.

She collapsed at his feet.

Her son wailed and withered. The darkness dissipated like fog burned away by the dawn.

Henry tossed the metal aside and hurried over to kneel by his wife. "Cass?"

She reached out, grabbed his arm. "The light... I can only see flashes."

"Keep your eyes shut. They'll recover."

"The Carmun—"

"She's gone, and her last son as well," Henry said. "I, uh, dispatched her." He grinned. "Very few things can survive having their head separated from their body. Hale taught me that."

"The shield broke." Cassandra clung to Henry. "I was so afraid."

"Yes, it broke. But so did her staff. She overestimated her power...and underestimated your strength reflected in the shield. Cassandra, we defeated her!"

Tears filled Cassandra's eyes, and she blinked and squinted past Henry. He followed her gaze.

The witch's body shuddered, and the ground shifted. The limbs of a young oak sprung from the ground, the tree shooting up to encircle the Carmun's remains. From the base of the tree, green life spread, rolling over the fields and swallowing the signs of destruction.

Chapter Thirty-Nine

Amy felt the shudder of relief roll through the land when Henry decapitated the Carmun. The undead collapsed, and the unnatural darkness dissipated. The first light of dawn shone over the smoking battlefield.

Telesm joined Amy, a light of triumph in his eyes. But his shoulders stooped. He looked much aged.

A chill walked over Amy's skin, and she sensed something near. Someone.

"Telesm?" she asked.

Telesm. The presence echoed.

"Ankhira?" Telesm choked. "You're here?"

I clung to the Carmun. I knew you would fight her, and I would be able to say farewell.

"I don't want this to be farewell. I was going to find a cure for you."

A faint laugh. *There are limits to even what you can do, my love.*

"I do not deserve to be called that. I did not appreciate... I didn't see... Don't tell me that I won't ever have the chance."

Of course you will. Even you will not live forever. And when you walk the Twilight Path, I will be there to greet you.

"I want to follow you now," Telesm whispered.

No, you don't. For all your show of a hard heart, you know you still have things to do here.

Telesm rubbed his face. "I am tired."

I know. And you will rest. But your journey isn't through. Mine was over long ago. But I made my sacrifice so you could go on. And now, I can truly rest, and when next I see you, it won't be merely a dream.

"No, wait!"

But the presence was fading.

A whisper touched Amy's ear, meant only for her. *Thank you.*

Telesm lowered himself to the ground. His shoulders shook, but he made no sound. Amy could feel his heartbreak. He sat and watched the field of battle with red-rimmed eyes.

The few who remained standing made their way to where Amy and Telesm watched: the changelings led by Lucien and Mary, with Fitzhugh and Richard trailing behind. Georgina, her eyes wide and glazed with shock, stood behind them. And the Weeping Woman had found her way to the changelings.

Henry, Cassandra, Jairus, and Domin—in human form—limped over.

"Is it really done?" Mary asked.

Amy smiled. "It is." She glanced down at the Grail, reading the uncertain images in the water. "You could drink from it too, if you'd like. Become a lady in the Fisher King's court. There will be much work to do, protecting Britain, and the Grail finds you worthy."

Mary looked to Lucien.

Amy studied the Grail. "You could both drink."

Lucien sighed. "I appreciate the gesture of faith, but I will stay with the changelings. They may need more guidance than Telesm alone can offer. Or my...or Fitzhugh," he added, glancing over his shoulder with a look of disdain.

Fitzhugh smirked but didn't argue.

"After all," Lucien went on, "the Carmun is dead, and we were even able to capture a Faerie Queen. They will be weaker now, and we will have many changelings to protect— especially when we work to free the changelings in the other courts."

"They will be welcome in my court as well," Henry said from behind them. A purple mark encircled his throat, rapidly fading. "But I will force no one to serve. Those who wish to learn to use their powers and live apart from the magical world will need a shelter."

Telesm sighed. "I never wished to be involved, or to be overrun by children." He smiled slightly. "But I see you will not give me any peace. Not yet, at least," he added wistfully.

Mary looked from Lucien to Amy, and then her eyes fixed on Cassandra. "I'm going to stay with Telesm," she said. "And Lucien. I might be strong enough to help them with the sanctuary, and I am already strong enough to help the lost ones who come to him. My path lies this way, not with you."

Cassandra smiled sadly. "I understand. I think...I think we will still see you at times?"

She looked to Henry.

He frowned thoughtfully. "The Fisher King's court is set apart, but it is there to be found by the honest-hearted who seek it. And of course, it must by necessity be tied to both the human and Fay worlds. Yes, I think this is not farewell."

Georgina pushed her way forward. "What are you saying? I didn't understand all of it. This is goodbye?"

Cassandra embraced her sister and spoke to her directly. "It is goodbye for now, but not forever. I will not see you often, but I will try, when I can..."

"I want to go with you!" Georgina said. "I don't want to be left behind again."

Amy glanced into the water in the cup. It showed her nothing. She shifted so Georgina could see her speak.

"Your heart is not yet certain."

Georgina looked at her in surprise. Defiance flashed in her eyes, followed by vulnerability. She looked at Cassandra and briefly at Jairus before returning a pleading gaze to Amy.

"But I will be so alone," Georgina said.

Amy put a hand on Georgina's arm. "Perhaps. But fear of loneliness is not a reason to commit a very long life to a service that will be difficult, dangerous, and will at times break your heart. The Fisher King's court is not a place of ease, but a place to try to heal the hurts done in Britain, to Britain, and sometimes even by Britain. We will be facing monsters of the Fay and the human varieties. You someday may decide it is the course for you, but you have to make the choice for the right reasons."

Georgina nodded, her eyes full of tears. Cassandra embraced her sister once again.

The Weeping Lady—Maude—stepped forward, her face dry for once.

"What will you do now?" Mary asked her.

Maude smiled at Mary. "I have doomed myself with my Lady, so I twisted her command and followed the changelings out of her kingdom. I have never felt so free."

"You cannot go back," Mary said. She glanced hopefully at Amy and at the Grail in her hands.

But Maude smiled. "If the Fisher King will grant me a boon, I will join the Wild Hunt."

"The...The Wild Hunt?" Mary stared at her Faerie mother.

"Yes," Maude said. "I have been a lost soul for many years. You helped to find me. Now, I would like to help others who are lost. The Wild Hunt does not have to be terrible—it can also be a solace for those who long to be found. And even the Dark Lady has no power over the Hunt while the Lord of Annwn holds the horn."

"You are certain?" Henry asked.

"Yes," Maude said, the word sure and strong.

"Very well."

Henry looked to the western edge of the sky, where the last star still shone before dawn wiped it away. A mass of clouds boiled up on the horizon, and wind howled. The clouds swept over them, bringing the echo of horses and hounds. And then the storm was gone as quickly as it had come, and Maude with it.

Mary watched it go, and then she nodded once, peace in her eyes.

Henry stepped toward the bridge, turning his face to the castle. It was calling them back. Amy heard it, too, the echoes of a horn only they could hear.

Cassandra embraced Mary and her sister and even Lucien, who looked quite taken back. And they parted ways. Amy was the last to cross the bridge, and when she looked back, it had vanished, cutting them off. She turned to the crumbling castle where Domin waited for her, and she smiled through the heartache of saying goodbye. They had a long work ahead of them, but Britain needed their light.

Epilogue

Two Years Later

Sheffield wasn't Jairus's idea of a holiday, in the cold and cloudy north of England, but it was nice to be back in the human world after spending months negotiating between Queen Mab and her changelings. A few of them chose to stay in the Faerie realms, given better living conditions in exchange for helping her rebuild after the Carmun's siege, but most were happy to find new lives with Henry or at Telesm's new sanctuary. The Fay were weakened—weakening further as humans built more with iron and steel—and they would be taking many fewer changelings in the future, mainly those who wished to join the Faerie world.

This quest, though, was more like his traditional work, hunting a monster troubling humans. He grinned and checked the charges on his shotgun and pistol. A ghost was said to be stalking the people of Sheffield, breathing fire, leaping great distances, and harassing pretty girls who walked in the park. Jairus had a pretty good idea of the "ghost" he was going to confront.

A woman's yelp drew his attention, and he ran toward the sound. He didn't think he would have to fight, but he still kept his gun handy.

He burst through the trees onto the path, and then stumbled to a stop at the tableau before him.

An extraordinarily tall man in a white suit—Spring-heeled Jack—stood with his hands in the air, and a young lady held him at bay with a birding gun and one hand and in the other... silver-plated chatelaine scissors held like a cross. Jairus cocked an eyebrow and approached cautiously.

"—Not very gentlemanly," the lady said. "Really, I expect— No! Don't mumble like that. I can't hear you at all."

Jairus's mouth pulled into a grin. He knew that voice.

Making certain he was visible, he walked forward, his hands raised to show he was no threat.

"Mr. Hale!" Georgina Weaver called. Her face lit up, but she quickly scowled and prodded her birding gun at Spring-heeled Jack.

"Miss Weaver." Jairus positioned himself so Georgina could read his lips. "I thought I was coming to the rescue, but it appears I'm not needed."

"Yes, you are," Spring-heeled Jack called, his tone pleading. "I just wanted a little kiss, and this crazy lass stuck me with a pair of silver scissors. Then she pointed a gun at me!"

"Sounds like you're getting what you deserve," Jairus said. "Miss Weaver, I'm not at all surprised that you know how to handle this fellow, but what are you doing in Sheffield?"

"Oh, Anne—my little sister—told me where I could be

useful. I've decided I like hunting monsters, you see. I was tired of being scared and wanted to stop the types of creatures that were scaring others."

"And your family...?"

She grinned. "They think I'm working as a governess teaching painting! After all, they believe that Cassandra married Mr. Stewart and left for America, and they're just as happy to see me on my own. Sophie and Robert are introducing my other sisters into society." She straightened her shoulders. "My painting *is* quite good now, though. That's how I support myself."

"I have no doubt it's good." Jairus smiled back. "But what did you plan to do with Jack?"

"Make him swear to reform. The Fay have to do as they promise, I've learned."

"They do, but Jack isn't Fay. He's half fire elemental."

Georgina sighed and lowered her gun. "That must be why he could see me." She displayed the little ring with its pearl on her finger. "Telesm never asked me to return it, and it has proven quite useful."

Jairus laughed.

Jack started to move away, but Georgina raised her gun again, freezing him in place.

"He's still nervous about iron shot, I see," Georgina said.

"Well, being shot would hurt him." Jairus gave Jack a look of mock sympathy. "She has you, I suppose."

"Aren't you going to 'elp old Jack? After all we've been through together?"

"You mean, like betraying Domin? Not really an endearing memory—none of them are." Jairus pulled out the Penny Dreadful he had brought tucked into his coat: *Spring-Heeled Jack, The Terror of London*.

"Oy! That one's about me! I told you they wrote books about me. It made me bold to come out of 'iding."

"But is that all you want to be?" Jairus asked. "The Terror of London? An unpleasant memory who meets a well-deserved end?"

Jack's mouth twitched into a frown and he blew out a ring of smoke.

"The world's becoming a less friendly place for magic folks," Jairus went on. "Most of the Fay are retreating to their courts. The solitary Fay are weakening, going into hiding or allying themselves with the Fisher King."

"What's that to me? I'm not Fay."

"No, but you are magic. The world is changing. What's your part going to be in it?"

"I'm no Knight of the Grail," Jack said spitefully.

"No, you're not. But as long as you're the Terror of London, people are going to keep hunting you with newer and better weapons. One of these days, they'll find one that works, and then old Jack is no more."

Jack glowered. "What am I supposed to do then?"

Jairus pulled out another Penny Dreadful, this one showing a nobleman-turned-highwayman rescuing a maiden from a band of thieves. "People do love a hero. Especially one with a tortured past. They're very unlikely to take shots at a character like that."

Jack took the Penny Dreadful with a thoughtful expression.

Georgina lowered her gun and looked to Jairus.

He smiled and motioned with his head for her to walk away with him.

"Will that work?" she asked when they'd left Jack behind.

"Will he reform, you mean?" Jairus asked. "I think it

appeals to his ego. And there isn't much place left for him in the world."

Georgina nodded. "I'm not sure this world is the right place for me, either."

"You do seem to have taken to monster hunting," Jairus said, glancing at the holster she'd fashioned for her birding gun.

"I can't ignore what I know is out there. I did try for a while, but I dream of things, and they come out in my painting. The Fay may be fading from the world, but they've touched my life, and it changed me."

Jairus didn't say anything. He would not mind seeing Georgina more often, but he didn't think it was his place to offer or to ask.

"I would like to see Cassandra again," Georgina said. "Is she well? And her baby? I received her letter..."

"Little Owain. Yes, I christened him. He's a healthy lad."

Georgina looked up at him. "Will you take me to the realm of the Fisher King?"

Jairus took a deep breath. "The Fisher King foresees dangers for Britain in the years ahead, and he welcomes those willing to serve, but there's no turning back once you choose that path. It's painful at times. We see so much suffering, and we can't always repair it. Sometimes we just have to...to bear it."

Henry had definitely aged since he became Fisher King, more from worry than from time.

"I can bear suffering," Georgina said, touching her ear. "I've already experienced my share of it."

"Then are you certain you want to guarantee yourself more of it? You could live a peaceful life in this world, even hunt monsters from time to time to keep things lively. You don't have to choose hardship."

"I've had two years to think it over, and this is what I want.

Not for my sister or for..." Georgina met his gaze for a moment, her eyes wide as they locked with his, and Jairus felt a thrill at the connection. Then she looked away, her cheeks reddening. "Or for anyone else. This is for me. I don't seek hardship, of course, but I want to know I have spent my time and energy making the world more of what it ought to be. This is the path I'm meant to walk."

Warmth and a feeling of rightness poured through Jairus. "Then, Miss Weaver, I would be happy to escort you to the Realm of the Fisher King."

He offered her his arm. She took it without hesitation.

They walked back to a large outcropping of rock. It might look like nothing to most people, but Jairus saw the faint gleam of magic that marked the way back to his home.

He guided Georgina through the narrow crack that served as a bridge and past the fields of fog that would confuse anyone not meant to find the island that moved where it needed to be in the landscape.

Cassandra stood outside the rebuilt fortress talking to one of Mary and Lucien's changeling girls. The child was good with ice magic and wanted to become a page to the Fisher King. Domin practiced swordsmanship with another changeling while Amy teasingly cheered on his young opponent. Henry stood with the white stag, its leg now healed so it could bring him news from throughout his kingdom. Young Will showed him a new trick with his fire magic. White banners flapped from the high tower, and songbirds flitted in the trees.

Owain clung to his mother's skirt, thumb stuck in his mouth. He grinned at Jairus and tugged on his mother's hand.

Cassandra glanced up, then looked again. Her face broke into a grin, and she hurried forward, throwing her arms around Georgina. The sisters embraced, tears streaming down their cheeks. Amy smiled and gave Jairus a nod of approval. The Grail magic could see Georgina even if Telesm's ring protected her from the Fay. They would have a Grail ceremony that evening, he wagered.

"How did this happen?" Cassandra asked, breaking away to look between Jairus and Georgina.

"She was hunting Spring-heeled Jack. Caught him, too." Jairus beamed.

Cassandra laughed, then her face grew more serious as she studied her sister. "I am so happy to see you, but are you certain this is what you want?"

Georgina nodded. "I've been hunting monsters on my own. Wouldn't it be better to do it with people I care about?"

"It would." Cassandra pulled her sister close. "Welcome home."

And Jairus smiled at those words, too. He was looking forward to getting to know Georgina Weaver better. It had been a while since he'd danced with a pretty girl. Guarding the land wasn't an easy path, but it was better with people he cared about at his side. It was hope and love that gave them all the strength for their journey.

This concludes the Iron & Thorns trilogy. Thank you for reading. I hope you enjoyed the story.

If you would like an exclusive bonus chapter about Henry's adventure while visiting the workhouses in London, you can sign up for my newsletter to download it at BookFunnel, https://BookHip.com/ZNTQHPR

And please remember to leave a review!

Notes on Lore and Lammas

As I have throughout the Iron & Thorns series, I drew the lore for this book from Celtic and broader northern European folklore, though I have sometimes mingled it or put my own twists on it.

The legend of the Carmun is from Irish mythology. As in this book, she was supposed to have been a witch (from Athens originally) who, along with her sons Darkness, Violence, and Evil, brought blight and battle to Ireland and nearly destroyed the island. Three supernatural (Tuatha de Danann, or Fay) male heroes and a sorceress defeated her with poetry, satire, and magic. Given the importance of words in Faerie lore, I found their choice of weapons very interesting. Her sons left the Carmun as a hostage and were banished from Ireland. The Carmun was buried in a grove of oaks in Wexford, and was supposed to have died of grief, but a festival was held on Lammas or Lughnasadh (August 1st) to remember and appease her, which suggested to me that perhaps she wasn't considered completely gone.

The Fisher King is one of the more obscure figures from Celtic and Arthurian legend. He's a little different in various retellings, but they agree that he is the guardian of the Holy Grail and that he has an injury that also causes his land to suffer. Most also include a question that the hero must ask to cure the Fisher King. Sometimes the Fisher King is alone, but other times, he has a court, possibly including a father and/or a daughter.

The presence of an elder and younger Fisher King in some stories suggests that the title may be passed on. It was my own invention to suggest that the role started with Bran the Blessed (who had a cauldron with healing powers somewhat like the Holy Grail, though without the Christian symbolism relating to the Last Supper or the blood of Christ), moved to King Arthur, and then to Owain Glyndŵr, the would-be liberator of Wales who vanished in 1415.

The idea that the Fisher King must be of royal blood and have a claim to the throne came from the old myth that the well-being of the true king is tied to the health of the land and its people—just as the Fisher King's injury harms those.

Domin's ex-flame, the female warrior Bradamante, and her magical spear that always strikes its opponent are part of Carolingian legend (stories and myths of Charlemagne, called The Matter of France, as opposed to Arthurian legend or The Matter of Britain). Most of the rest of Telesm's weapons, like the flaming sword and the staff or club Lorg Mor are from Celtic lore. Though J.R.R. Tolkein's *Lord of the Rings* made a certain ring of invisibility so famous that the trope has been retired (justifiably, as it's a masterpiece), Celtic, Norse, and European lore was full of rings of invisibility, so I gave Georgina a variation on the theme.

Thank you for reading *Fierce Magic*! If you enjoyed the lore, I hope it inspires you to read some of the original myths and legends and ask your own questions about where the stories came from and what they meant to the people who told them.

Also by E.B. Wheeler

British Fiction:

Born to Treason

The Royalist's Daughter

The Haunting of Springett Hall

Wishwood (Westwood Gothic)

Moon Hollow (Westwood Gothic)

A Proper Dragon (Dragons of Mayfair 1)

An Elusive Dragon (Dragons of Mayfair 2)

A Subtle Dragon (Dragons of Mayfair 3)

Cruel Magic (Iron & Thorns 1)

Wild Magic (Iron & Thorns 2)

A Haunted Masquerade (A Haunted Season)

Utah Fiction:

No Peace with the Dawn (with Jeffery Bateman)

Letters from the Homefront (Utah at War)

Balm for the Heart (Utah at War)

Bootleggers and Basil (in *The Pathways to the Heart*)

Blood in a Dry Town (Tenny Mateo Mystery 1)

A Company of Bones (Tenny Mateo Mystery 2)

Nonfiction:

Utah Women: Pioneers, Poets & Politicians

Mysteries of the Old West
Mysteries of the Middle Ages

Juvenile Fiction:

The Bone Map

Alejandra the Axolotl and the Big Mess

Acknowledgments

It took far longer than I had hoped to finish the Iron & Thorns series, but I wanted to do justice to the characters and their stories, so thank you to my readers for their patience. My thanks to The Writers' Cache for their support and critiques as I worked on this book, and especially to my early and beta readers Dan, Emily, Karen, Lauren, and Melanie for their detailed feedback. I also appreciate the many experts and reenactors who have shared their knowledge about historical details in person and online so I can make the world of Iron & Thorns as accurate as possible. As always, a heartfelt thank you to my husband and kids for their encouragement and support.

About the Author

E.B. Wheeler is the author of over a dozen books of history, historical fiction, and historical fantasy, including Whitney Award finalists *Born to Treason* and *A Proper Dragon*, and YA Fantasy Whitney Award winner *Cruel Magic*, as well as short stories, magazine articles, and scripts for educational software programs. She has a B.A. in history with an English minor from BYU and graduate degrees in history and landscape architecture from Utah State University. In addition to writing, she sometimes consults about historic preservation and teaches history, and she loves gardening, folk music, reading, and exploring the West with her husband and kids.